Hocus Pocus '14

Spooky Tales with a Twist

Volume One

Published by Flintproductions

eBook –   ISBN 978-1-909785-304
paperback – ISBN 978-1-909785-311

front cover illustration by Jake Harvey & Angela Oltmann

www.angieocreations.com

www.debbieflint.com   Flintproductions

Hocus Pocus '14

Spooky Tales with a Twist

INTRODUCTION

This anthology is a collection of short stories and short novellas, with a mystical twist. They are spooky rather than gory. From haunted house to fallen angel, devious spirits to soul stealers, these tales will give you thrills and chills.

Thirteen supernatural spine-tinglers - some a little more tingly than others...

Enjoy – and do check out the authors' links to their other writing. Many are award winning, others are best sellers – see if you can spot the new voices too.

Specially created for Hallowe'en 2014 and the October 31st online 'party' on Facebook:

'Hocus Pocus 2014.'

The Authors

Adrienne Vaughan, Lizzie Lamb *from New Romantics 4* writing group.

Debbie Flint, Carolyn Mahony, Mary Jane Hallowell, Litty Williams *from The Ladies of Posara writing group.*

Jane O'Reilly, Alison May, Jules Wake (and Debbie, Carolyn and Adrienne) *from genius author Julie Cohen's* writing workshops.

S. A. Edward (and Debbie) – *from Arvon's Totleigh* Barton writing retreat.

Lynda Renham, Tina K. Burton and Tracy Burton (not related – spooky!) brought together by the mystical powers of Facebook.

Edited by Debbie Flint and M J Hallowell

Hocus Pocus '14

Spooky Tales with a Twist

Contents

Seed of Doubt

By
Adrienne Vaughan

Seed of Doubt – a short story by Adrienne Vaughan

Thomas could see black spiked turrets poking into the pale sky, as the coach passed through the vast gateway, rattling along the leafless tree-lined avenue and on towards the house.

Determined to remain unimpressed, he gripped the seat, as the murmuring of his fellow travellers became a gasp and turned into an excited babble. The coach swept by the lake and swung round to take in the full view of the magnificent gothic pile, before juddering to a halt on the gravel. The East and West wings draped either side of the main house, sweeping backwards as if to formally present the glittering façade of glass and golden stone that was Moorcroft Hall.

Smiling 'welcomers' in polo-shirts bearing the Moorcroft Crest, ushered them up a mountain of steps and into a reception hall the size of half a football pitch. A fireplace, which could accommodate five full grown adults standing in a row, was ablaze with a forest of logs, the gleaming floor reflecting the galleried landing above. A shimmering staircase spilled to the ground, as a gossamer figure sailed daintily earthwards, sunbeams bursting in all directions as it sashayed towards them. They blinked, speechless.

"Welcome, welcome, newest friends only just met," the sparkly, gossamer-clad figure boomed, breaking the spell as it tip-toed around their defensive semi-circle, touching each arm, confirming that it was indeed solid matter, possibly human, sex as yet to be determined.

"I'm Willoughby, your host for what's going to be a truly memorable weekend," the now named Willoughby beamed, revealing disconcertingly brilliant teeth. "Reception drinks are being served in the morning room. You no doubt all got to know each other intimately on the bus, and those with single rooms might want to double up already, who knows?" Willoughby laughed appreciatively at his own, apparently huge joke, fox trotting towards an open doorway with silent footsteps. "Let's do the formal stuff first, and agree our programme over a nice glass of chilled Chablis." He pronounced Chablis as *chabless* and referring to the notes on his clipboard, tutted a bit, as he realised this was not the 'Soooo Don't Want to be Single!' group he thought it was.

Thomas hung back, waiting for the last of them to pass through to the other room and then as quietly as the polished floor would allow, tuned on his heel, pulling the squeaky wheelie suitcase behind him.

"Ahem," a feigned cough echoed. "This way sir, you'll be fine when you know what's what," Willoughby was standing in the doorway. The man half-turned back, unsure. "Sir, please, the programme is about to begin."

The room beyond grew silent. He pulled the squeaky wheels back across the floor. "You must be Thomas," Willoughby shook his hand. Thomas nodded, the hand he was holding was ice cold.

Later, sitting on the bed in the small room one of the 'Welcomers' had made a great fuss of taking him to, even guiding him round the tiny bathroom – at one point he thought the poor chap was actually going to demonstrate how to flush the loo - Thomas could just see out of the window.

His room appeared to be in one of the Hall's many turrets. His turret faced the rear of the house; if he stood up he could make out a vegetable patch in a walled garden and on tip toe, the corner of a greenhouse. He thought he saw a man, bent over, dressed in overalls but the light was fading and he was weary. The day had grown more grey and his view, considering the grandeur of the house and its landscape, positively gloomy. He kicked the squeaky, wheelie suitcase. Perhaps when they were all in bed he could call a taxi and go home.

He must have dozed off. There was a tapping noise, a creak and a shaft of light seared the darkness. Panic pounded in his chest, where was he? A lamp snapped on.

"Sorry to disturb but you didn't come down for supper. Something on a tray, will that suit?" Willoughby was hovering at the foot of the bed. Thomas could taste perspiration on his upper lip. "Just this once mind, you'll have to join in tomorrow. I know it's hard but just take that first step, it'll be worth it, you see."

Everything on the tray was freezing cold even the soup, yet the ice cream had melted, a swirling splodge of raspberry in a creamy frame, like blood dripped into milk. Thomas felt his stomach lurch and pushed the tray away. He fumbled in his pocket for a sleeping pill, swallowed it down and pulling the eiderdown over his head, stayed like that until dawn.

As soon as Thomas opened his door the following morning Willoughby appeared, wearing what looked like a translucent tracksuit.

"Ah, there you are, excellent, breakfast and then straight into our first session, Bereavement for Beginners." Thomas stifled a sigh and followed the glowing figure downstairs.

Sitting in the corner of the palatial former drawing room for the dreaded first session, Thomas could see across the courtyard to the edge of the walled garden. He recognised the greenhouse he had spotted from his turret window, a man with white hair appeared at the gateway, pushing an ancient wheelbarrow. The man stood up, straightened his back and smiled, a big broad grin straight at Thomas and then trundled off into the distance. Thomas watched him leave with longing.

It felt like a meeting of Alcoholics Anonymous, with members of the group volunteering to stand up and recount personal experiences. Some had been tearful, choked with emotion, while others had been desperate to pass on their pain. Thomas felt nothing, he just sat there wondering if the woman conducting the session had ever lost so much as a button, let alone a life partner. He was desperate to escape and so while the others chatted mutely over coffee, he quickly slipped away and out into the crisp March morning.

He drew a long, deep breath of air and gripping his nostrils blew hard as if to dislodge a blockage. Sniffing, he could smell burning, tendrils of smoke drifted a soft musky scent towards him through the gap, where the gate to the walled garden stood ajar. Stealthily, he crossed the frosty stone flags, pulling the gate behind him and, leaning against it, closed his eyes. When he opened them, he could see the old gardener through the greenhouse. The man looked up, crinkly eyes twinkled as grubby hands beckoned him in.

"It's you I saw, in there, staring out the window, wishing you were somewhere else," the man said. Thomas nodded.

"What's it this time? Teach Yourself Charisma? Write a Best Seller in a Weekend? Or How to find your Perfect Partner?" there was a smile about the man's mouth.

"Bereavement and Beyond," Thomas picked up one of the pots, nearly dropping it as the man's booming laughter ricocheted around the glass.

"Bet that's a total riot, got to be one of the best yet, what will they think of next?" No sympathy, no word of condolence. "No wonder you look so desperate. You never know, you might discover your charisma, find your perfect partner and write a best seller about the whole bloody thing," he chortled throatily to himself, emptying the last of the earth from the pots into a large tray, sifting it through with his fingers.

"My daughter, Denise, booked it, it was her idea, she insisted I came," Thomas said dolefully.

"A bit of a bossy boots is she?" the other man asked.

"She's just worried about me, I've been a bit weird since her mother died."

The man was picking tiny lumps gently out of the soil, transferring them into individual containers, then covering them tenderly with moist, black peat.

"What are you doing?" Thomas asked.

"Giving 'em a second chance. Sometimes things are best left, quietly in the darkness. If there's life there, it'll come back, eventually," the man rubbed his chin, giving Thomas the once over. "You're not a gardener?"

"No, my wife looked after that side of things. I work away a lot, not much time for gardening."

"Gardening doesn't take time, it's other things take time away from gardening," the old man was watching him with shrewd eyes.

A bell clanked across the courtyard. Thomas looked up.

"Better get back to your bereavement buddies, what's on the agenda this afternoon, embalming for beginners?" the man grinned. Thomas shrugged. "Come back at tea time, I've got a flask'll do you more good."

"Oh, what's that then?"

"Blackcurrant vodka."

Thomas momentarily cheered.

It was easy for Thomas to duck out at four o'clock, Willoughby had given them an 'unstructured' hour to help deal with any guilt relating to the dearly departed. The gardener was in the greenhouse, warming himself by a rusty stove. He waved Thomas in and handed him a mug of jewel coloured liquid. Thomas sipped, sweet nectar burned his throat and warmed his chest instantly.

"Swig it back man," the gardener insisted, "Plenty more where that came from. Good wife was she?" The gardener asked after a while.

"I thought so," Thomas took a generous refill. "Until she died anyway."

The old man signalled for him to continue. Thomas took a deep breath.

"Clearing out her things, I found stuff, letters and photographs, some old, some not so old, but all from people I didn't know."

"You mean people you didn't know about. Men?"

Thomas nodded.

"How many men?"

"Three or four."

"Were they graphic, these letters? Had she been intimate with these men, were they lovers?"

"Not really clear, nothing graphic, more flirting, talking about dinner dates, dancing, going to the movies together, that sort of thing," Thomas was surprised he was just blurting it all out. Something he had not been able to even think about, let alone talk about. Something that had been lodged in his chest, like a lump of granite.

"Didn't mean much then sounds like, just the company of the opposite sex and a bit of flattery more than anything, and you did say yourself, you work away a lot. She was probably just a bit lonely. You'll have lots more letters and pictures of happy family times together, I'd imagine." It was a statement. "What's the problem, do you feel betrayed?"

Thomas felt sure he should be uncomfortable having this highly personal conversation with a stranger, but he nevertheless he answered.

"No, that's the problem, I don't feel anything, no grief, no anger, nothing," Thomas said, flatly.

The gardener poked the stove. "Guilt then?"

"For what?" Thomas was shocked. "I've never been unfaithful."

"There's more than one way to stray. A mistress doesn't have to lie abed to take your heart or your soul. Other things can do it just as well, work, business, a hobby. Doesn't take much to leave a woman, even if you're still with her," the gardener poured more drinks.

Saved by the bell. Thomas quickly departed, glad to leave the old man to his twaddly, homespun wisdom.

After supper and before the session 'Rediscover Laughter' Thomas found himself alone in the greenhouse. The neat rows of pots stood silently awaiting the reawakening of the seeds inside. He lifted one to gaze at the surface and see if there was yet any sign of life and as he reached across, a fat envelope thudded to the floor. His wife's collection of memorabilia, snaps and scraps of fanciful romance with other men, letters, photographs, ticket stubs. He had been carrying it around with him since he found it in the old suitcase, at the back of the wardrobe. She had always loved a romantic hero. She liked to go dancing, out for Italian meals, popcorn at the movies ...no real hobbies to speak of, except gardening, she loved to grow flowers, roses were her favourite, corny but true.

Suddenly, Thomas bent to the ground and snatching the bundle up, lifted the lid of the stove and thrust the envelope inside, pushing the papers against the embers with the poker until it smouldered and burst into flame; devouring the words and smiling faces of memories that did not belong to him; memories and photos of a woman he had always assumed did.

"Well done, that was just going out I reckon," the old man was standing behind him. He proffered a mug of the blackcurrant vodka. Thomas who had never been a drinker, knocked it straight back, hoping it would dissolve the granite.

The next morning Willoughby and the 'Welcomers' were lined along the steps, shaking hands and saying sincere goodbyes to everyone.

"I hope that helped," Willoughby looked deep into Thomas' face.

"Dunno if I'm honest. I liked the old gardener though, nice line in blackcurrant vodka."

Willoughby arched an eyebrow. "So, it was you then. I wondered who he would choose this time."

Thomas tilted his head. "Choose?"

"Oh yes, he always picks one we can't help does old Protheroe. Cost effective too, no salary to find for a counsellor from the other side, a spirit guide in more ways than one, that's what we call old Protheroe," he gave Thomas a brief hug. "I'm so pleased for you."

Thomas sat at the back of the coach, straining to catch a last glimpse of the walled garden as they drove away, he thought he could see him, he was sure he waved. But maybe not.

"Did it help, Dad?" Denise was anxious, her father had been so cold, so unfeeling since mum died, he had hardly said a word, she really was at her wits end.

"Nah, I hate all that new age claptrap, you know I do!" Thomas said, he had just finished framing an old photograph, one of himself and his wife, taken years ago. She looked pink and shiny, they had been dancing, in a competition, they were quite good back in the day. He placed a rose from the garden in a champagne glass beside it. Standing back, he was pleased with his work.

"Make any friends? Decide on a new hobby?" Denise said, hopefully.

"Might try gardening," Thomas said, giving the girl in the photograph a brief smile.

THE END

Stranger than Fiction… from Adrienne Vaughan

"When I married my husband he took me to where the family came from in Herefordshire and told me that Arthur Conan Doyle's Hound of the Baskervilles should have been the 'Hound of the Vaughans' as the great Conan Doyle wrote the story while staying at Clyro Court, the ancestral home of the warlord Black Vaughan.

We arrived with our elderly, black (of course) dog, Wodehouse (after my favourite author PG) and our two puppies, Winston and Wellington. I could barely carry the key to our room it was so big, but when I was told we had a massive four poster bed in a vast suite, I could hardly wait to see it.

Climbing the sweeping, staircase, with full galleried landing and a plethora of portraits gazing down at us, Wodehouse suddenly froze, every hair on his and my body stood to attention, and as sure as I sit here now, someone breathed warm air on the back of my neck. The puppies started to tremble, and Wodehouse threw back his head and howled. I had never heard him do that before and he never did it again. He stopped, we looked at each other, and grabbing both the puppies up in my arms, I quickly changed my mind about seeing the room, as we flew down the stairs to join my husband chatting happily with the owner in the bar. Needless to say, we all slept together in the four poster, talk about a 'three dog night!'

Spooky…!

Adrienne Vaughan – About the Author

Born in Leicester and brought up in Dublin, Adrienne Vaughan has been making up stories since she could speak, as soon as she could pick up a pen she started writing them down. It was no surprise she wanted to be a journalist; ideally the editor of a glossy magazine, so she could meet and marry a rock star!

Today, she runs a busy PR practice and writes poems, short stories and ideas for books in her spare time. She is a member of the Romantic Novelists' Association and a founder member of the indie publishing group The New Romantics 4.

Adrienne lives in Leicestershire with her husband, two cocker spaniels, Agatha Christie – the rescue cat and a retired dressage horse called Marco.

The sequel to The Hollow Heart, titled A Change of Heart is available now, and the final book in the trilogy Secrets of the Heart will be published in autumn 2014.

Publication could be delayed however, if she gets the call to be the latest, if rather mature - *Bond girl!*

KEEP IN TOUCH

Twitter - @adrienneauthor

Email - adrienne@adriennevaughan.com

The Hollow Heart
http://viewbook.at/TheHollowHeart

A Change of Heart
http://viewbook.at/AChangeofHeart

Letter for Ray

By

Carolyn Mahony

Letter for Ray – a short story by Carolyn Mahony

'My Darling Ray,

As I sit here writing this letter to you, we both know that my life is nearly over, and suddenly I am feeling so old and weary. Too weary indeed to carry on concealing from you the truth about the terrible thing I did so many years ago.

I'm sorry that I'm not brave enough to face you openly with these revelations, but my life with you has been so complete that I want nothing to mar the short time I have left with you. I'm therefore going to leave this letter with our solicitor, to be passed onto you after I've gone. I hope that in time you might come to understand and even find it in your heart to forgive, the terrible crime I committed on this day forty five years ago - and the continuing lie I've lived ever since...'

My pen falters in its writing and I gaze unseeingly out of the window, the years rolling away as the memories of that day flood back and fill me with remorse. It isn't a new experience. I've lived with guilt long enough to know it's not a comfortable bed companion, and it sometimes rears its head at the most inconvenient of times. But today I'm going nowhere. No visitors are expected and I can face my demons in the sure knowledge that I won't be interrupted. It's something I need to do.

Do I believe in an after-life? I still don't know. But my desire to believe is overshadowed by the certain knowledge that if hell exists, that will surely be my destination. In days, possibly hours, my day of reckoning will come and I could be face to face with the sister who died as a direct result of my actions.

There was no excusing it. I'd known that at the time and I know it now. But I've always clung to the hope that wherever Paula was out there in the universe, she maybe had the power to understand me better than I understood myself - could see that I'd done it out of love for Ray – my husband. Whilst it was no justification, it had been the catalyst to spark off that moment of madness.

And I'd tried – God, how I'd tried – to make up for it ever since.

A chilling sense of foreboding swamps me as I lie propped up in my bed gazing out of the open window, and I pull the bedcovers more firmly around me. It's the same chilling feeling I'd experienced as I'd entered my sister's room – the one she always used when she stayed with us - and found it empty.

She'd been so distraught after the dreadful row we'd had, and I'd been so angry I could have killed her. That anger and resentment burned deep as I went to her room that night and wondered where she could be. I'd been sure that like me, she'd have been unable to sleep and I wasn't prepared to let matters rest. Ray was due back from France in the morning and I knew if I was to keep him, I had to convince my sister that she had to walk away - give him up.

I'd been shocked though not necessarily surprised, when I'd found out about their affair. Paula was so much better than I, so much *nicer* - of course it was only a matter of time before he was going to realise that.

But he was mine. Not hers. And what had really shocked me was that my own sister – my *twin* sister – could do such a thing.

In no mood for compromise, I looked around the empty room, wondering where she could be. Her softer nature would also be her weakness, I realised. I could see that she was tormented by guilt and I would play on that, as I had all our lives.

Something drew me over to the window to look down at the lake in the beautiful grounds of our house. Perhaps it was the kindred spirit of two souls intertwined since birth - linked in the way only identical twins can be - that told me she'd be seeking solace from her troubled thoughts in the peaceful serenity of the gardens as she often did. Gardens I thought she loved because of their link to me. Not because of her link to Ray.

Or perhaps it was the uncanny sixth sense we'd always shared - just as we shared our blonde locks, blue eyes and perfect teeth. That sense had clearly let me down in recent months – I'd been aware of the growing jealous rivalry between us but had never for one minute suspected the reason for it. And I'd been as guilty as she of that – I'd got used to being the stronger one. The winner.

A brief flash of movement over by the far side of the lake had me mindlessly rushing out of the room – my one burning desire, the need to confront her and resolve this situation once and for all.

Fifteen minutes later, shocked and wet, I slid numbly back into my bedroom and closed the door silently behind me. I leant against it in frozen disbelief.

It hadn't happened, I thought hysterically. It surely hadn't happened? But there was no escaping the fact that it had, and as I looked down at my still wet hands, they served as a gruesome reminder of the terrible scene I'd just left behind me … my sister's lifeless body floating face down on the cold, barely moving surface of the water.

I was shaking from head to toe. I wanted to scream but no sound would come, and instead I sank to my knees and rocked back and forth in silent agony. I loved my sister. Why hadn't I saved her?

Because I loved Ray more.

I'd always been the selfish one but up until that day I could never have imagined how far I would go to preserve my own happiness.

When she'd walked into that lake, screaming at me that if she couldn't have Ray then life wasn't worth living, I'd started in after her and we'd struggled. But then I'd asked myself why? Why was I trying to stop her when she was going to destroy my life? I felt emotionless as I let go of her arm and watched her walk deeper into the water. *Go then* … this unexpected solution was my right, my due - and I would take it, I thought, as I watched her head submerge below the surface.

But now the blood was coursing through my veins again - reality was sinking in. My sister was dead and I'd done nothing to save her. How could I? How could I have let her do it? It *had* to be a crime that I'd watched someone commit suicide and done nothing to prevent it. God knew I hadn't wanted it to end like this. And so much of what she'd accused me of in our argument was true. I *was* selfish, I *was* careless of others' needs – I was indeed a narcissistic butterfly. I realised that now, with an anguish that tore at my heart, where previously I'd have scoffed at such claims.

No wonder my husband had chosen her over me.

And now it was too late to change anything. For not only had I been the cause of my sister's death, but as a result I was about to lose everything I held dear – the wonderful lifestyle, the beautiful house, my freedom. But more than all of that, I'd lose Ray. And that would break my heart. I wrung my hands and paced the room. Then stopped dead. Slowly, tentatively, an idea was unfolding. It seemed impossible. Could I get away with it? Yet what did I have to lose? I shuddered at the thought of questions, courtrooms, prison. An empty bed beside me – the world knowing what I'd done. Paula was dead but if I could only hold my nerve there could be a way out - and maybe even yet, her death might have a purpose. One that suited me.

With calm deliberation I wrote a note, left it on Ray's pillow and crept into the guest room that Paula had been using. I changed into her nightclothes – a perfect fit, as I knew they'd be – and put my own wet clothes in the washing machine.

A few other tweaks, mostly to my hair, and even the mirror didn't betray me. Then I climbed into her bed and waited. By the time the distraught housekeeper knocked on my door several hours later to break the tragic news of 'my' death, a cold logical stranger had inhabited my body.

I would become Paula.

Ginette would be no more.

Too easily I began to spin the web that was to hold me in its grip for the next forty-five years.

No one had any reason to doubt my story. Why should they, when the suicide note in Ginette's writing had been found on Ray's pillow?

The Inspector had been sympathetic, commenting kindly that the loss of a twin must surely be even harder to bear than that of a normal sibling, and my eyes had shed rivers of tears – unbeknown to him, fed by fear, shame and guilt.

I furnished him with as many facts as I could – including the name of the Paris hotel where I knew Ray was staying. Then I took my leave. I headed for Paula's cold, silent flat where I guessed Ray would soon be contacting me. I showered in her bath products, covered myself in her body lotion and changed into her clothes. Then I waited, rehearsing, rehearsing, rehearsing.

Even so it came as a shock when the doorbell rang much later that evening, and looking out onto the London street below, I saw his white Mercedes parked outside as if it belonged there.

I drew a breath. The moment of truth.

Opening the door I was shocked at the haggard expression on his face, though I knew mine must look exactly the same.

'God, Paula.'

The name sounded strange on his lips; the way he said it made something snap in my heart - but I would need to get used to that. I longed for the reassuring comfort of his hold but was glad that he didn't take me straight into his arms.

Instead he moved stiffly over to the cabinet and picked up the photo that always sat there. My sister and I, when we were seventeen – ten years ago – the identical grinning faces showing not a care in the world.

His eyes filled with tears as he placed it tenderly back down and looked at me.

'I told her, you know,' he said in deathly quiet tones. 'I just couldn't bear deceiving her and living this lie any longer. It's all my fault. If I'd had any idea she'd do anything so drastic...'

His voice broke and he shook his head despairingly. 'I just can't believe she'd do such a thing.'

His hands shook as he ran them agonizingly through his hair, his normally vivid blue eyes staring dully into space. 'Did Ginny tell you? That I'd told her?'

I nodded bleakly, the hurt of the terrible things we sisters had said to each other still raw in my mind. I was afraid to say anything. Afraid I might give myself away. But I burst into tears and fell into his arms as I took the risk and spoke.

I told him how 'she' had phoned asking me to go over there the day before. How I'd known straight away from the tone of her voice that something was seriously wrong, and how, without her even having to say it, I'd known that she'd found out about the affair.

My hands started to shake quite genuinely and my knees buckled so that I was forced to sit on the sofa for support. I could feel myself going white – going cold - shutting down. Yes, I could stay this way – that would work. For the moment. Maybe forever. No one would expect a twin to be the same again, surely?

Ray sat down next to me and slid his arm comfortingly around my shoulder.

'It's ok, it's ok,' he soothed, playing with my hair the way he had in our courting days. I could feel his eyes boring into me and my heart skipped a beat.

'Look at me,' he said, almost brusquely.

I forced my terrified gaze to meet his. Had he recognised me?

But he kissed me tenderly on the lips. 'I wouldn't have had this happen for the world,' he said quietly, 'but don't think for one minute I'm going to let it change things between us. Things won't be easy but in time we'll make a good life for ourselves. You'll see.'

I exhaled sharply and sobbed some more – deep, deep sobs of relief as much as sorrow. And as I stared doubtfully into his eyes I realised he was right. We *could* put this behind us. My sister and I were like peas in a pod, everyone said so. And if with different makeup and a switching of the parting in my hair, my own husband didn't recognise me, then surely it wouldn't be too difficult a task convincing everyone else?

He didn't deserve the treatment I'd dished out to him in the four years we'd been married - my pleasure-seeking self-centredness, my declaration that I didn't want children, my careless disregard for his feelings.

I closed my eyes and prayed to God for forgiveness of what I was about to do. I thought I could smell jasmine – the scent of my sister's perfume, and for a moment Paula's face flashed in front of me – her usual gentle smile obliterated by the reproach in her gaze. I shook off the image. She would not have died in vain, I vowed to myself. If I could pull this deception off I was being handed another chance – the chance to really make something of my life with the man I loved. And if the price of getting his love in return was that I had to pretend to be my sister, then so be it.

The smell of jasmine grew stronger, nauseating me. But there was no going back. The gap between Ray and I had become way too wide for him to consider staying with me had he known that it was I, Ginny, and not Paula who was seated beside him right now. But I would make it up to him. Yes, that's what I'd do – I'd spend the years ahead of us making it up to him. And to Paula.

And so it was that through more than four decades... incredibly ... still no one knew. I'd fooled them all.

After a shaky start, I'd absorbed my sister's identity so wholly and completely, that even I sometimes forgot who I really was. I'd had a few close shaves of course – it isn't easy taking over someone else's life, no matter how well you know them - but quitting my sister's job had been the biggest action I'd needed to take, and I'd done that there and then. No one had thought it unreasonable.

As for my numerous lapses of memory, especially in the early days, they were conveniently attributed to post traumatic stress disorder at losing my identical twin – a diagnosis that has served me very well over the years.

Marrying Ray for a second time had felt bizarre - and this time I gave my vows with a solemnity that had been lacking before.

But if ever I was tempted to feel complacent about what I'd achieved, or feel that I'd got off lightly, I'd just remember that the light of love in his eyes was meant for my sister, not me. In a strange way I took comfort from that. It was my punishment. My just desserts for what I'd done.

But now – now with increasing age and illness - my over-active conscience can no longer be suppressed. Stupid maybe, but if I'm about to meet up with Paula I know she would want it to be with a clean slate. She would want me to tell Ray the truth. I surely owe them both that.

Of its own volition, my pen flows freely over the pages as I pour my life's confession onto the stark white paper. When I'm finished I lie weakly back on my pillows. I feel a little better for the confession. Isn't that what the psychotherapists always say – write it down and it will help, even if you don't send it?

My pen hovers uncertainly over the final signature.

Despite everything, Ray and I have been happy these last forty-five years. We have two lovely children. Do I really want to destroy all that? Taint their memories of me? Do I?

But it's the one selfless act I can do to try to make amends to Paula. Wouldn't she say I owe it to her to clear the slate? So that Ray finally knows the truth of what happened that day?

Still I pause. A breeze flutters through the open window. Even though it's a warm day, I feel a chill in the air; sense a presence in the room.

And there it is again. The scent of jasmine – faint at first and then stronger - until it overwhelms me with nausea. I can't see my sister but suddenly I'm taken back to all those times in our childhood when we connected instinctively, when we knew without words that the other was there; what she was thinking or doing.

She's here in this room, waiting for me. I can feel it. My heart quickens.

'Paula?' I whisper. My fear of what awaits me is increasing. I know without any doctor telling me that today will be the day I die. The day I face my reckoning. I also know that if I'm to have any chance of redeeming my soul I must leave the confession for Ray.

My eyes drop weakly to the pieces of paper in my hand. The sickness dissipates slightly. I can feel Paula willing me to do what is right by her and Ray. She wants me to tell him. She knows about the enormous burden of guilt that's been cloaked around him like a heavy shroud all these years – that his wife committed suicide because of his affair. How much easier would it be to bear that load, if he knew his lover had died because his wife had let her? But he would surely hate me for it. In his eyes I'd be relegated from tragic suicidal wife to callous, cold-blooded murderer. And Paula would have won.

I can't do it.

Very carefully, I shred the letter into strips and drop it into the bin at the side of my bed.

I hear a hiss and a screeching sound. It's like nothing I've heard on earth before, and I know it's the sound of my sister's rage. I can see nothing. Only feel.

And what I feel chills me to the bone.

But it's too late. It's too late. I feel the panic rise as a light begins to engulf me. I struggle to breathe.

'Paula!' I cry.

But there is nothing. I know she's gone as I feel my soul being sucked into a swirling void.

Something is waiting for me - reaching out with cold finger to grasp me. But it isn't Paula.

THE END

Carolyn Mahony – About the Author

Hello everyone. A brief introduction to who I am - just in case you're interested. I think I can best be described as a retired domestic cook, cleaner and bottle washer. Now that my family have grown up and moved on I finally have the time to do what I absolutely love - putting pen to paper and writing my stories. I've been writing for as long as I can remember – my first literary masterpiece was an attempt at a Georgette Heyer style Regency Romance at the age of fifteen. Unfortunately, I didn't get past the third chapter but that was the start of a love affair that my husband describes as the 'third person in our marriage'.

My debut mystery/crime novel - Cry From The Grave - was released at the end of last year and I've been thrilled at the generous feedback I've received. People have been very positive in their reviews, and that gave me the confidence to plough on and write another novel in a similar genre (this time more of a romantic suspense, to be released by early 2015). I've never written a short story before so Hocus Pocus proved to be something of a challenge. I hope you enjoy my contribution but I know I'm up against some superb authors, all of whom have done a terrific job with their stories.

If you'd like to take a look in more detail at who I am, this is the link to my website – www.carolynmahony.com Do sign up to my mailing list and you'll receive advance notification of when my next novel will be released. You'll also have a chance to win a free copy of Cry From The Grave, so give it a go – you never know!

Carolyn Mahony – KEEP IN TOUCH

Twitter - @carolynmahony

Facebook – www.facebook.com/carolyn.mahony.3

Cry From The Grave

http://amzn.to/1eNtrLb

Have fun with your reading and enjoy our Anthology!

Heaven Must Be Missing An Angel

By
Jules Wake

Heaven Must be Missing an Angel – a short story by Jules Wake

When she was little, Amy thought sunbeams were magical. As she got older, she didn't give a toss until five minutes ago when she discovered they're actually the equivalent of a celestial lift-shaft.

Unfortunately like a lot things up there, Heaven hasn't quite got technology taped. As transportation systems go, sunbeams are pretty rudimentary – along with uncomfortable and unreliable. Turned out she came back to earth with one hell of a bump, although landing on top of a tall dark stranger wasn't a total write off and by the looks of things he lived in a very swanky pad.

If he lost the pout he'd have been a hell of a looker. And would 'they' just quit with the tug on the big toe every time she blasphemed or whatever. It hurt. This afterlife gig wasn't turning out to be much fun.

Was it her fault she'd landed on him? You try flying on learner wings – it's Top Gun without stabilisers. A serious head rush - and she was an expert on those.

OK, she hadn't *landed* 'landed' on him, just kind of fallen on top of him when he'd surprised her.

She wasn't expecting to arrive back on earth in a kitchen, especially not one like this with its uber cool Star Wars, Darth Vader vibe going on. Handy really because she had the munchies; he had a fridge full of food – so what was his problem?

If she could have cleaned out the fridge and vamoosed it would have been fine but clearly the guy was brave because he'd decided to investigate.

'You shouldn't go round creeping up on people,' she said watching him rub his ankle. 'And where is this? And why is there no chocolate in your fridge?'

His face went through outrage to disbelief then back to shirty. 'Excuse me, but this is my flat and you're breaking and entering.'

Boy he was stupid. 'You ever see a burglar dressed like this?' Amy gave a twirl. The whole get-up was seriously over the top but it was real old school up there - tradition, tradition, tradition. And the rules … Jeez.

'I hate to tell you this,' said Mr Sulky Chops pursing those almost cute lips, 'I don't know how you got in but you've got the wrong place. This is Duchy Mansions -'

'Harrogate?'

That was a surprise. Back on home turf.

'The fancy dress party is somewhere else,' he said.

'Very funny. Seen these babies?' She gave the two-ton wings a waggle.

'Impressive ...' Doubt crept across his face as he studied the tall white columns of feathers and then looked down at the floor. Where her feet should have been.

He paled.

Amy smirked as he shook his head and rubbed at his eyes. Being able to hover a couple of inches off the ground was kind of cool, although he now looked completely spooked by it, but at least it made him pay attention.

'Told you. I'm your Guardian Angel.' She gritted her teeth as the invisible string around her toe tightened with a strong yank from 'beyond.' What? Hadn't they heard of poetic licence?

Once he'd got over the shock, which took a couple of stiff drinks, it turned out his name was Ben.

'Since when do angels go in for B and E?' He frowned, his face still looking on the white side.

'I'm not burglarising you ...' She looked round with a practised eye, 'you got naff all to pinch.' Most of it was too high end and distinctive. Although the iPad would fetch a bit and the nifty docking station was worth something. 'I'm on a mission.' Now that sounded more like it - a Charlie's style angel. Maybe she also had super powers and could kick ass.

'What? James Bond in a frock?'

Oooh, Mr Sulky Pants had found sarcasm.

'What's your mission? Feeding the homeless from my fridge?'

He had her there. Just what the *he...ck* was her mission?

Not the most promising start to her celestial assignment. Of course she hadn't paid attention, what did they expect? If school had been a pain in the proverbial five years ago, Heaven's version was even worse. Lots of long drawn out lectures, all prosy and preachy. *D-U double L.* The only bright side, and very bright and shiny he was too, came in the shape of Gorgeous Gabe. Gabriel to those in the know – now he was a serious hottie. But he had to go and spoil things with his Redemption morality crap.

Thank *Go...* OK, OK ... Thank *...fully* there'd been a convenient hand-out at the end of that last lecture. Unfortunately the bugger weighed a ton and was brick ugly – you'd have thought in Heaven the manuals would come with a nice bag – say Gucci or something. Anyway it was far too heavy to be carting round. Bottom line was she had no freaking idea what she was supposed to do here. And once upon a time she wouldn't have cared but ... something stuck in her head, an annoying insistent buzz and she had a quick flashback of Gabriel's face, earnest and ...

Oops, not going there.

She had a vague memory of tearing out the last few pages and stuffing them in that girdle-with-pocket thing around her waist. She patted herself. Sure enough there they were. She yanked out two parchment pages, which fluttered to the floor. She managed to grab one but Ben was quicker.

'Sarah,' he read from the other one, 'it's ... a recipe? Chocolate tart?'

She snatched the paper from him. 'Oh *sh* ... sugar.' A memory rocketed through her brain. *Christ in a handbasket.* 'Ow!' She hopped up and down, clutching her toe through her biblical leather sandal.

'Mean anything? This note?' he asked, his nose quivering like he was some kind of blood hound on the scent of a clue.

Oh, yeah it meant something all right. Sarah was her saintly, sanctimonious sister. Sarah, who would have looked much better than Amy did in this get up. Sarah, the perfect damn angel – golden hair, insipid blue eyes and a bit on the plump side. Amy took a quick glance at her own arms, *yup* still lovely and thin.

Now it was all coming back to her.

'I'm supposed to find my sister.'

Her heart sank. *Find Sarah.* Now wouldn't *that* be a bundle of laughs. Amy would much rather just stay here, getting to know Mr-Increasingly-Better-Looking-All-The-Time.

Ben's face softened. 'Sarah's your sister?' It was as if he felt sorry for her.

'Yeah,' Amy said, her chin in the air. She refrained from adding, 'the boring bitch.' Somehow she didn't think he'd approve.

'So? Do you know where she lives?' he asked.

'I guess.' She shrugged. Like she kept tabs on Sarah! 'Near here... somewhere,' she said, recognising The Stray outside his window.

'So have you lost her address?'

Chr... Gosh he was persistent. 'No, I just haven't been to her house for a while.'

Living in the squat had been easier. No one watching you coming and going.

'What about your parents?' Ben had that kind, sympathetic-without-pity look on his face.

'They died. Fifteen years ago.'

Ben swallowed, looking uncomfortable before he said, 'Didn't you see them? You know ...' He nodded upwards.

She laughed without mirth. 'You're kidding. I'm still this side of the gates – not allowed in until I've proved my ... something or other.' It came to her in a flood of images. She needed to find Sarah. If she didn't, she'd be stuck in that classroom forever more. *Christ* – ow! That tug on her toe really hurt – she might as well have gone straight to hell.

He looked thoughtful. 'So your sister's alone. We'd better find her.' He paused and turned. 'And what about the recipe?'

She shrugged and rolled her eyes. 'Not important.'

Amy felt a smidge guilty sending Ben striding off up the path. Bless him, he thought he was being a knight in shining armour, doing her a massive favour. He had no idea, the poor sucker. She could guarantee Sarah wasn't going to be pleased to see her. Miserable cow. But needs must. There was no way she wanted to stay in that *blood...* blessed classroom.

She plodded towards the front door, her wings dragging heavily at her back, feeling the familiar depression that still lurked in her mind at the mere thought of Sarah.

'Hi, you don't know me but I'm here about your sister.' Sarah's eyebrows raised, and Ben flashed his easy confident smile at her. Amy could tell he was taken by her, from the sudden widening of his pupils. Funny how she noticed things like that, now. Not much of a super power, though. Poor guy, he was clearly entranced by Sarah, by the cloud of blonde hair, back-lit by the hall light as she stood in the doorway clutching the frame, her knuckles white.

'My sister?' Sarah's voice went flat, the original enquiring spark in her eyes snuffed out by Ben's words. 'You'd better come in.'

Hiding on the other side of the porch, Amy gave Ben a quick shove. 'You go, break it to her gently before I appear. Probably best.'

He gave her an uncertain look and followed Sarah into the house, and into the kitchen.

Unnoticed by either of them, Amy crept into the hall, hiding in the shadow just beyond the door frame.

From there she could see that old familiar kitchen, still cluttered but not untidy. Nothing had changed. Nothing. Her heart twisted as if pinched by invisible fingers. Pottery chickens danced along the dresser, along with a mixed collection of colourful china plates and mugs. Quirky without being kitsch. The four inch red and orange hen on the far left had been a birthday present from Sarah a couple of years ago, when Amy still found that kind of stuff cute. In fact most of the chickens were originally hers, and nearly all were presents from Sarah. Amy was surprised she'd kept them.

Sarah offered Ben some coffee and moved around the kitchen, her movements sure and relaxed. Of course, she made him 'proper' coffee, in a cafetière, before taking a moment, as she always did, to choose just the right cup for her guest. Amy's mouth quirked. Her sister was big on looking after people.

Once Sarah handed the coffee to Ben, she sat down opposite him, her hands clutching the body of her cup, as if incubating it. Thinking.

'I'm sorry ... I don't know how well you knew Amy but ... she's dead.' Sarah sighed, her blue eyes looking down at the table, instead of meeting Ben's gaze.

Surely she'd been happy to be rid of her pain in the butt? The let down she called sister? After all, Amy had given Sarah nothing but grief for the last few years.

But now she noticed how drawn Sarah looked – dark shadows under her eyes, gaunt. Amy frowned. She hadn't expected Sarah to look so very tired... and sad.

'I ... er ... I know, that's why I'm here,' Ben said at last.

For a moment Amy almost felt sorry for her sister – until she saw her sit up straighter, a mulish expression snapping into place on her face. Dear old Sarah, girding her loins, to do the right thing. Oh, yes her do-good sister was great at that.

What tale was she going to spin Ben? Suddenly Amy just wanted to get him out of there.

'Your sister ...' Ben looked towards the hall.

If he wanted her to appear as if by magic, he could whistle. She wasn't moving, not with Sarah looking all old sourpuss like that.

Sarah's lip curled. 'Don't tell me. She owed you money. Rent? Bills? Or did she just steal from you?' Then her blue eyes clouded. 'What do you want?' Sarah shrugged. 'My sister's gone. She made some mistakes. Whatever you're owed, I can repay it but it'll take some time.' She drooped over her coffee.

Ben, clearly taken in by her little act, covered her hand with his. 'Hey, I'm sorry but that's not why I'm here?' He looked confused now.

Out in the hall, Amy winced, her wings feeling heavier than ever. She could see it, the dumb bastard was going over to the dark side.

'Amy, your sister … I didn't even know her name … she's here … she's an angel.' There was a question in his voice as if he couldn't quite believe what he was saying.

Rather surprisingly, prissy Sarah's manners vanished, and she burst out laughing. Helpless giggles at first, quickly turning to tearful sobs and then just when she seemed in danger of outright hysteria, she grasped her mug and glared at him.

'What do you *want*?' she snapped.

'Look.' Ben stood up and paced, his hand pushing through the flopping bit of hair at the front. He looked confused and all Hugh Grant. It was quite cute, really.

'I know it sounds unbelievable–'

'Unbelievable. Totally … I think you should leave. Now.'

'Look, I know …' He turned round as Amy stepped into the kitchen. 'See …' He pointed but Sarah gave no sign of seeing her. 'Here …' He pointed again.

Sarah's face tightened but tears glimmered in her eyes. 'I don't know what game you think you're playing but please just leave.'

Ben glared at Amy, shrugged and turned to go.

Great. Just great. He was giving up already.

'Wait!' Amy called out, 'Give her the recipe.'

'The recipe?' His face screwed up in disbelief.

'The what?! What recipe?' Sarah's voice cut through the air with the precision of a guillotine. Even Ben jumped at her tone.

He pulled the folded parchment from his pocket and handed it over.

Sarah's face paled as she smoothed out the creases. 'Where did you get this?' she whispered.

Ben glanced uncertainly back at her. 'From your sister. I know … it sounds mad but she… just turned up – in my flat.'

'And she gave you this … to give to me?'

He nodded, crossing his fingers. Sarah saw them and shook her head. 'Ben, you didn't know Amy, did you.'

'No, like I said, never met her - until she turned up at my flat. As an *an-gel.*'

'An Angel …? Amy …?' Sarah stopped and smiled. 'I had her down as heading straight to hell. Well, what do you know.' Her face lit up with a golden smile. *Christ,* the bitch almost sounded as if she cared. 'Good for her.'

'Don't you want to speak to her? See her?' Ben was looking hopefully at the door. Hoping that she might come to his rescue – prove he wasn't totally barking.

'No.' Sarah smiled again. 'It's enough to know she's at peace.'

Ben looked uncertain. 'But …'

'She had a troubled life. We were twins–'

'Twins!'

That surprised him, Amy almost giggled at the look on his face. You'd have thought he'd swallowed a horse whole.

'Still looking like a walking skeleton?' asked Sarah.

Cheeky cow. She was just jealous.

'That's what heroin addiction does.' Sarah shook her head. 'She never ate properly except ….' She stroked the folded parchment. 'I tried to help her but …' Sarah's face crumpled and tears started to slide out of her eyes.

Hypocrite. She was the one that did the throwing out. Changed the locks. Just like that. What kind of sister does that? And now there she was pretending to be all sad and contrite.

'It got so bad. The stealing and lying. Then ...' Sarah's voice hitched, with just the right amount of drama. 'It sounds so pathetic now ... this was Mum's recipe. Neither of us liked dried fruit, so she always made this Chocolate Tart for us at Christmas. I used to make it for Amy when she was ... ill, trying to feed her up. She was so thin. One day .... she was mad because I wouldn't give her any money, I tried to make her stay at home. She ripped the recipe out of my notebook and set fire to it.' Sarah gave a mirthless laugh. 'Stupid, after all she'd put me through, that's when I lost it with her. Lost it completely.'

Too right she had. Yelled and screamed like an effing banshee. It was just a bloody recipe.

'It was the final straw ...' Sarah said. 'She needed help. My own sister needed help and I threw her out.' Sarah laid her head down on the table and began to sob quietly. Ben, the big sucker, went round and put his arm around her.

'You know Sarah, you did the right thing. Drug addicts don't play by the rules, and they take advantage of those that do. You couldn't win whatever you did. Amy had to *want* to help herself.'

Dizziness overwhelmed Amy. Ben was agreeing with Sarah. *The bastard.* What did he know? A flicker of self-doubt rattled her wings. She hadn't been that bad. Had she? But like a film reel, all the terrible things she'd done began to unfold in her head. A hot spurt of shame filled her, like a fireball gathering pace until she was incandescent with it. And then she remembered burning the recipe, the flames licking the bottom of the sheet of paper – the horror on Sarah's face as she watched her sister wilfully destroy a precious memory. Amy was on her way to hell after all. And, she thought with horrible certainty, it was exactly what she deserved.

Merciful cold doused the heat and she found herself back in that bloody class room.

'Well done Amy. Unorthodox approach but it did the trick.'

She blinked uncertainly at Gabriel, her mouth dry. Boy, and she'd thought Ben was a looker. Gabe was seriously hot, even in the duff Jesus sandals. And then she remembered. Her instruction had been to find someone for Sarah, stop her being lonely. She grinned. She had a strong suspicion that Ben and Sarah might just be perfect for each other. Sarah deserved some happiness in her life and some one good and decent to share it with.

Mission accomplished. Or was it getting a little warm in here once more…?

THE END

Jules Wake – About The Author

Despite early lofty ambitions, the path to published novelist took a wide diversion when after reading English at the University of East Anglia, Jules Wake found herself in the glamorous and deeply shallow world of PR, which she rather enjoyed, and spent a number of years honing her fictional writing skills on press releases.

After taking a creative writing course and finding no local writing group, she set up the Tring Writers' Circle seven years ago. As a result it was incumbent upon her to set a good example and actually write, which was rather fortunate as with a genuine allergy to cleaning, she finds writing offers the perfect displacement activity.

Her first novel *Talk To Me* was published by Choc Lit early 2014.

KEEP IN TOUCH

Twitter - @juleswake

Blog -   www.romanticallyinclinedblog.wordpress.com

Website www.juleswakewriter.co.uk

Talk To Me

Available on Amazon

http://www.amazon.co.uk/Talk-Me-Jules-Wake/

The Last Leg

By

S. A. Edward

The Last Leg – a short story by S A Edward

I stored Jay in joint size pieces in my large freezer at the back of the lean-to – the one we had built with the kitchen extension.

I've been busy over the last few months: chopping, grinding and tending to my extended vegetable garden.

This last leg – Jay's last leg, is for this special meal I've got planned for Fiona tonight. It's her favourite dish, see – lasagna. I found it in a book of recipes she gave me a couple of Christmases ago.

Now let me see, *'Two and a half pounds of ground beef'.*

I ain't got no scales, but I've been cooking long enough to know what two pounds of meat look like. Being in the freezer's made it easier to peel the skin off.

I've tenderised and grounded the meat – the old fashioned way. The chopped onions burn my eyes. I quickly drop them in the oily pan with the crushed garlic and *'add the minced meat, to brown'.*

The sizzling mixture of spices and seasoning take over the kitchen. They'll help give the mince that special kick and really add some flavour. This leg won't be climbing into bed with anyone, I tell myself – not unless it's in their stomach. Ha-ha.

'Now stir in the chopped tomatoes and tomato sauce.' That's it. Add the *'quarter cup of chopped parsley,'* fresh from my vegetable garden – the bit where I've buried his eyes.

I know the thirty minutes the recipe says won't be enough to cook that tired old leg, so I'll just give it a little longer.

More than eighteen years of my life I gave him. And I did so love him. But when a man doesn't come home every night cos your bed ain't got the calling it used to, you've got to sharpen your tools, start digging around. It didn't take me long to find out whose bed he was finding warmer than mine and that was just too much to bear.

'Heat until bubbling, stirring occasionally'.

Me and Fiona was close. Close enough for me to drop in on her and pick up a few clues, like Jay's special scent all over her duvet cover, and his washed underpants in amongst the clothes in her laundry basket. I knew she was up to something even before those discoveries. I'm smart. Always have been.

'Reduce heat and simmer...should be like soup'.

Oooo. Smell that. My simmering stew. You'd never know. Would you?

Now let me see. *'Mix cottage cheese and parmesan cheese'* into a bowl with *'two table spoons of parsley flakes...salt...pepper...Italian seasoning'*. Oops, don't forget the *'pinch of sugar'*.

My sheets of noodles are ready – I'll just get the dish. Oh shit, sounds like she's here already.

Fiona has a bottle of wine in her hand.

"Come in. Come in, Fi. Take your coat off. Make yourself at home." She gives me a warm hug. I smell the layers of foundation she always piles on her face. We part and she hands me the bottle.

"Oh, thanks. You know you didn't have to."

She tilts her face up into the air and her narrow nostrils open slightly. She says something smells nice and wants to know what it is.

"Your favourite," I say, noticing the blonde streaks she's had added to her hair.

A smile spreads over her coloured lips. "Lasagna!" we both say together, like we're singing the chorus of a song on a girl's night out.

I look at her straight white teeth. Her dimples that add sparkle to her face.

"I'm in the kitchen," I say, hanging her coat on the banister, and let her lead the way. Her jeans, as usual, hug her size fourteen body tightly, and I feel untidy, with my tracksuit bottoms and baggy tee shirt, smelling of well – lasagna.

She offers to help.

"Oh, no. That's okay," I start saying. "Well, maybe you can make the salad."

She says she'll make her special dressing – the one she knows I'm fond of.

I open the bottle of wine. It's red. I pour her a drink without asking cos I know she'll never refuse it. It's juice for me. I never drink – not anymore. I let her sip her wine while I get the salad things out of the fridge. She stands opposite me at our breakfast bar and watches as I layer the baking dish with stew, noodles and a sprinkling of cheese.

She's wearing a pale purple top, with a knot at the cleavage. I notice the top of her boobs are all exposed. She wants to know how I'm coping. We haven't seen much of each other for a while – since Jay's disappearance. I pretend not to notice her taking large sips of her wine in between chopping up the yellow and green peppers.

I put the dish in the oven and reduce the temperature by four degrees, then sit watching her mix her special dressing with vinegar wine, olive oil, black pepper and garlic.

When she's finished, I suggest we move to the comfy seats in the front room. She swings off her stool and follows me.

"So what 'ave you been up to then? It's been a while, eh?"

She says she's been okay, but very busy. Joined a gym, started swimming too and that I should come with her one day, as a guest. My eyes fall on her neatly polished toe-nails.

"It's good to take care of yourself," I tell her.

She lies and tells me I look well, and that I must miss Jay.

"Of course", I tell her, "always wondering about him," and get a quick flash of his drunken body falling to the side of the bath after the third bounce of my Perspex rolling pin against his head.

She says she's sure he'll be in touch one day. I agree then excuse myself to go check on the oven.

"Ready to eat?" I call from the kitchen, and she appears offering her help again. I suggest she gets the bread, plates and cutlery while I put the hot dish on the table and get the salad out of the fridge.

We sit opposite each other at the table and I start to butter my bread while Fiona picks up the large serving spoon and digs deep into the steamy dish. Some of the sauce spills onto her fingers as she puts a portion on my plate.

"Not so keen on meat anymore," I tell her and see me bent over in the bathroom, washing splashes of blood off the tiles.

The strong scent of the cooked meat, seasonings and melted cheeses escape into the air around our noses. She says it smells really great – the flavour rich. I smile, "Mmm," I say and pick up some salad.

I watch her slide her fork laden with lasagna into her mouth and chew away at Jay's leg. Munching on a slice of sweet pepper, I look at Fiona's mouth opening and shutting and the movements of her jaws as they bite down on the flesh of the man we both once had and I think about the days and nights I've spent imagining him and her wrapped in each other's arms, laughing at me.

There's a knock, then a ring from my front doorbell. We stop and look at each other.

"Think it's for me," Fiona says dropping her cutlery on her plate and wiping the greasy purple lipstick from her mouth with a piece of kitchen paper. "It'll be Mic, my fiancé," she says, her eyes bright with excitement. "I asked him to pick me up from here. Didn't think you'd mind."

I get up to follow her and met them in the hallway.

"Mic," Fiona says, opening her hand in my direction, "Meet Les – my dearest and best friend."

The smell of the aftershave, just like the one I'd brought Jay back from Dubai – his special scent – almost knocks me out in the hallway.

THE END

S.A. Edward – About the Author

S. A. Edward lives in London. She writes short stories, novels and other 'in-betweenies' which have been described as 'out of the ordinary'. Two of her short stories, *'The Bump'* and *'Cuts'* came runner up in 'Darker Times Publishing', (Jan) 2014 Flash Fiction competition http://www.darkertimes.co.uk/winners.aspx

KEEP IN TOUCH

You can read more of her short stories here:

'Short-story.me' -

http://www.short-story.me/featured-stories/545-an-okay-day.html

Firstwriter Magazine' issue 24 and Alfie Dog Fiction –

http://alfiedog.com/products-page/s-a-edward/

S. A. Edward blogs at: http://www.saedward.com.

Lovespelled

By
Jane O'Reilly

Lovespelled – a short story by Jane O'Reilly

I knew the moment I walked in that the house was where I needed to be. That it was the place that would shake me out of the funk that had settled on me lately. I wore it like an itchy cardigan, constantly irritated, but somehow unwilling to take it off in case I got cold. I needed a change, and I was sure that Circe House was it.

The flat on the second floor had plenty of dust, a leaky tap, and a grumpy landlord who lived upstairs. What more could a girl want? I have to admit, I'd seen other flats that were cleaner, closer to work, that didn't have ancient, peeling lino in the kitchen, or pink bathroom suites. But something about Circe House pulled at me. Something always had. Even as a kid I'd make sure to sit on the right side of the school bus so that I could press my face to the window and desperately try to catch a glimpse of it through the thick muddle of trees that hid it from view. My mother said it was probably haunted. My grandmother said it was lonely. I liked her version. I romanticised as only an awkward fifteen year old can, imagining a dramatic, tragic love story developing between the Master of the house, and a young, poverty stricken servant. Only he could see her true beauty. He swept her into his arms, and did...things to her.

When the flat came up for rent, I leapt at the chance. I paid the ridiculous deposit. I didn't even haggle over the rent, though I wished I had after I forked out fifty quid for cleaning products and used them all up on the first day. But it had some compensations. The view out of the kitchen window for one, showing a world outside which was nothing but trees - in the middle of a private wood, dark and scowling, like some sort of gothic fairytale. I fantasised about running through the trees at dawn, in nothing but a white nightgown, as evil chased me, like one of those women from the novels my grandmother had favoured. This was the place where my life was going to become exciting. Where things were going to happen to me, strange, wonderful things.

Unfortunately, reality soon killed off the dream.

The hot tap on the pink bath dripped. And dripped and dripped and dripped. The pipework banged and the toilet made strange howling noises in the middle of the night, and after three days, I was ready to commit homicide, or suicide, or something.

Instead, I phoned the landlord. 'What?' he said, when he finally answered the phone after seventeen rings.

'It's Becca Murphy here,' I said, biting back the urge to tell him not to be so rude. He wasn't one of my pupils, he was my landlord. Best to keep my teacher voice under wraps – at least for the first five minutes. 'In the flat downstairs.'

'I know who you are,' he said.

'The hot tap on the bath won't stop dripping,' I told him. I used my most charming voice, the one that I used on car salesmen and traffic wardens and big, scary dogs. 'I was wondering if you could fix it.'

'No,' he said. 'I can't.'

Charming voice *nil*, landlord *one*. I switched to my work voice. The one that made fifteen year old boys quiver in their short trousers and big shoes. 'You are the landlord,' I told him. 'It is your responsibility to fix it.'

'I'm aware of my responsibilities,' he said. 'Please don't ring me again during the day.'

And then he hung up.

I stood there and stared at the phone for a foolishly long time.

'Well,' I said. I didn't know quite what else to do. My hands ached and my knees were raw from all the cleaning I'd done. I couldn't sleep with all the strange noises and my landlord was clearly a bit of a git.

I couldn't exactly give him detention and ring his mother. I was going to have to find another way to deal with this. I couldn't move back to my old flat, because it had already been rented out to someone else, and I doubted very much that Mr Grumpy upstairs would give me back my deposit and the rent I'd already paid. And more than that – I'd been so excited about moving in here, even though everyone warned against it. Everyone apart from my grandmother, that is. She'd merely smiled and gone back to tending what I was sure was deadly nightshade growing in her garden, and said 'good.'

I endured the dripping tap for another three days, by which point I was ready to commit multiple murders, starting with Mr Grumpy. He'd said not to phone him during the day, and I'd stuck to that, just. It had helped that I'd been run off my feet at work. It helped that Halloween was only a few days away, and all the children were distracted by thoughts of ghosts and witches and love spells. We'd ditched the standard texts and were sneakily reading Harry Potter. I'd set the Year Nines the task of writing a spooky story. Year Tens I had asked to write a script for a ten minute horror film. I dreaded to think what awaited me when I looked at those. Year Eleven I'd asked to write a spell of their choosing, complete with detailed instructions.

Their pile of books was on my desk in the living room. I decided to have a look at a few of them while I tried to psych myself up to deal with my recalcitrant landlord. It wasn't that I was afraid of him, as such, it was just that he had asked me not to ring during the day, and I didn't want to be the bad guy in this.

I sat myself down, flicked through the first couple of books. They were predictable – a spell to make your enemy puke slugs (thank you Harry Potter), another to awaken an army of flesh eating zombies. The third one, though, that one caught my attention. It had been written in beautiful, flowing italics, the page decorated with swirls of coloured ink. Not smelly gel pen or glitter, but beautiful artist's inks, in shades of teal green and rich purple. I checked the name on the front of the book. Molly Bell. A strange girl, with waist length red hair and spooky green eyes. I recalled that her mother was a nurse, and she had two younger sisters. They all looked exactly the same. Strong genes in that family.

I turned my attention back to her book.

A spell for the heartsick, it said. *Use carefully, and these words will bring to you what you most desire. Speak them out loud, say them softly and with hope, and it will be yours.*

The plumbing chose that moment to howl like a banshee.

What the hell, I thought. So I bent my head, and I took a deep breath, and I read the spell out loud. I read it again, just to be sure. I poured every bit of my frustration, my exhaustion, my annoyance in to it. I thought about all the things I wanted. I thought about some things I pretended not to want, the things I had thought this house could give me.

Then I picked up my pen and wrote, 'Beautiful work!' on the bottom. I gave it an A, and a merit stamp, even though Year Elevens generally claimed not to care about such things. I closed the book, set my fingers to the next one.

But I didn't open it. I'm not sure what happened, exactly. There was the strangest smell, like very old lavender from the bottom of a drawer, and burning candles, and blood. A sudden gust of cold air rushed past me, as if someone had opened a window on a snowy day. I sucked in some air. It chilled my lungs.

Then it was gone. For a moment I just sat there, my heart racing. Everything looked too bright, the way it does when you're scared. I told myself not to be so stupid, that I was probably imagining things.

And then I heard something. Or rather, I didn't.

The tap had stopped dripping.

I pushed the pile of books aside, got to my feet, and went into the bathroom. I stared at the tap.

Definitely not dripping.

And the reason it wasn't dripping was because the damn thing was running.

I set my hand on top of it, tried to turn it off. It wouldn't stop. Steam rose up from the bottom of the bath, where the scalding hot water pooled before making its way slowly down the drain. *Great*. Just great.

I turned and left the bathroom, and I was halfway to the phone when my temper got the better of me. I marched upstairs, stamping with every step. The stairs were old, polished, creaky, uncarpeted. I sounded like a herd of elephants. Mr Grumpy didn't want phone calls during the day? Fine. He could damn well deal with me face to face, instead.

I'd be lying if I said that I knocked politely. I didn't even come close. I hammered on his door like I was trying to break into his flat. Actually, I hammered on it like it was his head. And then I kicked it, just for good measure. I was about to kick it again when it was snatched open, and I got my first look at my bad tempered landlord.

We stared at each other, for a moment. And then it began.

'What?' he yelled at me.

'My bloody tap, that's what!' I yelled right back. I planted my hands on my hips. I found myself wishing that I'd brushed my hair. And maybe put on makeup.

Maybe then he wouldn't have looked at me like I'd just crawled out from under a rock. But given that he was wearing dodgy striped pyjamas, the old fashioned kind with the buttons all down the front, and he hadn't even managed to fasten them properly, maybe I wasn't the one who should be worried about my appearance. He had messy dark hair, and he needed a shave, and he was glaring at me. It was hard to figure his age, though he was younger than I'd expected.

'Fine,' he said. He slammed the door in my face.

I blinked. I lifted my hand, about to hammer on it again, when it opened. He was still wearing the pyjamas, and his hair was still a mess, but he had a big spanner in his hand, and he'd put on a pair of thick rimmed glasses. He moved out into the corridor.

I stood there, staring at him like a dim-witted fool. For all the scruffy hair, and scruffy pyjamas, there was just something about him, something oddly familiar, through I couldn't put my finger on what it was.

'Tap,' he said.

'Right,' I said. I turned on my heel, remembered I was angry, and stomped all the way down the stairs, down to the middle floor, and my flat. I marched straight through to the bathroom, not bothering to wait and see if he was following me. I knew he was. I could feel the back of my neck prickling. I thrust out an arm and pointed at the tap. 'There.'

He moved behind me. The bathroom was small, and thanks to the enormous seventies suite, complete with bidet, there wasn't much room. I felt his breath skate across my cheek as he looked over my shoulder.

'It looks perfectly fine to me,' he said.

'But...but...' I moved closer to the tub, bent over and reached for the tap. I twisted it. It turned easily, sending a stream of steaming water cascading down. Off, on, off, on. I straightened up, turned. 'It was broken,' I insisted, folding my arms.

'Hmm,' he said. He was still holding the spanner, still wearing the awful pyjamas. 'Look, Ms Murphy. I'm a busy man.'

Yes, I thought. The sort of busy man who is still in his pyjamas at two o'clock on a Saturday afternoon.

'Don't bother me again,' he said.

And with that, he walked out. I was still standing in the bathroom, fiddling with the tap, when I heard the slam of the door, and his heavy footsteps as he made his way back upstairs.

'Well,' I said. I straightened up, eyed the tap with distrust. Everything about it, from the cracked ivory top marked with a faded H, to the wide, gaping mouth that spat out water, seemed to mock me. It was a strange sensation, a tingling of the skin, an odd feeling of awareness that I couldn't seem to shake.

I felt almost as if I was being watched.

Carefully, quietly, I backed out of the bathroom. I went back to the kitchen table, back to my pile of books, and spent the rest of the afternoon working through them. I barely read the words on the page. I scribbled in green ink, made endless, meaningless comments.

But all the while, I was listening. I listened to the sound of the birds chirping outside, and the wind caressing the trees, and the hush, hush of my own breathing. I bared my arms, waiting for the touch of cold. I breathed deeply, trying to pull in the scent of old lavender and burning candles.

There was nothing.

The plumbing stayed silent, and the floorboards too. It was almost as if the house was holding its breath. Which was ridiculous, of course, because houses don't do that.

I didn't sleep that night. I couldn't. My brain wouldn't be still. I spent most of Sunday in a daze, finishing my marking and ironing my work blouses, clogged with exhaustion.

But on Monday morning, I stood in front of the beautiful ornate mirror in the bedroom, and gave myself a stern talking to. 'Pull yourself together, Becca. You're just not used to the house. That's all.' And if in that moment the air seemed to smell of lavender, and burned candles, it was only my imagination.

Somehow, I managed to survive the day at work. I may not have been completely present during the staff meeting, and I may have handed out Year Seven exercise books to Year Eight, but I made it to half past three. I drove home, picking up fish and chips along the way. It was definitely a fish and chips sort of day. Outside, the sky was a soft shade of grey, and crispy, orange leaves danced along the pavement. As I turned off the road on to the narrow track that led to the house, everything seemed to dim. It was the oddest thing.

I gripped the steering wheel tighter as the trees seemed to lean closer, their semi naked branches reaching for me. Ahead, I could see the house, the sandstone darkened by years of dirt from the local mills. And there it was again, the sensation of being watched.

The smell of lavender was unmistakeable.

I jammed my foot on the brake. My little car skidded to a halt, the back end bucking. And then the engine stalled.

'No!'

I twisted the key, pumped the accelerator. Nothing. Absolutely nothing.

I twisted it again, harder this time, willing the damn thing to start.

I sat there, trying to breathe, trying not to, the smell of lavender and burning candles heavy in the air now.

And then someone opened the door. I may have sworn a little. Or even a lot, as I looked up into the face of Mr Grumpy. 'What the hell is wrong with you?' he yelled.

'What do you mean, what the hell is wrong with me?' I yelled right back. 'You're the one yelling!'

'Because you nearly knocked me off my bike! Why weren't you looking where you were going?'

'Because...' I began. Then I stopped. Probably best not to tell him it was because I'd thought the trees were trying to attack me. 'I *was* looking!'

'I don't think so!'

I unfastened my seatbelt and glared back at him. His face was flushed, and the stubble and the glasses were gone, and his eyes were very blue. I shook that thought away. I made to get out of the car. Fortunately he moved before I had to ask him to. We stood there, glaring at each other, our breath misting in the air.

I broke first. I glanced across at his bike, which was black and looked flashy and expensive. Shame he hadn't invested some of that money on the plumbing. I considered pointing that out for a second.

But I had nearly run him over. All the adrenaline seemed to leave me then, as fast as it had rushed in. 'I...do you want a lift?' I asked.

He raised an eyebrow. 'I'm not sure that would be wise.'

'I'll have you know, I'm a very safe driver!'

'Despite evidence to the contrary,' he replied. 'Either way, I'm a terrible passenger.' He moved away, picked up his bike, mounted it. 'Have a good evening, Ms Murphy.'

And then he rode off, his rear light flashing. I watched him go, wondering how on earth I'd managed to miss him. He was wearing a high vis vest over his jacket, for goodness' sake, and the bike had more lights than a Christmas tree.

I got back in my car. The engine started first try. I put it into first, and cautiously crawled the rest of the way to the house. I parked up, grabbed my bags from the boot, and my fish and chips, and went inside. The plumbing was back to banging and rumbling, and I found the noise oddly comforting. I ate my fish and chips, and watched something dreadful on the TV. I must have fallen asleep on the sofa, because when I woke, it was the next morning.

I went through the motions for the next two days. Go to work, shout at Year Ten, confiscate phones from Year Eleven, wonder why Year Thirteen had to be so enormous, discuss The Fault in Our Stars with distressed Year Nines who didn't think they would ever get over it. I didn't see Mr Grumpy. I didn't smell lavender, or burning candles. I slept, too.

I began to wonder if I had imagined it all. Maybe it was just the stress of moving. Chocolate chip cookies always helped with that, so I bought some, and ate them all in one sitting. I don't know if I felt less stressed, though I definitely felt a bit sick. I wallowed in the bath, and willed the hot tap to drip.

It didn't. My car behaved itself, too. It was all very normal, and I told myself that was a relief. I absolutely did not spend any time thinking about my landlord, and his surprisingly blue eyes.

On Wednesday, I drove straight home. I had some lesson planning to do, and I wanted to make a start on cleaning up the fireplace in my living room. I was sure that under the grime were beautiful Victorian tiles. I could see hints of them in places, touches of red, of blue. I ate a quick dinner of beans on toast, finished up my work, then changed into my cleaning clothes and got to work. It was hard, sweaty business, and the dirt wasn't too keen to be parted from the tiles beneath. I'd emptied out three buckets of filthy water and was on my second cloth when the smell hit me.

And then everything went dark.

In the middle of a city, nothing ever gets truly dark. There are always streetlights, and car headlights, and all night petrol stations. But here, in the middle of the wood, there was none of that. Night had fallen while I'd been scrubbing away, and I hadn't noticed. The sky held a faint tinge of inky blue, but it wasn't enough to make anything visible inside my room.

I scrambled to my feet, my heart racing. 'Who's there?' I shouted. 'What is this?'

I didn't get an answer.

I staggered forward, kicking the bucket over as I fumbled for the door. It was too dark, too dark, and the smell, that hint of lavender and burning candles, it so strong that it burned my throat. Either I was going mad, or there was something very strange going on. The window rattled. And I could have sworn I heard footsteps.

I was out the door and running up the stairs to Mr Grumpy's before I could stop myself. I hammered on his door. I hammered long and loud and hard enough to wake the dead.

He opened the door. The pyjamas were back, as was the messy hair. 'What?'

I wasn't sure what I was going to say next. *My bloody flat is haunted* was up there. Instead I went with 'the power is out!'

'No, it isn't, he said.

'Yes it is!'

It was then that I realised that the light in his hallway was on, and that's why I could see him so clearly.

'Well, it's off in my flat,' I blustered. 'It's very dark.'

He sighed. He rubbed a hand over his face, and then he looked at me. 'The fuse box is in the basement,' he said. 'I'll sort it in the morning.'

'I can't have no electricity until the morning!' My voice had taken on a definite undertone of hysterical female.

'Afraid of the dark?'

Yes, when it smells of lavender, and it's filled with weird noises. 'No,' I said stubbornly.

He sighed again. 'You might as well come in.'

I hesitated. Then I thought of the dark, and the noises. I followed him inside his flat. 'I got you out of bed, didn't I?'

'Yes,' he said, as he led me through into his kitchen. I was surprised to see that it wasn't much of an improvement on mine. But it was at least clean, and I took the seat he offered me at the table, and the cup of tea. He made it the correct way, in a pot.

'Sorry about that,' I said.

He leaned back against the worktop, one big hand wrapped around his own mug. 'Are you?'

'Yes!' I protested. Though actually, as I thought about it, I wasn't so sure. It pained me to admit it, but I was curious about him. Very curious. He lived up here all alone, and he kept all sorts of odd hours, and he did have the bluest eyes.

'Hmm,' he said.

I looked around the kitchen. 'So what do you do?' I asked him. 'When you're not sleeping, that is.'

'I work at the hospital,' he said.

That explained the weird hours, if he worked shifts. 'Oh,' I said.

'In the ER,' he said. 'I'm a doctor.'

Bonus points for Mr Grumpy.

'My name is Jamie, by the way.'

I choked on my mouthful of tea. 'Yes,' I managed. 'I'm Becca.'

We sat a few minutes longer, drinking our tea and not talking. I was grateful for that. 'So how long have you lived here?' I asked, when I couldn't stand it any longer.

'Five years,' he said. 'Since I inherited the place.'

'Five years?' I couldn't hide my surprise. 'Have you had other tenants?'

'No,' he said. 'You're the first.'

A few more minutes of silence, as we both pondered that. And so it went for well over an hour, as we cautiously, carefully got to know each other a little better. It turned out that we had quite a lot in common.

Not least of which was Molly Bell. 'She's my niece,' he said.

'She's very bright,' I said, not wanting to get on his grumpy side again, when I'd only just found his good side.

'She's a pain in the arse,' he replied.

I couldn't disagree.

'This might sound crazy,' he said, 'but she likes to interfere.'

'What do you mean?'

'Never mind,' he said. 'It doesn't matter.' He pulled open a couple of drawers, found a torch. 'Come on,' he said. 'Let's get your electricity sorted.'

We made it to the bottom of the stairs. I'd left my front door open. Light blazed out into the hallway.

'It was off!' I insisted. 'It was!'

'Becca,' he said. 'If you wanted to get my attention, there are easier ways.'

I turned, ready to give him a sharp retort.

And then he kissed me. It was warm, and determined, and there was a certain magic to it. I could feel it, coursing through me. When he straightened up, I didn't know what to say. I just stood there, staring up at him.

'Next time,' he said, 'don't invent a domestic disaster. Just ask'.

'I didn't invent it,' I protested, even as my muddled brain screamed at me to shut up. 'It was just like all the other times. I could smell lavender. And candles when they've burned themselves out. Then everything went weird.'

He froze. For a moment, I thought he was going to tell me I had some terrible medical condition and had only two weeks to live. He was a doctor, after all. But he didn't. He said something even worse. 'This isn't going to work.' He rubbed a hand over his face. 'I think you should move out.'

Then he turned and made his way back upstairs.

I pressed my hand to my mouth. My brain couldn't process what had just happened. One minute, I'd been experiencing the kiss I'd waited for. The kiss I'd wished for, when I'd read that spell from Molly Bell's exercise book. When I'd let those words float in the air, and I'd thought of the things I kept secret, the things I never told anyone, the secret, private wishes I hid away.

When I'd wished for magic, I hadn't expected to actually find it.

I went back inside my flat in shock. I sat on the sofa, with all the lights blazing, and tried not to cry. Then I made myself go to bed. I made myself get up and go to work the next morning, Thursday. I didn't smell lavender. I barely functioned. That evening, I dragged the boxes out of the cupboard and started to pack them. I hadn't had time to get rid of them. I'd barely had time to unpack, so there wasn't much to do.

This time, the scent of lavender crept up on me slowly. It wasn't the fast punch of the other times, but a subtle creep, so that at first, I thought I was imagining it. It grew stronger. I tried to ignore it.

'You can't make me go back up there,' I said. My hands stilled on the box I was currently filling with kitchen bits and pieces. 'It doesn't matter what you do.' Cold, unseen fingers trailed across my cheek. 'You might as well give up,' I said, trying to sound a lot braver than I felt. The back of my neck prickled. But I wasn't going to surrender to it, not this time. Some wishes are not meant to come true.

And anyway, I didn't believe in magic. *I didn't.* Even though a small voice inside of me cried out as I thought that, and called me a liar. I forced it down. Maybe once, I'd believed. But I was an adult now. And this was just a house, and he was just a man. There was no such thing as magic.

Is that what you believe? The magic whispered inside my head. *What you truly believe?*

'Yes.' I gripped the box tightly, as I betrayed myself. 'That's what I believe.'

There was a moment of still, of silence. The scent of lavender surrounded me, drowned me, filled me.

And then it was gone.

I felt oddly empty, as if my insides were hollow. I wanted to cry, but there were no tears. There was nothing. Just a deep, unshakeable feeling that something was missing. I went to bed, and for the first time in days, I slept. It was deep and dreamless, though when I awoke I felt like I hadn't slept at all. I dragged myself to work. I don't remember what lessons I taught that day. I'm pretty sure they were dreadful. All around me, I could hear the whisper of magic. It was as if, now that I had acknowledged it, now that I had denied it, I could see it everywhere.

It followed me home, taunting me. At Circe house, it was everywhere. It almost seemed to be seeping out of the walls. I packed up the last of my boxes, and started the process of loading up my car. I'd have to arrange a removal firm to come and collect the rest at some point next week. For now, I just wanted to be away from here. An aged aunt had offered to let me stay for a few days, until I found somewhere else to live. 'Never liked that house,' she'd said, as she sniffed down the phone. 'Gives me the creeps.'

I was so busy thinking about this, and feeling sorry for myself, and trying to ignore the magic oozing through the gaps in the floorboards that I completely misjudged the stairs. I would probably have been alright, if I hadn't been carrying a box full of books, and if I had thought to drop the box and grab for the handrail.

But I didn't.

I regretted that when I finally came to a halt at the bottom. I eased my phone out of my pocket, my hands shaking. 'I need an ambulance,' I croaked, when the call connected a few seconds later. 'I fell down the stairs. I think I've broken my ankle.'

I sat at the bottom of the stairs, with my phone in my hand and the burst box and loved, yellowed paperbacks scattered all around me, until the door opened, and the paramedics strolled in, wearing green uniforms and kind smiles. They scooped me up, and pushed me into the back of an ambulance decorated with pictures of pumpkins and fake cobwebs.

'It's Halloween,' I said, surprised.

'Yes, love,' they said. And then they dosed me with painkillers, and I talked a lot of nonsense, and before I knew it, I was stretched out on a bed in A&E. A nurse with short red hair and a firm bedside manner took details from me. 'Oh,' she said when she saw my address. 'You'll be my brother's tenant.'

I blinked at her. Everything was a tad hazy. 'He doesn't like me,' I said.

'Did he tell you that?'

I blinked some more. The cubicle was just as it should be, with curtains that didn't reach the floor and didn't block out the sounds coming from whoever was in the next one. The hospital smell was exactly as it should be. But this woman...she reeked of magic. I'd stopped bothering to pretend that I didn't believe in it. The drugs were helping me with that. 'I read a spell,' I said. 'I didn't mean to.'

'Ah,' she said, and stared at me. 'You're Molly's teacher, aren't you?' And then she shook her head. 'Blast that girl,' she muttered. 'Never knows when to stop interfering. She knows he doesn't trust magic. Or women who are touched by it.'

'What do you mean?'

'I don't think I'm the best person to explain this,' she said. She scribbled something on my notes, then tugged the curtain open and disappeared through them, yanking them closed behind her.

I lay there, propped up on the crunchy pillows, wondering what on earth she'd meant. Whatever the paramedics had dosed me with was starting to wear off a little, enough for me to be able to string my thoughts together. I glanced down at my foot. It was already starting to bruise, and it was swelling up impressively fast.

And there was magic leaking out of it.

I sat bolt upright, gripping the covers tightly. Maybe the drugs hadn't worn off as much as I thought. Because although my grandmother had always told me I was full of it, I'd never really believed her. I'd never dared to.

The curtains twitched.

Then Jamie walked in. He was wearing blue scrubs, with a stethoscope around his neck, and a wizard's cloak. As you do. 'Becca,' he said.

'What the hell is wrong with me?' I asked. I somehow knew he would be able to tell me, that I wouldn't need to explain what I really meant.

'You're a witch,' he said, as he picked up my notes and looked at them.

'Oh,' I said. Then, 'excuse me?'

He sat on the edge of the bed, taking care not to move my foot. 'There is probably someone else in your family who had magic,' he said quietly.

The answer to that was obvious. 'My grandmother.'

He nodded. 'Sometimes it can skip a generation.'

'But I never had any magic! I tried, when I was a kid, but there was nothing.' And the other kids had called me weird, and my mother had pulled her disapproving face, and I'd stopped.

'You always had magic,' he said. 'I knew it the day you moved in.'

'How?'

'Because....' he flushed, looked away. 'Do I have to spell it out?'

'Yes.'

'Because the men in my family are fated to fall in love with witches,' he said.

I stared at him.

'It never ends well,' he said sadly. 'All we want is a quiet, normal life, with a quiet, sensible wife. But no.' He turned to me then. 'What do we get? Interfering, nosey wives determined to fix everything. Throwing magic around left right and centre, and getting themselves into all sorts of trouble. I didn't want that. But you wouldn't let it go. You kept coming up to my flat, looking so pretty and smelling of magic.'

'I didn't mean to,' I pointed out. 'But all sorts of weird things kept happening. That was hardly my fault.'

'When you read Molly's spell, what did you wish for?' he asked. The question caught me off guard, and for a moment, I didn't know how to answer.

'I wished...' I bit my lip. I'd never told anyone this. 'I wished for magic.' I hung my head. 'And I wished for love. That sounds so lame.'

'Not really,' he said. 'Witches are particularly difficult to love. They're stubborn and annoying. Which is why I've spent my whole life trying to avoid them.'

'Don't you want to fall in love?' I asked him.

'Of course I want to,' he said. 'But I want to know that it's real, and I can't know that if I let magic push us together.'

He was looking at my foot.

'Magic didn't have anything to do with me falling down the stairs,' I told him.

He turned his head, staring at me with those bright blue eyes. 'Are you sure?'

'Yes! I just...fell. Because I'm a clumsy fool, and because I haven't been able to think straight since you kissed me.'

'You haven't?'

'No,' I told him. 'Have you?'

'I haven't been able to think straight since you moved in,' he admitted. 'You're bloody annoying.'

'Well,' I said. 'I don't think that has anything to do with magic.'

'Becca,' he said patiently. 'It has everything to do with magic.'

'I don't see how,' I replied.

'Because if it didn't,' he said, 'you would annoy me, and that would be it. I wouldn't spend all my time thinking about it. And I wouldn't miss it when you stopped. I wouldn't...' He paused, as if he wasn't sure he wanted to say it. 'I wouldn't have wished you would carry on.'

We both looked at my foot, then, which was hot and throbbing.

'You're going to need an X-Ray,' he said. 'You're probably going to need a cast. You'll be on crutches for weeks. You're going to annoy the hell out of me.'

'What about the magic?' I asked, my voice little more than a whisper. 'You hate magic. What are we going to do about that?'

'I guess I'll just have to learn to live with it,' he said. Then he moved closer, slid his fingers back into my hair, tilted my face up, and kissed me, and it was everything I had wished for, and more. It was real, and it was right and it was wrong, and I knew the instant he surrendered to the spell of it.

And it was magic.

THE END

Jane O'Reilly – About the Author

Jane O'Reilly once saw a ghost in the toilet of her student house when she was at University. It was a woman in a long grey dress. She didn't use that particular bathroom much after that. These days, she writes award winning contemporary romances and smutty erotica.

KEEP IN TOUCH

Twitter - @janeoreilly

Website - www.janeoreilly.com

Amazon PAGE - http://www.amazon.co.uk/Jane-OReilly/

Clarissa

By
Lynda Renham

Clarissa – a short story by Lynda Renham

'We can't possibly afford it Frank.'

There was an air of dismissal in her voice and Frank's heart sank. She turned back to the washing machine with a flick of her hair, implying there was nothing more to be said. He felt himself simmer with anger. She talked to him like she spoke to Danny when he pestered her for a new bike, or Charlie when he was whining for more pocket money. He hated her 'that's all there is to it' attitude. He'd be damned if she'd take that attitude with him.

'I've checked our finances and I think we *can* afford it,' he said, keeping his voice firm and steady. Why did he have to say 'think we can afford it'? Is he the man of the house or not?

'Oh, you have, have you?' she snapped sarcastically.

Kate stopped filling the washing machine with dirty laundry and turned angrily to her husband. Frank felt himself falter and much to his shame his tone became pleading.

'Kate, a good car is essential, you know that.'

'But Frank, it's much more than we said we would spend.'

'It will be worth every penny. Come and see it for yourself.'

Kate sighed.

'I'll come and see it but it won't make any difference. We can't afford it. I won't change my mind.'

Frank had to stop himself from punching the air. He had won. He could hardly contain himself. He strolled to the back door, every muscle in his body itching to run, jump and explode with happiness.

'See you later,' he said casually.

Only when he was halfway down the street and safely out of her view did he allow the explosion to erupt. He jumped up and down and glorified in his light-headedness. Life was finally looking up, and not before time. He walked gaily along the street, his step bouncy, a gait not normally associated with Frank Longhorn. He was well-known for his stooped posture and his slow walk; the walk of a man who had given up on life. Or as Frank thought, life had given up on him, but now everything would change. Once he was with her, life would be altogether different.

*

Two days later and looking at Kate's horrified face, Frank realised he'd counted his chickens before they were hatched. Her mouth opened and closed and she stared at the car in disbelief.

'Isn't she beautiful?' he breathed, drinking in the loveliness before him until he felt quite breathless.

Kate swallowed and said, 'Damn you Frank Longman, have you gone totally insane?'

She pulled her eyes from the hideous sight in front of her and turned angrily on her husband.

'You brought me all this way to look at a piece of junk? I'm really beginning to believe that you're losing your mind Frank. It's an old relic.'

'It's a classic,' stammered Frank.

After giving him a filthy look Kate turned and stomped out of the garage.

'You're making a big mistake Kate,' he called after her.

'I made my big mistake a long time ago,' she snapped.

Frank didn't hear his wife. He only had eyes for the beautiful shiny vision before him. Frank could feel her enticing him, her warmth reaching out to him. He knew he had to be enveloped in that wonderful body. Her voice whispered softly and tenderly to him.

'Take me, take me.'

'Well mate, you interested? You sure been looking at 'er a lot this past week, needs a lot of work mind you. Nice little motor though if you've got the time to give 'er.'

Frank jumped at the voice. The salesman smiled, his eyes wide and piercing. 'What?'

The salesman made a 'looks like we've got a queer one 'ere' face.

'Wanna buy 'er do ya?' he repeated.

Frank looked at the car longingly. Oh, he wanted her all right.

'Yes,' said Frank resolutely. 'I'm going to buy her. I'm going to buy Clarissa.'

He felt sure he heard the car purr.

'Who?' asked the salesman, shuddering a little as though he had a cold chill running down his back. 'I know people get attached to their cars but naming them before you've purchased them...' He narrowed his eyes at Frank. 'Your wife didn't seem too keen.'

'Clarissa,' Frank replied.

'That your wife?'

'No, that's this beauty.' Frank's smile seemed to make the salesman shiver. Frank stroked the bonnet with trembling hands.

'Sure mate. I call it a Cortina meself but whatever. You sure you don't want something a bit more modern? I've got a nice little Clio, a good runner ...'

'No,' said Frank sharply.

'Right, come into the office and we'll do the paperwork. The sooner the better, then you and Clarissa can drive off into the sunset.' And he led the way back across the showroom with an urgency in his step.

*

A little while later Frank walked into the house. The past two hours had been heaven. He had never been so happy. He and Clarissa had spent time together, gliding along, her purring relaxing him. It had been sheer bliss. He couldn't remember when he had last been that happy. She had wrapped her smooth body around him and he had felt warm and safe. They had cruised along, oblivious of everyone else. Frank had caressed her gently, getting to know every part of her. Now they were home, the two of them together - forever. They cruised up to Frank's driveway where standing at the gate - staring in astonishment - was Kate.

'Don't worry Clarissa, it will be all right,' Frank whispered as he climbed from the car.

He approached Kate with a beaming smile on his face. Kate stared hard at Clarissa and then followed Frank into the house, slamming the front door behind her.

'Take that thing back Frank,' she said firmly and waltzed past him into the kitchen.

The house was strangely quiet.

'Where are the children?' he asked and then remembered it was Saturday.

'At my mother's of course, where do you think they are?'

How would I know, Frank thought. *You never tell me anything these days.*

'I can't take her back Kate,' he said quietly.

She laughed.

'Don't be ridiculous. Of course you can. It's a car Frank, not a lost child. There is nothing wrong with our other car, aside from a few dents.'

He stared at her. She's never understood him.

'You don't understand. I need her,' he said.

Kate threw her weight behind the fridge door and slammed it shut.

'Don't be so ridiculous Frank. What is wrong with you?' she said rolling her eyes. 'Where are the keys?'

She marched back into the hall and for a second Frank froze. What is she doing? He heard the jingle of keys and forced his stunned body to follow her.

'No,' he shouted. 'Leave her alone Kate.'

'You're mad,' she cried, reaching the front door.

He lurched himself towards her.

'I said no,' he shouted, pulling her back by her jumper. He felt her struggle but his only thoughts were for Clarissa. He grabbed Kate, pulling her from the front door and dragging her back to the kitchen. Kate's feet slipped beneath her and she cried out.

'Frank, for God's sake. Will you stop it, you're hurting me.'

She let out a piercing scream which made Frank's ears ring

'Be quiet,' he hissed.

'Let me go,' Kate cried, scratching his arms.

Frank kept on pulling. She couldn't take Clarissa back. He wouldn't let her. Kate's screams echoed in his ears. Somewhere he could hear Clarissa calling him. She must be frightened, desperate to have him near. Kate must never touch her. Not now, not ever. Kate kicked out and hit his shin. He looked down at her snarling face and suddenly found his hands were encircling her throat.

'Frank,' Kate gasped, clutching at his hands. 'Stop it or...'

She made a gurgling sound and Frank watched as her mouth grimaced. He felt her legs buckle.

'Yes, yes,' breathed Clarissa. Frank could hear her in his head. *'Just you and me, do it Frank. Do it for me.'*

'Frank, Frank,' it was a choked sob from Kate.

'Don't stop, oh don't stop,' breathed Clarissa. *'Do it for me. Don't stop.'*

He could hear the excitement in her voice and it sent a shiver of excitement along his own spine. He was in control. Kate was still begging to be released. But it felt too good. He squeezed some more, and smiled as her nails tore into his flesh. He could hear Clarissa breathing heavily with excitement and he squeezed again wanting to please her. It was the most excited he had felt in years.

'She won't take you,' he whispered.

'Yes, Frank, do it for me.'

'Frank please, please stop. I'm sorry. Please Frank.' But the more Kate begged, the harder he squeezed.

He was the one in control now. 'You won't take Clarissa now, will you,' he panted.

Kate's eyes bulged and he watched in fascination. There was a buzzing in his head and he couldn't hear Clarissa clearly. But she was telling him to do it, he was sure she was. He would do anything for her. From somewhere in the distance he heard a thud. He realised it was Kate's body that had fallen to the floor. He looked down at the bulging eyes and the purple marks on her neck. He stepped over her, giving her a last disdainful look.

'I warned you,' he said, walking casually to the front door.

*

Clarissa purred as he approached her. He stroked the bonnet tenderly and then started the engine. He drove her carefully into the garage and parked her behind their old Volkswagen.

'That will go tomorrow too,' he said, climbing from the driver's seat. 'I'll get rid of them both and then it will be you and me,' he smiled.

Clarissa purred happily and whispered.

'The body Frank, you need to get rid of it.'

He shook his head. Yes, he needed to get rid of it. Get rid of Kate once and for all. She never understood him. He made his way back to the house. The ringing of the phone stopped him in his tracks. His heart began to race. The ringing jarred his nerves. Beneath his feet were the car keys that had slipped from Kate's hand during the struggle. He remembered Kate pleading and felt a tingle down his spine. He put his hand on the phone and strained to listen for Clarissa.

'Answer it,' she sang softly.

He lifted the receiver.

'Hello?'

'Frank?'

It was Kate's mother.

'Yes.'

'Are you all right, you sound strange.'

'I'm fine.' He struggled to steady his voice. 'I was outside.'

'Is Kate there?' her tone implied she wasn't interested in talking to him.

'She's gone shopping,' he said.

'Gone shopping,' she said incredulously. 'I thought she was coming to collect the boys.'

His mind raced.

'Can you keep them overnight? I was hoping to take Kate for a romantic dinner.'

'That's thoughtful,' she answered and he could hear sarcasm in her voice. 'That *will* surprise Kate.'

Frank had an overwhelming desire to squeeze his hands around his mother-in-law's throat too.

'Yes well. See you in the morning then. Thank you.'

He slammed the phone down. He'd collect the kids tomorrow. Take them all on a nice holiday. The boys and Clarissa, after all he had some time owing at work. He ran out of the front door, taking deep breaths as he went. He sighed with relief at the sight of Clarissa and fifteen minutes later he had decided what to do.

He hadn't anticipated how heavy Kate was. Just dragging her body to the cellar door had left him panting. How often had he told her to diet? It was obvious she was overweight but she just wouldn't stop stuffing her face. Well, she won't eat anymore now, will she? He smiled at the thought. All the same, she was still making him a struggle. If dragging her to the cellar door left him feeling like this, what would he feel like after taking her down the cellar steps? Supposing he should have a heart attack carrying her down there? I'll have to take it slowly, he told himself.

He began the slow task of carrying her body down the cellar steps. The musty smell of the cellar hit him, making his head spin. Kate's body seemed to get heavier and heavier with each step. Even though it was cool he wiped the perspiration from his face. He could feel it running down his back and saw his T-shirt was stained with sweat. He lugged Kate down another two steps and stopped to catch his breath. Every step had seemed harder than the last. He looked down at the few steps that were left. There was a buzzing in his head and he swayed slightly. He was finding it hard to breathe. Perspiration trickled into his eyes and he wiped it away. Why did she make him do this? Finally, he was on the last step. He dropped Kate and she fell with her head lolling to the side, the purple marks on her throat standing out more than ever. Suddenly he couldn't get any air into his lungs. He was gasping, struggling for breath. *No, no, nothing must happen to him now. Everything was perfect. Clarissa was waiting for him.*

'Frank it's all right.'

It was Kate's voice. No, it couldn't be. Frank turned his aching head towards his wife, his heart beating frantically. He stared at her and her bulging eyes stared straight back at him. Frank screamed.

*

'Mr Longman, please try and calm down. Nurse, give him the injection please.'

The voice was calm and reassuring. Was it the police? Had he passed out in the cellar? Slowly, hesitantly, he opened his eyes.

'There you are. Back with us at last.'

A doctor leaned across him.

'We were getting a bit worried about you,' he smiled.

'Where am I?'

Be careful, he thought. Don't give yourself away. Did they find Kate? Where were the police?

'You're in hospital Mr Longman. Do you remember coming in? We operated on your ulcer. You've taken quite a while to come round.'

Ulcer, what did he mean? Frank tried to understand what the doctor was saying. He wanted to ask about Kate and check that Clarissa was safe. He looked at his hands. No handcuffs. Did they miss the body?

'Kate?' he whispered.

'Here I am, darling.'

No purple marks, no bulging eyes.

'Clarissa?' he said softly. What had she done to Clarissa?

Kate laughed. 'Dreaming about another woman? I don't know,' she clucked.

Frank began to cry. Tears fell like rain onto the pillow.

*

The next day Kate came to collect him from the hospital. After Kate had given the staff chocolates and Frank had thanked everyone, they made their way to the exit.

'Home then,' said Kate cheerfully.

Frank murmured something and blinked as the bright sunlight attacked his eyes.

'I have a surprise for you Frank,' smiled Kate soon after as they reached the car park.

'That's nice,' Frank replied dully.

He lifted his head and there in front of him stood Clarissa. The sun was shining brightly onto her shiny body. Frank shuddered.

'Oh no,' he gasped, 'It isn't possible.'

He heard Clarissa purr, her body shimmering with desire for him.

'*Just a trial run,*' she whispered. '*Next time will be different. Next time it'll be for real.*'

THE END

Lynda Renham – About the Author

Lynda Renham writes romantic comedy novels and has a growing fan base. She has been likened in style to Sophie Kinsella but writes with a down-to-earth humour. Lynda's novels are popular, refreshingly witty, fast paced, and with a strong romantic theme. Lynda lives in Oxford, UK. She has appeared on BBC radio discussion programs and when not writing Lynda can usually be found wasting her time on Facebook.

"Lynda Renham is right up there with chick-lit royalty! I'm not talking princess either, for me, the Queen of Chick-lit". – *Booketta Book Blog*

KEEP IN TOUCH

Twitter @Lyndarenham

My webpage is www.renham.co.uk

The facebook author fun page is

https://www.facebook.com/pages/Lyndas-author-fun-page/

Amazon –

http://www.amazon.co.uk/Lynda-Renham/

Orange Blossom

By
Mary Jane
Hallowell

Orange Blossom – a short novella by Mary Jane Hallowell

PART ONE

I gave a startled cry. I lifted my head from his shoulder, opened my eyes and tucked a stray strand of long brown hair behind my ear. Suddenly, I peered into the gloom and focused my gaze on the door.

'What's the matter?' Harry asked, as he caressed the back of my neck.

Despite the semi-darkness of the curtained room, he could see a certain fear must have registered on my face.

'Some-one just tried to open the door. I saw the handle turn.'

'Perhaps it was the cleaning lady. What's she called?'

'Maggie. She never comes on Wednesdays, she cleans on a Friday, ready for the week end. And anyway she comes at eight in the morning, not midday - if she can't make it she always lets me know.'

'Who else could it be?'

'Hugh,' I whispered so softly he had to strain to hear me. My lips were trembling. Thank goodness some sixth sense had made me lock the bedroom door behind me as we had entered, even though I knew we were quite alone in the house. For a split second I wondered why I had done so. Could it be a guilty conscience? Then all thoughts of guilt had been swept away as I felt his hand on the back of my neck as he slowly unzipped my dress.

Now, sitting up in bed I pointed to the clothes he had hurriedly discarded not half an hour ago, and thrown carelessly across the chair which stood in front of my dressing table. He glanced at me, and sensing the tension in my body, threw back the bedclothes, and leapt out of bed. He went over to the chair, picked up his shirt and pulled it over his head.

'Come on darling, it's nothing,' he said still in a low tone, but trying to lighten the situation. He turned around to face me. 'Even if it is Hugh, at least I'm half dressed!'

'Oh, for God's sake, don't joke. Make yourself decent.'

He finished dressing in silence. He fumbled with his shoes and dropped one of them on the floor with a loud thud. My alarm was infectious, making him clumsy. I slipped out of bed and reached for my silk kimono, the one Hugh had brought me from Japan on the latest of his many trips to the Far East.

'You'd better go now.'

'How shall I get out?'

'Through the door of course. How did you think you were going to get out? Fly through the window like Tinkerbell?' I could barely conceal my impatience. 'I'll go out and see if the coast is clear. It can't possibly be Hugh — he's in Edinburgh overnight. I dropped him off at King's Cross station to catch the 7.30 train this morning.'

We spoke in whispers still. Wrapping my kimono tightly around me, I walked quickly to the en suite bathroom. Again, some intuition had made me lock the door in the bathroom which led onto the landing. Suddenly I caught my breath, and put my hand to my throat. I glanced quickly at Harry and he followed the direction of my horrified gaze. We saw the white china knob of the handle slowly turn. We had heard no one walk along the landing, and it was terrifying to see that silent motion. We stood there, two figures frozen, like those living statues you sometimes saw in a park, or in the street.

My knees shaking, I walked back to the bed and sat down heavily. I must have been as white as a sheet, and underneath his tan he was quite pale too. I looked at him, willing him to somehow make this whole ghastly situation disappear.

He pulled himself together and tried to put the best spin on the state of affairs. 'It can't possibly be your husband,' he repeated as if to re-assure himself as much as anyone. 'It must have been your cleaner. If it was Hugh surely he would have banged on the door, or shouted, if only to make sure you were all right. Yes, it must be Maggie.' He was warming to his theme now, getting into full flow, gaining more confidence. 'He never comes back in the middle of the day, does he?' I shook my head. 'And you actually saw Hugh board the train?'

'No, I just dropped him at the station.' I stood up and walking over to my dressing table, I picked up a silver backed hairbrush and pulled it through my hair. Suddenly I turned and looked at myself in the mirror, then swung to face him. 'Thank God, I've just remembered. When I got back here this morning I saw that he had left some papers on his desk. He was working on them till late last night, and I thought they might be important, so I called him on his mobile and he *was* on the train. How stupid of me to have forgotten! Panic over.' I breathed a deep sigh of relief. 'Hugh said the papers weren't important, and thanks anyway, and that the train was nearly ten minutes late in leaving. But I must say this has given me quite a fright.'

I was right. It had given me a deep shock, and I was surprised to find myself much more worried and shaken than I would have thought imaginable. I gave him the shadow of a smile. 'We can't stay here forever. I'll go out and make absolutely sure the coast is clear. If it is the cleaner I'll say I was feeling ill and locked the door accidentally. Something like that, I'll make it up. You stay put.' I was feeling a lot more assured.

'Are you sure you don't want me to come with you, in case it *is* an intruder?'

'I'll be all right.' I said tersely, giving him an impatient look.

I unlocked the door, and stepped quietly out onto the landing, standing motionless, straining to hear any sound. Nothing. I padded softly in my bare feet, and stood at the head of the stairs, then slowly ventured down until I was in the hall.

'Hugh? Is that you?' There was no reply. 'Is anyone there? Maggie, is that you?' No answer. I went through the half open door of the sitting room and looked about. Everything was just as I had left it, the fashion magazine I'd been reading when Harry had arrived was still open at the page, my half-drunk cup of coffee, now cold, on the side table.

I went back into the hall to check Harry hadn't thrown off his coat and left it lying about but, if he had one, he must have left it in his car. Thank God for that. I knew his car wouldn't be parked outside the house, even if he could find a space. He always took the precaution of parking in the next road. I went down the hall, and into the kitchen. Again, nothing, it was just as I had left it earlier that morning, and Harry had refused a coffee when he arrived, so there was no incriminating dirty mug in the sink. I went back into the hall, and retracing my steps I stood at the foot of the stairs and called out.

'O.K. It's safe for you to come down. There's no-one here.'

He came quickly down the stairs and went into the sitting room. 'I do believe we must have imagined the whole thing. I could use a drink. Do you have any brandy? Never thought that you would drive me to drink so soon in the day, my darling.'

'Don't joke. You were just as shit scared as I was. Hugh's got some brandy I think. Look in that cupboard over there and help yourself.' I indicated with a nod of my head towards the far end of the room, to the antique mahogany corner cupboard. Harry crossed the room in easy strides, opened the door, reached inside, and pulled out a decanter half filled with brandy. He gestured towards me.

'No, not for me, it's too early. I'm going to have a cup of strong tea to steady my nerves.'

He splashed some of the golden liquid into a glass, and downing the contents in one, replaced the brandy in the cupboard. Standing by my side he pulled me towards him, and gently kissed me on my forehead.

'I'd best be going. When will we meet again?'

I was anxious for him to leave. I wanted to be alone, and to take stock of what had happened in the last hour. 'I'm not sure. Perhaps it would be better if we left it for a week or so, after Hugh returns. I want to be absolutely certain that everything's all right, and it will give me time to check it out with Maggie and see what she has to say, if anything. I'll give you a ring.' I smiled at him. He took me in his arms and kissed my lips. I looked into his deep brown eyes which crinkled irresistibly at the corners when he smiled. God, he was good looking. No wonder I had fallen for him.

We turned and walked hand-in-hand to the front door. He stepped outside into the pale sunlight of the February afternoon. 'Good bye my love, and don't worry. Everything will be all right.' With that, he ran jauntily down the steps. I closed the door, went back into the sitting room and watched him through the window until he rounded the corner, and disappeared from my sight.

Later that night I was lying on the sofa watching television when I heard the key turn in the front door, and Hugh walked slowly into the sitting room.

The minute he entered and I saw the set of his shoulders there was no doubt at all in my mind that he knew. He knew everything. He *had* returned to the house when Harry and I had been in the bedroom. Our eyes met as he stood in front of me, and as I saw the cold, black, lifeless look in them, an icy chill ran down my spine. He sat down slowly in the chair opposite me almost as if he was sleepwalking, his gaze steady. When was he going to say something?

I could bear it no longer, I had to break the awful silence. It took all my self-control to speak in a normal tone. 'You're back early. I wasn't expecting you home until tomorrow. What happened?'

'My meeting was cancelled at the last minute. I managed to get off the train in Leeds and I caught the express train back to London almost immediately. Funny thing was, I realised I needed those papers you phoned me about after all, so in a way the fact that my meeting was cancelled was quite fortuitous.' He did not look at me as he spoke.

I glanced at him sharply, waiting for him to say more. What did he mean by 'quite fortuitous?' Was that his way of informing me he had returned to the house that afternoon and then discovered I was not alone? A flash of quick anger and contempt swept through me. If that was the case why did he not confront me, accuse me openly, why did he not demand to know what the hell was going on? I longed for him to be a man, not a mouse and run away.

I noticed he was deathly pale, but the expression on his face was inscrutable, and his voice sounded strained, forced. For a moment I thought that was going to say more. He rose from the chair. 'I'm going to take a shower.' He turned and walked slowly from the room, and I heard his steady, measured tread as he went upstairs. Was that it? Was there to be no inquisition?

I swallowed hard. This time I did need a drink and opened the cupboard and poured myself a small brandy. The strong liquid burned my throat, and I spluttered slightly. I retraced my steps and sat back on the sofa. My head was still spinning, but I felt a slight sense of relief. Was

Hugh going to leave it at that? Perhaps, I thought, he didn't want to make a scene. Men hate scenes, and Hugh hated scenes more than most.

And, unbelievably, that was all that was said.

I knew that he was madly in love with me. Everyone said how much Hugh adored me, how he worshipped the very ground I walked on, so surely he would never contemplate divorce? I knew I took him for granted, and took for granted the lovely house and the very comfortable life style we had – the expensive holidays, my credit cards paid off every month, and no questions asked. All this he provided and more, and I was very happy to accept it as my due. The very thought that my comfortable life might be in jeopardy shook me to the very core of my being. What a fool I had been in risking all this by having a fling with Harry. He wasn't worth it, and it certainly wasn't worth losing all this. It simply wasn't. I would have to be a lot more careful in future.

Of course I wasn't what was called 'being in love' with Hugh. But equally, I didn't wish to cause him any unhappiness, or to humiliate him in anyway. The last thing in the world I wanted to do was to hurt him. So I adopted the attitude of 'least said, soonest mended,' and I hoped and prayed this mess I had got myself into would simply disappear.

But it didn't disappear, not completely. Not, as I've already mentioned, that Hugh made any reference to Harry, or even hinted, far from it, but it was his attitude towards me that had definitely changed. I was sure about this, and it was not just my imagination, nor the consequence of a guilty conscience.

The first time I noticed the change in his manner was when we were having dinner with friends two or three days after the 'Harry' episode. Whenever we were out in a group at dinner, at a party, he always gave me little, smiling glances during the course of the evening. This particular evening however, I noticed he never once looked at me. I thought he looked pale, and his eyes appeared coal black. He made no effort to join in the conversation as if the last thing in the world he wanted was to be there. He looked unbearably miserable.

Of course he knew; of that there was no doubt in my mind. I supposed he was furious with me, and, I presumed, with Harry. At least Harry had had the grace to lie low for a few days. I had already decided what to say if Hugh confronted me.

There was no use in denying it, he wouldn't believe me. I had told him of the relationship between Harry and myself when I agreed to marry him. Anyway, it wasn't a secret, everybody knew we'd been together for five years, for heaven's sake.

And I had severed the relationship with Harry immediately, before Hugh and I had announced our intention to get married. But now, nearly two years down the line, what did Hugh expect? He was away so much, travelling to all those godforsaken places, leaving me alone for weeks on end. Harry and I were still good friends, and I enjoyed his company. All right, we shouldn't have slept together, but it wasn't entirely my fault. Hugh shouldn't have left me by myself so much - while the cat's away, and all that. I knew for sure that if it did come down to an open confrontation between Hugh and Harry, I wouldn't see Harry for dust.

But why hadn't Hugh said anything? Perhaps it was because he would hate the scandal and gossip intensely. He was such a private man, and would loathe the thought of *nudge, nudge, wink, wink* if, say, we went into a wine bar. The whispered asides, 'You know about Flora and Harry, of course?' For some-one who hated drawing attention to himself as much as Hugh, it always struck me as somewhat ironic he should choose to be a lawyer. After all, he had to appear in court for his living, and he was always attending high level conferences where he had to make speeches in front of hundreds of people.

There was one other thought that struck me, and that was that men especially could be quite vain, and Hugh would hate to think that anyone knew what was happening in his private life, and that his wife had been found in bed with her ex-lover by her husband! So, to keep the *status quo,* for the sake of our marriage, Hugh chose to ignore the situation. Perhaps he had even forgiven me. As I looked at him across the dinner table that evening at that moment it happened my gaze met his. There was no forgiveness in it.

When Hugh and I married we had only known each other a short while. Looking back, I wasn't sure when it was we first met, and it was only after we'd been engaged for a few days that he told me we had met for the first time at Stamps, a trendy new club not far from the West End.

The fact we had met in a club surprised me, for Hugh wasn't the club going sort, much more the serious type, reserved and very self-controlled. Not a person at all to lose himself in a riotous evening getting wasted, and strutting his stuff in the latest and most fashionable club in London.

He was tall and slim, and obviously kept himself fit. He was well dressed in a conventional way, not the latest fashion, that was not his style, but classic. He did not have what you would call film star good looks, but his appearance was pleasing enough with his straight nose, well-shaped mouth and regular features. He had a good head of hair, very dark, almost black that was just beginning to grey around his temples, but in no way did it age him. In fact it was just the opposite, it gave him a rather distinguished air. His best features by far were his eyes, for although they were quite deep set and almost black, he had thick, dark lashes which any female would die for. Sometimes, when I happened to meet his glance, his eyes were dark and impenetrable, almost dangerous, in that there was no way you could guess what he was really thinking. If the eyes are the gateway to our souls, then Hugh kept the door to his soul very firmly shut. He was intelligent, well educated (a First in Law from Durham University), and he was very well off. He had a first class job with one of the top five legal firms in the City. He was also madly in love with me.

For the last few months we had mixed in the same group of friends, though not as a couple and we were definitely not thought of as an 'item'. I always regarded him as a person who was on the periphery, the fringe, but it didn't matter. An unattached male was always useful in balancing the male/female ratio. It seemed to me that he had never particularly sort out my company, so I was mildly surprised when, one evening as I was on my way home from work, I bumped into him in the King's Road, and he stopped me.

I was just about to pop into Sainsbury's to get something for my supper – yet again I had no food worth speaking of in the flat. I was late leaving the office, tired and hungry when a voice behind me shouted, 'Flora, wait, have you got a minute?' I spun around and saw it was Hugh Fenton.

'Oh hi,' I replied. 'Yes, what is it?' I hoped I didn't sound too off hand, but after all I was in a hurry and it had started to rain. He pulled me over to the side of the pavement where we were in less danger of being shoved around by the milling crowd.

'I know it's your birthday next week, and I wondered if you would have dinner with me that night, that's if you're free.'

I looked at him in astonishment. How had he known it was my birthday, and why would he care? Whilst I hadn't deliberately hidden the fact I would be another year older, I hadn't exactly broadcast it to the world either, although naturally my close friends and family knew. For a second I hesitated, although I knew I had no special arrangements for that evening. In fact I was very upset with Harry because he had refused to come to my flat for dinner to help me celebrate; he had told me that he had a long standing engagement that night which he wasn't going to cancel. It had led to a furious argument.

So, I found myself replying, 'That's very kind of you, thank you very much. As it happens I'm not doing anything special on my birthday, I'm celebrating at the weekend. So, yes, I'd love to have dinner.' It would serve Harry right when he found out I had another date. It might even make him jealous.

Hugh looked at me with that intense, impenetrable look. It was possibly the first time I had really noticed his eyes. 'That's wonderful,' he said. 'I'll pick you up at your house about eight.'

It had started to pour down harder now, and the rain was dripping into my upturned collar. I was even more anxious to get home, so I didn't ask him how he knew where I lived. 'Great. O.K. I'll see you then. Looking forward to it. Ciao,' and with that I escaped into the crowd before he could delay me further.

The following week passed as uneventfully as ever, and my job working for a big national charity was boring and tedious. I had gone to work there as a temporary project manager five years ago, and I was still there. On the night of my birthday dinner as I hurried home after work I found I was almost looking forward to the evening. At least I'd get an extremely good meal, and it would be a change not to have the usual argument with Harry over whose turn it was to pay. I had no doubt that Hugh Fenton would be the perfect gentleman in that respect.

I showered, changed and the doorbell rang exactly as the hands on my kitchen clock pointed to eight o'clock. I ran down the hallway and opened the door.

'Good evening Flora,' Hugh said, as he stepped into the rather cramped hall of my small flat.

'Hi,' I replied, wishing that he wouldn't sound so boringly formal. 'Come in.' He stood awkwardly on the threshold for a second, then he said, 'Happy birthday. By the way these are for you,' and handed me the most lovely bouquet of very pale cream roses, creamy peonies, sweet smelling stock, hydrangeas, and pale green frothy *alchemilla mollis*. The effect was stunning.

'Oh Hugh! What lovely flowers. Thank you so much, it's very sweet of you. I'll just go and put them in some water.' I went into the small kitchen frantically looking for a vase. 'Do go into the sitting room and take a seat. That's if you can find anywhere to sit. It's rather untidy, I'm afraid. Would you like a drink? A glass of wine perhaps?' I asked, hoping there was a bottle in the fridge.

'No thank you very much. If you don't mind we'd better get going. I've booked a table for eight thirty, and I don't like to be late.' No, I thought to myself, I bet you don't, and I wondered what sort of evening I had let myself in for.

I plonked the flowers in water, and went back into the hall where Hugh was still standing exactly in the same spot where he had come in. 'Here, let me help you,' he said as I picked up my wrap and pulled it over my shoulders. He held the door open for me as we left the apartment, went down the front steps, to where he had parked his Mercedes.

It only took around twenty five minutes to drive to the restaurant which was quiet, discreet and very expensive. The maitre d' greeted Hugh by name, and showed us to the best table in a corner where we would not be noticed or overheard by anyone. The menu was hand written in black ink on thick cream card, and there were no prices shown. The sommelier came, and after a brief discussion, he left and reappeared with a bottle of Bollinger. Vintage, naturally.

This was obviously an evening where no expense was going to be spared, and I happily went along with the waiter's recommendation when discussing the menu, and ordered English asparagus, quails' eggs with white truffle to start, followed by warm lobster salad with a cardamom, lime and mango vinaigrette. For pudding - I wasn't going to hold back tonight - a passion fruit sorbet.

The champagne was poured, cooled to just the right temperature and I looked appreciatively as the pale gold bubbles filled my glass. I took a sip of the delicious wine and settled back in my chair. Hugh raised his glass in my direction. 'To you Flora, and wishing you a very happy birthday.' I raised my glass in return.

We made small talk, or rather I led the conversation, as Hugh didn't speak much and then our meal was served. I chattered on in what I hoped was a light and entertaining way. At last we finished our meal, the last of the wine drunk, and coffee ordered. 'Would you like a liqueur?' he asked. I shook my head, while he ordered a brandy.

It arrived and he sat silently, and seemed strangely abstracted as he swirled the amber coloured contents around in the brandy balloon. What a peculiar creature he was I thought, and wondered why he had bothered to ask me to have dinner with him at all. Suddenly, he looked up from his glass.

'I have something to say to you. Something I want to ask you.' His voice was low and intense, and it trembled slightly. I looked at him. 'Really? What?' I was only mildly curious. He might have been about to ask what I thought about some particular television programme. So I practically fell to the floor when he said,

'I want to ask you if you'll marry me.'

My mouth opened and my jaw dropped. I must have looked a fright. I looked at him in utter amazement. I wondered if I had heard him correctly. I was, literally, speechless. He saw the astonishment on my face, and he gave a wry smile.

'I hope I haven't completely shocked you.'

My mouth was still open in an "O", and I heard a voice, my voice, replying, 'Marry you? What on earth for?'

'For the reason that most people ask some-one to marry them, because I'm desperately in love with you.'

'I had no idea you loved me. You've never shown it.'

'I'm very good at hiding my feelings, and I'm not very good at saying things which mean a great deal to me. I want you to know that I fell in love with you the first time I saw you.'

'But I hardly know you. Hugh, I'm very flattered but ...' My voice tailed off as for once again I was lost for words.

'You don't have to give me an answer immediately. I know this has come as a great surprise, but take your time and think things over.'

'But I don't know you, I don't know you at all.' He gave me that intense look of his, and our eyes met, and this time I did see in them a passion and tenderness and love that I have never before seen in anyone, and it inexplicitly moved me and excited me at the same time.

'As I said, I'll give you some time to get used to the idea. Perhaps after a while it won't seem such an outlandish idea. I'm happy to wait, but don't keep me waiting too long, please.'

I did not say anything, but two thoughts were rushing through my head. In the last month my two very best friends married their long term partners, and although they swore that nothing would alter our friendship, this was not the case. The status quo had subtly changed, and our relationship was different. We were still the best of friends, but I knew that their husbands had now taken first place in the friendship stakes, and that was as it should be. I didn't resent this, but I mourned the change.

Also I knew for sure that my five year affair with Harry was going nowhere ... fast. And when the age of thirty is looming on the horizon, I knew that I wanted that permanent commitment from someone. Being an older single woman didn't appeal to me, although it was perfectly all right for some, and they lived happy and fulfilled lives, it was not for me. It was simply not my scene.

So I took a deep breath, and smiled my sweetest smile. 'I think perhaps I would like some time to think things over.'

It was over another expensive meal that I agreed to marry him. This time he had taken me to a delightful country hotel on the banks of the Thames. After lunch we sat out on the terrace watching the river flow slowly by and listening to the birds. He sat by my side, and took my hand in his.

'Flora, you've had some time to think over my proposal, and although I think I am a patient man, I would like to know what you have decided. I'm going to Japan very soon for three weeks, and it would mean the world to me to know that you were here waiting for me when I return.'

I had, in the interim, thought very seriously about his proposal. After all, I reasoned, why not? He could offer me security, love, a very nice life-style, and an escape from the drab, going nowhere existence I was leading. We had more in common than I had at first appreciated. We came from similar backgrounds, we shared the same friends, and to a degree, interests. All right, he was probably more of an opera or ballet buff, while my tastes were not all that highbrow, more clubbing and the occasional rock concerts. We lived in London, and both wanted to continue doing so; our ages were compatible. He was nice looking, had very good white teeth (I have a 'thing' about good teeth, and dental hygiene in particular, and Hugh obviously went to an expensive West End dentist), and he adored me. I knew I had come to a momentous cross road in my life.

Almost before I knew what I was saying, I replied. 'Thank you Hugh I'd like to say yes. But, in fairness to you, I must make one thing quite clear – I will marry you but only if you agree that we do not have any children. I have never wanted children, and in any case I don't think I'd make a very good mother.'

When a girl is fast approaching her thirties it makes her realise that another decade is looming, anno domini and all that. Not that I was worried about the gynaecological clock ticking away with regard to having children. It was simply the thought of having children, and the whole pregnancy scene, filled me with horror. That had never appealed to me. Not that I disliked kids, far from it. But the physical aspect of child bearing, all that pushing, panting, the whole bloody, messy business appalled me. It would be even worse if you elected to have a caesarean section, as I had read some women did. The thought of losing my figure was something that I never wanted to contemplate. However much you exercised or dieted after having children, the tell-tale tummy bulge was always there afterwards. No, children were definitely not on the agenda. I had to make that perfectly clear. It was my body, and the thought of another being implanted inside me and over which I had no control well, I couldn't contemplate it.

Hugh listened carefully to what I had to say, but made no objection though I thought I detected a slight shadow had crossed his face. Then, as the penny dropped and he realised I had accepted, he gave a gasp of delight. 'So it's a "yes" then?'

'I suppose so.'

Six weeks later we were married.

I knew him very little then, and now, although we had been married nearly two years, I knew him very little more. I was touched by his kindness, his consideration, and surprised by his passion.

We had a three week honeymoon in Italy, and after we had made love and I lay in his arms, he would become sentimental and oddly emotional for one who was normally so self-conscious, reserved and controlled.

On a day to day basis he was extremely attentive, very polite always helping me in or out of the car, holding the door open for me, that sort of thing. It appeared to me that he treated me more like a treasured object, as though I was a piece of rare Chinese porcelain, and not as other men treated their wives as a friend, a buddy, and an equal. He put me on a pedestal, and at times I felt the bonds of marriage strangling me.

At first it amused me to be so treasured, and I was flattered, but as time went by it began to grate on my nerves. Sometimes I would deliberately provoke him to see what reaction there would be, but invariably he humoured me and let me have my way until I wanted to scream. I often wondered why he had fallen so deeply in love with me.

He gave me a wonderful life, a lovely four bed-roomed house not far from the Embankment, with a small but very pretty garden at the rear. I left my job, which I was delighted to do, and I suppose I became a 'lady who lunched.' I shopped to my heart's content, had lovely holidays two or three times a year, went to the hair and beauty salons every fortnight, and had all my bills paid. I had household help, and if ever we did any entertaining that involved more than having friends in for supper when we sat around the kitchen table, we always engaged professional caterers. I was spoiled, treasured, adored. Eventually, I was bored beyond belief.

Life with Hugh became so predictable I longed for a little excitement, for danger. I was in the proverbial gilded cage, and I wanted to break free, and it was then I resumed my affair with Harry.

At first we were very discreet, but as time went by I became reckless, almost as if I was tempting fate and I wanted Hugh to find out. At least it would provide me with some excitement, but then there was that unfortunate incident in February when Hugh had come home early and had caught Harry and me, well, not exactly *inflagrente delecto*, but in a very tricky situation. That had shaken me immensely, and I appreciated what I was in danger of losing; and so the weeks passed, each of us tiptoeing around each other, as if we were executing the steps of some grotesque minuet of long ago.

Then in late summer Hugh announced that we would take a short break in Devon, to a place called Kilworth Barton, and he was adamant that we go and stay. I decided there was no way I was willing to rock the boat even further by refusing to go, he might think that I was just looking for excuses to stay in London and see Harry, and nothing could be further from the truth. So I duly packed my bag, set off down to the West Country, and it was then that my life changed, forever.

PART TWO

The first thing I noticed was how Kilworth Barton nestled comfortably into its surroundings, and how the lush green colour of the lawn to the front melded into the landscape. The old house rose effortlessly, the grey of the granite blending in with the surrounding grey of the hills, and above it the grey skies. Even the rain which was now falling gently on my upturned face was grey, and almost invisible. Putting my suitcase down for a moment, I glanced down at the paper I held in my other hand, a copy of the email which gave the directions to the bed and breakfast. I had printed these earlier that morning before I left London for the journey to the middle of Devon.

'Located in the wildest part of central Dartmoor, Kilworth Barton is possibly the most remote bed and breakfast in the area. For walkers there are footpaths radiating across the moor in all directions, while non walkers can enjoy the tranquillity of the gardens and rest in a sun lounger to watch the cattle, sheep or Dartmoor ponies graze just outside the garden gate.'

It was certainly true, this spot was really remote, and picking up my overnight bag I made my way down the gravel path to the front door and banged on the iron studded oak front door. As I reached the door, I realised that it was open slightly, and I tried to push it open further, but it was firmly stuck, and would not budge. Then, from deep inside a woman's voice shouted 'Helloooo – come on in please, I'll be with you in a minute.' I put my bag down, and with both hands pushed the door even harder. This time the door did open, and I almost fell into the house.

The grey flagstone floor felt cool beneath my feet, and the hall was dark and at the far end I could barely make out a flight of stairs. Suddenly a door on my left opened and a tall, slim pleasant looking woman of about forty stood in front of me, wiping her hands on her apron.

'Hello, I'm Cassie French, you must be Flora Fenton.' She held out a slightly floury hand. 'Sorry about this,' she said dusting her hands, and indicating to the flour. 'I've been making scones. Welcome to Kilworth Barton. I hope you had a good journey down, and you didn't have too much trouble finding us.' It was more of a statement than a question. She turned, and from a recess took out a rather battered visitors' book. 'If you could just sign this for me, and then I'll show you to your room. Is your husband with you, or will he be joining you later?'

I hesitated slightly, and I recalled the conversation I had had with Hugh earlier in the week.

I was going out to meet a friend for lunch, when Hugh had emerged from the kitchen, tea cloth in hand, and stopped me just as I opened the front door.

'By the way Flora, sorry I forgot to tell you before, we're going away on Thursday. I've booked us into a bed and breakfast in Dartmoor for this week-end on a three day break.' I looked at him in dismay.

'But I don't want to go to Devon, and I especially I don't want to go to Dartmoor. You remember what happened the last time we went, it rained all the time, and it was miserable. I was miserable. Anyway, I've got things arranged for the week-end, you know I'm meeting my sister and I haven't seen her for ages. In fact, I don't want to leave London.'

'I'm sorry darling, it's too late. I've booked us in for three nights. It's all confirmed and paid for.' He looked at me with a strangely calm and enigmatic expression. As he spoke there was a new firmness in his voice which I had noticed he had adopted lately, ever since that unfortunate episode with Harry. Not that Hugh had ever mentioned anything, far from it, but his attitude towards me had, in some strange, imperceptible manner altered very slightly. He was still kind and considerate, and if I wanted anything, nothing was too much trouble, but in a subtle way he had become more assertive, less willing to please me, and it was as if the tables were slowly turning, and I was dancing to Hugh's tune. Not all the time, but I was conscious that at times the status quo was gradually changing. Strangely enough I found I quite liked it. I was gaining more respect for him, and he wasn't being such a doormat. It was challenging, and in a way exciting.

But this time I dug my heels in. 'I'm not coming. You'll just have to go by yourself, or cancel. You know you'll be much better off without me, you can walk to your heart's content. You know that's not my scene, and I'll only make us both miserable.'

'I'm sorry you feel that way, but it's too bad. You're coming, and that's that. Anyway, walking across the moor and the fresh Devon air will do you good. It'll help you to get fit.'

'I *am* fit!'

'You're coming to Devon with me and that's that ... if you know what's good for you.' I didn't like the implied threat. I looked at him sharply, and, not wishing for this to turn into a full blown row, turned and opened the front door and went down the steps to my car. As I walked away I could feel his eyes following me.

Then, to add insult to injury, last night and at the very last minute, he had informed me that a very important meeting had been arranged for the following morning, and I would have to drive down on my own. I was annoyed. I didn't want to drive the four hour journey in my own car, I would be much more comfortable being chauffeured by Hugh in his big Mercedes.

'I'll wait and we can travel together. It makes much more sense to only take one car.'

'I'm not sure what time I'll be able to leave. Anyway, I don't want you tiring yourself by hanging around. It's much better you go on down, settle in, have a rest, and I'll join you later.' He said this in his new tone that would brook no argument.

Now, as I stood in the hall of Kilworth Barton, I smiled at my hostess. 'Hugh will be here later. Unfortunately he got held up at work so we decided to drive down separately. I was anxious to get out of London early and take my time driving here. I hope he'll be down in time for dinner.' I bent to pick up my bag, but before I could Cassie had beaten me to it.

'No, let me take this for you. You must be tired after your journey.' She looked at me in what I thought was a rather odd manner, then led the way down the dim hall and up the stairs. We reached the landing, and she ushered me along a narrow sloping corridor, stopping outside a white painted door. She clicked the latch and stepped aside to allow me into the room first.

The room was enchanting. Opposite the door set low in the wall, three latticed windows looked out to the front of the house, over the lawn and flower beds. To my right a large, high white enamelled Victorian bed took up most of the wall, complete with a faded patchwork quilted cover.

'Cassie, what a delightful room,' I said as I bent down to look out of the window at the garden.

'Thank you. I'm glad you like it. It used to be our bedroom before we began the bed and breakfast, and then we moved to be nearer the girls' bedroom at the end of the house.'

'You have children?'

'Yes, two, twins actually. They're almost seven.'

'How do you manage to run the bed and breakfast and cope with two small children?'

'With difficulty, especially in the summer when we are at our busiest. It's not too bad if there are other children staying, but although we've been fully booked for weeks, I've had no families to stay. The girls are away visiting my parents at the minute. Sending them to my mother helps ease the load, and as they are their grandparents they love having them.'

'We were lucky to get a room if you're so busy as my husband only booked last week,' I said. I bent to smell the little posy of tiny pink roses in a small white vase shaped like a swan that had been placed on the bedside table.

Cassie put down my bag. 'I think you must be mistaken. Hugh, I mean your husband,' she corrected quickly, 'booked ages ago, way back in February. He said it would be the first time he could get away as he had a very busy schedule for the next few months. I remember the booking as it was the first reservation I'd taken for the summer season and ...' She stopped abruptly as if she realised that possibly she had said too much. Maybe she noticed the bemused expression on my face. What did she mean, the room had been booked months ago? She must have mixed us with another booking I thought, and dismissed it from my mind.

'Anyway, it doesn't matter,' Cassie said changing the subject, 'You're here now and that's the important thing. This is your bathroom. Do be careful of the step down. I'm afraid the floors in these old houses are rather uneven.'

She crossed the room and opened another door to reveal a huge white cast iron bath standing on enormous ball and claw feet, with an old fashioned rose shower head above. Over a mahogany towel rail large white, fluffy bath towels had been neatly folded, and white crochet edged handtowels draped over them. A blue and white jug and bowl standing on the floor in the corner completed the effect which was fresh, wholesome and welcoming. 'Perhaps you'd like a nice relaxing bath, and there are tea making facilities in your room.' As we stepped back into the bedroom she added, 'Dinner will be ready about 7.30. I hope your husband will be here by then.'

'I'm sure he will be. I'm expecting a message from him any time soon to tell me he's on his way.'

A small frown crossed her pleasant features. She flicked a stray strand of hair from her eyes. 'I'm sorry but we don't have a very strong mobile phone signal. But if you go down the front path to the gate sometimes you can pick up one there.'

Cassie made her way to the door. 'Perhaps you'd like a little rest before dinner? Do let me know if there's anything else you need.'

I smiled. 'Thank you. I'm going to do just what you suggested – first I'm going to make a nice cup of tea, and then put my feet up.' Suddenly, I felt completely exhausted and even though the journey had been easy, the idea of a rest was very inviting.

Cassie hesitated, her hand on the door knob, as if she was going to say something else, then changed her mind. 'I mustn't keep you chatting. Have a nice rest. I'll see you later.' With that she opened the door, and shut it gently behind her, and left me to my thoughts.

Why had Hugh not told me before about booking to come here? It appeared as if he had deliberately not told me. Thinking about it, February was time the little 'incident' with Harry had occurred. Was Hugh playing some kind of game? The idea disturbed me for this behaviour was so unlike him, so out of character from the person I knew, or thought I knew. I had always regarded him as completely open and honest, without a devious thought in his head. Perhaps I didn't know my husband as well as I thought.

I sat down on the bed, and it was cosy and enticing. Kicking off my shoes, I climbed in and snuggled under the quilt. The smooth white linen sheet had a crocheted edge and above it the initials LJW were embroidered in the centre. The laced edged pillow cases were plump, soft and inviting. I laid back and closed my eyes.

The room was filled with a soft light, and there was a distinct fragrance in the air, warm and sweet smelling. At first I thought it to be lavender, but somehow I associated it with the warm scent of citrus blossom. I was struck by the complete and utter silence, as if I was the only person alive in the world. Somehow all my senses were heightened, my vision, hearing, sense of smell, all had been in a way enhanced.

All but the sense of touch – I could not feel the weight of the quilt on top of me, nor could I feel the cool sheet underneath. I rose from the bed, all traces of the previous fatigue had vanished. I moved effortlessly across the floor to the bedroom door, and stepped out into the passage, down the stairs, and opened the front door. This time the door did not stick, it moved with ease. There was no one else about, no sign of the other guests, or of Cassie. I was quite alone. I retraced my steps down the garden path, out through the gate, and turned left down a rough stone strewn path.

I was walking downhill, and the grey mist which had obscured the moor when I arrived had lifted. The sky was now cloudless, and an amazing electric blue. I walked on and on, without effort, almost as if I was in a dream, but this was no dream. I found myself walking towards the sea, and as I got closer I could smell the salty tang of the sea, and was aware of swirling seagulls, whooping and diving over my head, and the poignant sound of their cawing filled the air, whereas before the silence had been so profound.

I had reached the beach, and the tide was out leaving long stretches of flat, pale yellow sand exposed. The sea rolled in, now covering the empty stretches of shore with a swish and swirl of lace edged foam, now sweeping away leaving a glittering silver-like mass of sand in its wake. To my right the cliffs rolled down to the sea, while to my left the beach stretched on endlessly, passed Start Point and on towards Dartmouth and eventually the Exe estuary.

Not too far away I spotted a woman sitting on the beach. She was looking in the direction of two small children who were paddling in the waves. I could see she had on a pale yellow dress dotted with dark blue pansies, not dissimilar to the one I had bought for the summer, although I thought it rather cold to be wearing for this time of year. Her hair was brown, rather nondescript and shoulder length, again it was a similar in colour and style to my own, before I had the blonde highlights. I could hear the children's delighted cries coming from the sea as they shouted and laughed and frolicked in the waves, and they waved to the woman sitting on the beach who waved back.

Slowly, I walked over to where she sat. Some unknown instinct made me look back over my shoulder, and I saw that the incessant sea had wiped out all traces of my footprints in the soft sand, as though I had never walked across the beach at all. The wind was blowing gently about my head and blew my hair across my face and into my eyes. I had reached the place where the woman was sitting.

'Hello,' I smiled. 'It's a lovely day.' She did not turn to look at me, but I sensed she smiled, 'Are those your children over there?' I indicated to the two children who were still dancing around in the waves. Their squeals of delight as they splashed each other carried easily in the clear air, and the droplets of water caught the sunlight as if a waterfall of diamonds was cascading around them.

'Be careful you two,' their mother called to the children. 'Don't get too wet!' Then she addressed me. 'Yes, they're my girls, they're twins. We're down here on holiday. We thought we'd take an early break this year, before it gets too crowded.'

'So are we, down on holiday that is.' I glanced towards the children. 'They're having a wonderful time. Oh – to be that age again!'

She patted the tartan picnic rug on which she was sitting. 'Would you like to sit down? Take the weight of your feet.' She looked at my swollen belly.

'Thank you. How kind. You may have to help me up though!' I grimaced.

'When's the baby due?'

'In about six week's time. Towards the end of April.' I sank as gracefully as I could onto my knees, and then I shuffled along on my bottom next to my newfound friend.

'What a co-incidence. The girls' birthday is at the end of April – the 30th actually.'

'Would you believe it, that is exactly my due date. To tell you the truth my husband and I didn't plan on having any children ever. I'm not the maternal sort. I was horrified when I discovered I was pregnant.

What's it like? Having twins I mean. One baby must be hard enough work, but two ...' I broke off, appalled at the very idea.

'Oh, you get used to it. I can't pretend it isn't hard work, especially at first with all the night feeds. But it doesn't last forever, as they say.'

I continued talking to my new acquaintance, and out of the corner of my eye I noticed a man walking towards us, and approaching quite fast, and as he did he waved in our direction. But for us the beach was completely deserted. The shouts of the children still carried over the air.

'There's someone coming towards us waving. Do you know him?'

She glanced in the direction of the approaching figure.

'Yes,' she said, then she turned her gaze away, as if she were totally disinterested. 'It's my husband.'

We sat in a friendly silence, and I could feel the warmth of the sun on my face, even though it was only mid March. By now the man had reached us, and he stopped. He ignored the woman seated beside me, as if she wasn't there, and focused his gaze solely on me. I looked up into his face, but the bright sunlight shone directly into my eyes, blurring my vision. The man held out his hand and I took it, and he helped me to my feet.

It was then that my companion turned around and I saw her face for the first time. I saw the light brown, shoulder length hair, and at the temples amongst the brown the first strands of grey. On her forehead horizontal lines crossed her brow from one side to the other, crow's feet around her eyes, and I noticed a slight puckering around her mouth. She appeared careworn and tired. Then she stood up, and for the first time I was able to see her figure. She was certainly not overweight, though I would guess she could lose about ten pounds to regain what I would call a trim figure, and there was that tell tale bulge around her tummy – the legacy of the twins.

The wind blew her hair in front of her eyes, and she reached up to tuck the offending strands behind her ears in what was a very familiar gesture. It was then the lightning bolt hit me – I was looking at myself, but as I would look in about seven years' time.

I glanced at the man who was still standing by my side. He looked at me and smiled and his eyes were black and burned right into the very core of my being, like lakes of liquid jet.

'Hello,' he said. 'I've made it to Kilmarth in good time after all.'

It was Hugh.

The cup of tea beside me on the bedside table was untouched and had gone quite cold, so I went into the bathroom to empty the contents down the sink, and caught sight of myself in the mirror. I looked a mess, my hair was all windblown and my cheeks glowed as though I had caught the sun on my walk and I felt sweaty and sticky. I needed a shower to freshen up and then change before dinner.

I picked up my mobile phone to see if I had any messages, and there I saw I had one missed call which had gone straight through to the messaging service. It was from Hugh to say that he would be arriving at Kilworth around 7 p.m. In spite of what Cassie French had said about the lack of a signal, somehow this one had managed to reach get through. I must have fallen into a really deep sleep when I'd had my rest, for the mobile was right beside me on the bedside table, and I had not heard its shrill ring tone.

Refreshed after my shower I put on my new black silk top and my favourite black jeans. They had cost an arm and a leg, but were so well cut and fitted so beautifully especially around my hips and my thighs and did not bulge, and were worth every penny. As I zipped them up I noticed that they were rather tight about the waist, and I looked at myself in the mirror in alarm. Had I put on weight? I didn't think so, but was that what Hugh had meant when he made the remark about my fitness. I turned sideways and pulled in my stomach, to check again. It was then I had the flashback to the beach and I remembered, with growing horror, my swollen stomach, and how I had thought myself pregnant.

No, surely I was as slim as ever, but maybe I would have to watch my diet, cut down on the cappuccinos, and horror of horrors, go to the gym! I had always been one of those fortunate women who could, within reason, eat or drink whatever I wanted without the need to diet, or take strenuous exercise, and stay as slim as I had been at sixteen. Of course, not having had children helped.

Then I heard the floorboards creaking in the passage and approaching footsteps, the sound of voices getting nearer, then the low hum of conversation between Cassie and Hugh. I listened, but couldn't hear what was being said, and finally a rattle at the door. It opened, and in walked Hugh. He crossed the room and kissed me, then holding me at arm's length and he looked at me, smiling.

'Darling, you look marvellous, and you've got some colour in your cheeks already. I'm going to take a quick shower and change, and you can tell me what you've been doing over dinner.'

As with many old houses the dining room was rather dark and low ceilinged, and at the far end there was an enormous inglenook fireplace big enough for two people to stand in, with a huge granite lintel over. Although it was summer, there was a slight chill in the air, and Cassie had lit a fire. The setting sun streamed in through the low west facing window, and dust motes caught in the rays of the sun danced in the golden light.

As we entered the room I saw Cassie placing a little vase of fresh flowers on a table by the fire. The table was laid for two, and she looked up as we entered, and smiled.

'There's only you two booked in for dinner tonight, so you'll have the place to yourselves. Would you like a drink before dinner? I haven't a license to sell liquor, but I can offer you a glass of wine, compliments of the house. I have a lovely chilled Chablis or if you prefer red, there's a very decent claret. My husband Nick is in charge of the wine, that's his area of expertise. I just enjoy drinking it.'

'That's very kind of you, we'd love a glass. I'll have the claret, and Flora will have the Chablis, thank you.' This was the new Hugh again, ordering for me, whereas previously he had always waited for me to make my choice.

Cassie smiled. 'I'll just get your wine first, then we can talk about dinner.' She slipped out, closing the door.

Hugh looked about him, as if he were soaking up the atmosphere. He went over to the fire and held out his hands to the gentle glow. 'It's lovely being here again. I used to stay here when some people called Hunter owned this house. My parents came every summer for years, and ...' He stopped suddenly as if he had been about to say more, but suddenly changed his mind.

I looked at him in amazement. That was the first time he had ever mentioned that he knew the place, and that he had ever been previously. Why had he never mentioned it?

'Really Hugh, you've been here before? Why didn't you tell me?'

'I did Flora, I told you when I said I'd booked to come here. I said to you that as a child I came down most summers with my parents. You must have forgotten,' he said quickly.

I sat and stared at him. Was he going mad, or was I? We had never had that conversation. I started to contradict him, but I could see that it would evolve into one of those tedious 'Yes I did, no you did not' arguments between husband and wife. He leant forward to give the fire a poke. 'Forget it, Flora. It's not important.' He gave a half hearted laugh. 'You're getting very forgetful in your old age.'

Rather than make a scene, I thought it best to drop the subject. 'Sorry, I must have forgotten.'

Cassie returned with a glass of white wine for me, and an already opened bottle of claret for Hugh who had seated himself in one of the yew and elm Windsor chairs next to the fire. He stretched out his long legs, and smiled at our hostess, and raised his glass in a silent toast. As I sipped my glass of wine, I turned to Cassie.

'That's an amazing fireplace, it's so big you would be able to get three grown men standing inside it. Is this a Devon long house?' I remembered reading somewhere ages ago in one of those country living magazines an article about long houses.

'Yes, it's a long house, or as we call it a cross passage house, as you see it's built on a slope. The humans lived in the upper part here, and the animals across the passage, and downhill for obvious reasons!' she laughed.

I was intrigued, I had never really been interested in old houses before. 'How old is Kilworth?'

'We've had the National Park people here and they date the present house to around 1680. This is not the original building on this site though. There is a Kildermearth Barton mentioned in the Domesday Book.

'Barton' is the old English word meaning 'farm.' This place has been knocked about and altered to suit the times, and rebuilt over the centuries. And this is what we're still doing to houses today, so you see, nothing is new. It has all been done before.'

Despite the warmth from the fire, I sensed a slight shiver running down my spine. My next question came almost before I heard myself ask, with a small laugh, 'Are there any ghosts here?'

It may have been my imagination, but I thought I saw Cassie give a sly, sideways glance at Hugh. 'No don't worry,' she laughed. 'We've no ghosts here, none that I've heard of anyway.' Then, as if to deliberately change the subject she asked, 'What would you like for dinner? I can offer you something special tonight. One of our guests went to Exmouth today and brought back some fresh crab, caught this morning and with it you can have new potatoes and salad, all straight from the garden. Or, you can still have what was originally on offer, the local lamb grilled with rosemary, and I serve it with new potatoes, carrots and peas, again from the garden. Oh, and fresh mint sauce, of course. For pudding I have sticky toffee apple or a lemon syllabub. The sticky apple comes with clotted cream from the next door farm, strictly the non-fattening variety naturally!' she added with a wicked smile.

I heaved a huge sigh. It all sounded so delicious, I would definitely have to go on a diet after this. A decision. What to order, the crab sounded delicious. I took another sip of my wine.

'What a co-incidence that you should have crab. I had the most wonderful walk on the beach this afternoon, and after all that sea air that is exactly what I would like.' I said.

Cassie and Hugh looked at me in amazement, then with mutual expressions of bewilderment etched on their faces. For a moment no one spoke, and Cassie said in what I thought was an apologetic tone. 'Goodness me, you must have slept soundly when you had your nap. You couldn't have possibly gone to the beach. The coast is over forty miles away. You must have been dreaming.'

It was my turn to look astonished. I *knew* I had gone to the beach. I closed my eyes for a second, and the scene was set vividly before me. I saw the rough stone strewn footpath, and could feel again the small sharp rocks beneath my feet as I walked down the track which had taken me to the beach. I had smelt the sea, and had licked the salt from my lips. I had seen and heard the screaming gulls following the tide, and the small waders skimming the surface of the water. I had watched those two small children playing in the sea, and had sat and talked with the mother. This time I wasn't going to be told I'd got it wrong, I'd made a mistake, I'd forgotten. I was beginning to feel like some kind of nut case. I'd had enough. I took a deep breath.

'But I did go to the beach this afternoon, after my rest. I met a woman there, she was with her two daughters, twins, and we sat and had a long talk. You *know* I was there Hugh, you met me there, you ...'

My words faded away as I could see the incredulous looks on their faces, and Hugh interrupted me, and when he spoke there was concern in his voice.

'Are you sure you're feeling all right darling? I drove straight here from London, and arrived about an hour ago. You were still asleep when I went up to our room. I came downstairs and had a cup of tea with Cassie. You looked so peaceful I didn't want to waken you. How could I have possibly met you anywhere – let alone on a beach! Have you been taking something you shouldn't? You must know that we're miles from the coast. Cassie's right, you must have been dreaming.'

I was feeling slightly hysterical now, were they going mad, or was I? 'But you know I was there Hugh, you must. You met me on that beach.'

'Stop this nonsense Flora.' He sounded impatient and rose and went into the hall, returning with one of the brochures, which he thrust into my hand. 'Read it,' he ordered. 'Go on, read it. What does it say?'

I looked down at the leaflet and slowly read the words, 'Located in the wildest part of central Dartmoor ...' My voice trailed off and there was total silence in the room. Cassie gave an embarrassed laugh, 'I shouldn't be standing here talking, I should be in the kitchen cooking your dinner.' She left the room, tactfully shutting the door behind her.

Hugh reached over the table and patted my hand. 'Don't worry about it, you must have had a very vivid dream.'

I sat in silence, completely bewildered, and trying to get my head into some sort of order. If Hugh was attempting to undermine my confidence, he was succeeding. I knew I had been on the beach that afternoon. I knew it, didn't I? Surely it was no dream?

The meal Cassie served was delicious, but it was rather a silent evening. We spoke very little, and when we did our conversation was stilted as though we were strangers, making conversation because that was what one did, being polite. When we finished our dinner the twilight of the long summer evening still lingered. After we drank our coffee Hugh pushed back his chair. It made a scraping sound on the stone floor.

'I think I'll go for a little walk, stretch my legs and breathe some fresh air. Are you going to join me?'

Suddenly, an inexplicable weariness came over me, as it had when I had first arrived. 'No,' I said. 'No, I think I'll go upstairs to bed. I've had enough fresh air for one day.'

I walked slowly up the stairs, down the corridor to our room, and sat down on the bed with a thump. I kicked off my shoes. They were the same ones which I had been wearing all day, and as I did so a trickle of pale yellow sand spilt onto the carpet.

We breakfasted late the next day, and once again we had the dining room to ourselves. There was no sign of the other guests, and I thought they must have had an early start, and be very keen to walk across the moor.

Cassie breezed into the dining room with freshly percolated coffee for me, and a pot of tea for Hugh.

'Good morning, I hope you slept well. It's going to be a lovely day. Now, what would you like for breakfast?'

All I wanted was some fresh fruit and yoghurt, while Hugh settled for bacon and eggs. 'Have you any plans for today?' Cassie asked as she placed some toast in front of Hugh. 'All the other guests have gone walking.'

'And that's exactly what I intend doing,' said Hugh pouring himself some tea. He looked at me. 'What about you darling? I don't suppose you'll want to come hiking across Dartmoor. Why don't you stay here and put your feet up? Take it easy, you had a long day yesterday.'

'You're right. I'm going to sit in the garden and read, I'll have a wander around later, and walk into the village. Is there a pub there?'

Cassie nodded. 'The Half Moon. They make their own pasties, and very good they are too.'

'Fine. Hugh, why don't we meet there for lunch?'

Our plans made, our breakfast finished, we went our separate ways.

The day turned out to be hot and sultry, the oppressive kind where no breath of air stirs the leaves, and everything is motionless and still. It hadn't taken me long to walk into the village along a lane so narrow that only one vehicle could pass at a time.

I imagined the lane in springtime, when it would have been full of primroses and bluebells, but they had long since vanished, and even though the steep banks were dry and dusty they were filled with wildflowers, foxglove and campion, cheeky Red Robin, and golden rod.

I reached the centre of the village, a small square with a few whitewashed cottages clustered around, and there, set back from the green, was the parish church, an ancient granite building with a large squat Norman bell tower at the northern end.

I glanced at my watch, it was not yet twelve and the pub wasn't open. There was no sign of Hugh, so I decided to look around the church. The entrance was down a small path, and I clicked the latch to open the iron gate, and walked down the uneven stone path to the porch and pushed at the heavy oak door.

Inside, the church was quite deserted, cool and quiet, serene with the calm of centuries. To the east, through a large stained glass window above the altar the sun shone, lighting the nave. Over to my right and against a whitewashed wall there stood a huge granite cross and carved in it there was, which I could barely discern, an equal armed cross within a circle in the open jaws of a serpent.

I was studying this and trying to make sense of it, when I heard the church door click open, and a large woman carrying bunches of wild flowers bustled in. At first she didn't see me, then as her eyes grew accustomed to the gloom she saw me and came over.

'I see you're studying the Celtic cross,' she said, putting down the flowers in the nearest pew and stood beside me. 'Fascinating isn't it?'

'What exactly is it? What does it mean?'

'Nobody knows for certain, all we know is that the cross is really pre-historic. The cross within the circle is one of the oldest symbols used by man, an elemental symbol used long before Christianity. We think the circle represents the sun, the earth, possibly creation itself, fertility, the continuous renewal of birth, life and death. Eternity. The serpent represents the Life Force. It has all kinds of symbolism.'

She retrieved the flowers from the pew. 'I'm on the flower rota for this week. Aren't these lovely? And not a single bought bloom ... I foraged all this from the wild bit of my garden, only I didn't realise the wild bit was quite so wild.' She smiled. 'Are you staying in the village?'

As she spoke, I bent down and picked up a long foxglove stem that had fallen to the floor, and it was then I noticed the inscription carved on the back of the pew in front of me. It was the name of the house that caught my eye. It read:-

"In memory of John and Jane Hunter of Kilworth Barton."

I straightened up and handed over the foxglove.

'Yes, I'm staying with my husband at Kilworth Barton, just for a couple of nights. It's an amazing old house.'

'Oh, so you're staying with Cassie Hunter, or French as she is now. She's lovely, known her since she was a girl. Watch out she doesn't put you in the Orange Blossom room!'

I looked at her in amazement. What was she talking about?

'The Orange Blossom room! I'm afraid I don't know what you mean.'

'That's not what it's really called, the Orange Blossom room ... that's only my name for it. It's reputed to be haunted, no, don't be alarmed – haunted by a smell not a person. Some people have sworn they can smell orange blossom in there even though there isn't any. I think in a way that's rather nice, and certainly not scary. I'm sorry if I alarmed you, I just meant it as a joke. Now, I really must go and put these flowers in water, they're beginning to wilt already. It's been nice talking to you. Enjoy the rest of your visit. Oh, and do please sign the visitors' book before you go.' She turned and waddled away down the aisle and disappeared into the back of the church.

I stood a little longer in front of the cross, then made my way back towards the door. Suddenly, a faint voice echoed in my head. 'I used to come here and stay when some people called Hunter owned this house.' Hugh's voice and I shook my head from side to side to clear my head, and suddenly the atmosphere stifled me and I needed to breathe some fresh air.

As I stepped outside a shiver passed through my body, as if someone had walked over my grave.

That night at Kilworth Barton again we were the only ones having dinner, and afterwards I went to straight up to our room. As before when I climbed into the bed, I must have fallen into a deep, deep sleep for as soon as my head hit the soft pillow, there was nothing that I remembered.

At some stage much later, I was conscious that Hugh was in bed beside me, and I could feel the pressure of his arms as he folded them about me. The warmth of his body was strangely comforting, and I could feel my body trembling all over.

I had never thought of Hugh as a passionate man, but on our honeymoon in Italy he surprised me with the ferocity and the emotion of his love making such that I had never before experienced. I was surprised to learn how intense he really was. He had always been so self-controlled, but I had always put that down to his background and long training in self-control in the legal profession.

Tonight as he lay beside me he started to kiss me, and as tired as I was I felt aroused, and I sought his lips and returned his kisses with a desire and passion which amazed me, for I had never before felt so intensely this way. All my body was melting into his being, and I knew it was I who was uttering amazing words of love. I could hear myself moaning slightly, and suddenly I found my face was wet with tears. And he found my lips again and again, and the pressure and intensity of his touch shot through my whole body with an ecstasy I had never before experienced.

He lifted me off the bed and I felt once again the flames, and I was burnt to a cinder. What was he doing to me now? He was doing this and this and this, and from afar I heard a deep groan, and it was not only coming from me. Later, I clung to him, desperate to keep that moment, desperate and adoring.

I felt the angel breath on my cheeks, and a voice whispered softly in my ear seemingly from a great distance. "Let him kiss me with the kisses of his mouth, for thy love is better than wine."

Sometime later I awoke, and for a long while afterwards sleep eluded me, and I tossed and turned. The pale grey fingers of dawn crept into the room under the blinds, and at last unable to bear my restlessness any longer I rose and went into the bathroom to fetch a glass of water. I returned to my side of the bed and perched on the edge gently so as not to disturb Hugh. As I did so the bedroom door very slowly opened, and two small children crept in, whispering and giggling into the other's ear. Their long blonde hair fell over their faces and down on their shoulders, and their hands were playing with something which I could not quite make out. Whatever game they were playing it absorbed them completely, for they took no notice of me.

At first I thought the children must belong to one of the other guests, but then I remembered Cassie saying there were no children staying. The girls must be Cassie's daughters. They must have returned from staying with their grandparents.

I stood up and went over to them, shaking the nearest child gently on the shoulder. 'What are you two doing here, and why aren't you in your beds? It's far too early for you to be up. You must go back to your room immediately or we'll all be in trouble.'

They took no notice of me and continued playing with the object they held in their hands. It was a paper chain, the sort I used to make as a child, with one piece of coloured paper linked into another in a long continuous chain. They sat down on the floor and continued their game, ignoring me completely.

I was getting a little annoyed by now, so once again I whispered more forcefully. 'You must go back to your own bedroom now ... immediately.' Still they took no notice, so I bent down again, and as I did so I noticed they each had a garland of very small white flowers in their hair which smelt strongly of orange blossom. I touched the nearest child on her shoulder once more to make her aware of me, and it was only then when both the girls turned to me I could see their faces. I wished they had not done so for, as they turned their heads and I looked at them, apart from the shape of the head, I could see they had no features at all, no eyes, no nose, no mouth. There was nothing. A big black void. From a distance I could hear a horrified scream that seemed never ending.

I realised the scream was coming from me.

It must have been the first time I had ever been really ill, and I knew I was more ill than they dared tell me.

Days melted into weeks, and weeks became months. At times I was aware I was sitting in a chair by a window looking down onto a garden. The sunlight streamed in and it was only when I tried to open the window wider that I saw the iron bars that prevented me from doing so; and when I tried to lean out to breathe more air, they rushed at me and jabbed my arm with needles.

Sometimes it was daylight again, and once more the sun shone into my room and across my bed, and my eyes were dazzled by the white sheets. Sometimes it was night, and I was bathed in pale moonlight, cool and gentle, and the long shadows of silver grey danced about my bed.

People, doctors and nurses, came and went, and all the time I was aware of Hugh, his face above mine, concerned, and he faded in and out of my consciousness. Sometimes he was loving, kind, solicitous, and I was safe, and he would guard me against the demons that inhabited my body, he made them disappear, and for a while I was at peace. I knew that we spoke, and he held my hand before the darkness once again overtook my mind.

At other times I could feel the jet black of his eyes burning through me, his gaze hard and implacable, as if he no longer wanted my presence on this earth. It was then I twisted and turned and wanted to escape the shackles which bound me. But there was no way out, no escape, and the chains that tied me to this torture grew tighter and tighter. There was no beginning and no end, just one long continuous blur.

I was weak and frightened, pain wracked and bewildered. It seemed as if my whole body was inhabited by demons who plucked at me with hot knives, or squeezed me with hot pincers so it was all I could do not to groan aloud. May be I did so, for I was vaguely aware of cool towels being pressed to my brow, and my lips being forced open, and refreshing water trickling down my throat.

I did not know what was happening to me, and I was too weary and too defeated to ask. Then there was pain and more pain, and I could hear the sound of hushed voices as they spoke above me, and faces once again swam in and out of my consciousness.

Time passed, but I have no idea of how long. Eventually, people in white coats rushed into my room and I felt myself being lifted into the air as they swung me from my soft bed onto a hard narrower one. There were shouts, crashing, and bangings and I could feel the cold air rushing by my face, and as I looked up hard bright white lights were shining in my eyes, and they rushed me down a long corridor. Doors opened and shut, and again more doors opened, and someone put a clear plastic mask over my mouth and told me to take deep even breaths and whispered that everything would be all right. Then some-one else bent over me, a nurse with a dark green splodge in the middle of her face, and above the splodge a pair of kind brown eyes looked down on me, and she held my hand.

'Flora, you're doing very well. Everything is going to be all right. I want you to squeeze my hand, as hard as you can. That's fine, just a little harder. Good girl, that's wonderful. Now you'll feel a little prick in the back of your hand and I want you to count to ten,' came the voice from behind the mask.

I heard a voice from a long way away saying, 'One, two, three ...'

Then, another voice. 'We still can't understand it. This is the first case that I know where a woman who is proven congenitally infertile has got pregnant.'

Then later, much later, another voice. 'Flora, Flora, hello darling. It's me ... Hugh. It's all over. Well done, we have two beautiful daughters – twins.'

From: cassiehunter-french.@kilworth000.co.uk

To: hugh.@fentonynk.co.uk

Re: Congratulations

Delighted to hear of the twins' safe arrival, and that Flora is slowly recovering at long last. I'm so pleased that The Orange Blossom room worked its magic again, as you know it worked for me and Nick. (!!!) It's strange to think that when we were kids we'd go into that room and pretend we were asleep to try make "those children" come to us. Stay in touch and come and see us again soon – with the family!

Love

Cassie

THE END

Mary Jane Hallowell – About the Author

Mary Jane grew up in Sydney, Australia where she attended Queenwood School. Her journalist father was relocated to Japan when he became a foreign correspondent for a London newspaper, and Mary Jane lived in Japan and Hong Kong, eventually returning to the U.K to study radiography. Returning to Hong Kong, she worked for Qantas before joining BOAC as an air stewardess, and flying the world. Marriage to a service man and two daughters clipped Mary Jane's wings, but she always found time to write. Finally now settled in deepest, darkest Devon, Mary Jane has recently published her first full length romantic novel 'To Touch a Rainbow' and her short story 'The Thrill of the Chase' - both available on Amazon. She is co-editor of a short story anthology 'Hocus Pocus 14' for Halloween with Debbie Flint and other authors, and has contributed her own supernatural story 'Orange Blossom.' A Christmas Anthology, 'The Mistletoe Run and Other Stories' will be available as of December 2014.

KEEP IN TOUCH

Twitter @maryjhallowell

Facebook.com/maryjane.hallowell/

Amazon author page – Mary Jane Hallowell

Thrill of the Chase – on amazon

To Touch a Rainbow – on amazon

Jumping

The Queue

By

Lizzie Lamb

Jumping the Queue – A Short Story by Lizzie Lamb

The express lift whisked me up to the 154th floor and I stepped into an atrium bathed in shimmering blue and gold light. Late for my interview and slightly out of breath, I rushed over to the reception desk and announced that I was the 11.30 candidate.

'Ah, Miss Richardson, you're earlier than we expected,' the receptionist frowned and double-checked the schedule on her monitor.

'Sorry?' I could hardly believe what she'd said.

Arriving early for an appointment just wasn't part of my psyche. I was habitually late for everything. My unpunctuality went beyond the fashionable and veered towards the pathological. Of course, my long-suffering friends put up with me, but I knew that most people thought me disorganised, and - less flatteringly - ditzy and unreliable.

'No matter,' she smiled beatifically. 'Early or late, we're always pleased to welcome a prospective candidate to the... corporation.'

'Thanks,' I murmured, thinking that this was just the kind of place where I would fit right in!

I checked out her lapel badge.

Experience had taught me that addressing non-executive staff by their first name often got them on side. And if I came to work here, having a friendly receptionist to cover for me - should I be late once too often - would be a bonus. But her badge gave no clue as to her identity; it simply stated *P.A., R. Adise Incorp.*

'Here. Drink this.' I was startled out of my dream as she handed me a mug of hot chocolate. Its aroma made my stomach rumble. Running late for this interview had meant that there'd been no time for breakfast and I was now ravenous.

'How did you know...?'

'It's our business to know everything about - the people we interview.' Again, there was a slight hesitation in her voice. As though she was afraid of disclosing information that would give me an advantage over the other candidates being interviewed today.

The hot chocolate was delicious.

It made me feel like I'd had a shot in the arm or someone had wrapped me in a warm, loving embrace. I raised my hand to wipe the steam away from my glasses -and that whimsical thought from my mind, and made a startling discovery. My spectacles were missing and I seemed to have 20/20 vision.

How could that have happened? I looked deep into the mug as if it held the answer. 'What is *in* that drink?' I demanded. If the company wasn't marketing it, they should be! Maybe I could win brownie points by bringing it up at my interview.

A buzzer sounded on her desk and she took the mug from me. 'They're ready for you now.' She gestured towards a pair of massive deeply carved doors which swung open just at that moment, as though at her command.

Maybe it was the sugar high from the hot chocolate but I suddenly felt weird – high, almost. I had the craziest feeling that I was being propelled forwards, towards the giant doors, my feet floating several inches above the creamy white carpet. Next thing I knew, I was sitting in a deep armchair in front of a large desk. At the desk sat three executives, each holding a clipboard. My heart began to pound and the blood rushed into my ears. My breathing became laboured as though a heavy weight had been placed on my chest. And, as the doors closed behind me, the feeling of rapture and euphoria quickly dissipated.

'Welcome. Miss Richardson. Saskia.' The executives spoke in harmony, like a Greek chorus, their voices enthralling and mesmerising. Heads bent together, they flipped through my CV, whispering. But, the whispering did not appear to emanate from them. It was more like a single voice in my head, calling to me.

'Saskia.'

'We weren't expecting you.'

'You've jumped the queue.'

The chief executive turned towards me and – with a flash of recognition – it came to me. He looked exactly like the saint from the stained glass window in our local church: St Michael and All Angels. All he lacked was the lance in his hand and the dragon at his feet. Wordlessly, as though at his command, the other two executives turned towards me and I saw them clearly for the first time. Their faces were terrifyingly beautiful; their hair the colour of old gold, and their eyes a piercing blue that saw deep into my soul.

Now, I remembered... hurrying to work because I was late, sheep on the snowy road, the long skid, my car flipping over, the sound of breaking glass, the smell of petrol.

Then... *this*.

'I don't want – *this*!' I spoke the words out loud and held my hands in front of my face, rejecting 'them' and all they had to offer. Then suddenly everything changed. I felt myself being pulled backwards and the room, the executives – or whatever they were – disappeared down a dark tunnel and I travelled away from them towards the light.

The light being shone in my eyes by a paramedic.

'Saskia. Don't struggle we're going to lift this off you and you'll be able to breathe more easily, sweetheart.' Then she raised my head and slipped an oxygen mask over my nose and mouth.

'You got here just in time. A few minutes later and she'd have been a goner,' someone close by said matter-of-factly; clearly unaware that I could hear them.

'She's trying to say something... ' I smelled perfume as the female medic put her ear closer to my lips.

'Heaven...' I muttered.

'Heaven can wait darlin'. You're going to St. Michael's. St Michael and All Angels, A & E department. They're expecting you.' She took my hand in hers, gave it a reassuring squeeze and I knew that I'd been to the brink and had come back. From now on, hot chocolate would never quite be the same again...

THE END

Lizzie Lamb – About the Author

After teaching my 1000th pupil and working as a deputy head teacher in a large primary school, I decided it was time to leave the chalk face and pursue my first love: writing. In 2006 I joined the Romantic Novelists' Association's New Writers' Scheme, honed my craft and wrote *Tall, Dark and Kilted,* quickly followed a year later by *Boot Camp Bride*. I love the quick fire interchanges between the hero and heroine in the old black and white Hollywood movies, and I hope this love of dialogue comes across in my writing. Although much of my time is taken up publicising *Tall, Dark and Kilted* and *Boot Camp Bride* I have almost finished my third novel, to be published before the end of 2014. Plans for a third, fourth and fifth novel are in the pipeline. I have also founded an indie publishing group: **The New Romantics 4** with June Kearns, Mags Cullingford and Adrienne Vaughan. Our watch cry is: all for one and one for all – in the vain hope that D'Artagnan from the Three Musketeers will come knocking on our door.

KEEP IN TOUCH

Twitter: @lizzie_lamb

Website: www.lizzielamb.co.uk

Goodreads http://tinyurl.com/cbla48d

Boot Camp Bride - Romance and Intrigue on the Norfolk marshes

http://t.co/XSXdFBgIts

Tall, Dark and Kilted - Notting Hill Meets Monarch of the Glen

http://t.co/eobg1qn11

"when I'm not writing - I'm dreaming"

Haunted House

By
Alison May

The Haunted House – a short story by Alison May

'It doesn't feel right.' Melly stopped partway up the stairs and turned back to shine the torch on Max's face.

He was staring up at her, blue eyes catching the lightbeams, as he shook his head. 'Well it's just a regular house Melly.'

'So?'

'So regular houses don't get haunted. Mansions and castles and spooky historic pubs get haunted.'

She squeezed past him, back into the hallway, and flicked the switch by the front door to make the light come on. 'You're not taking this seriously.'

Her friend leaned back against the wall and shook his head. 'Not really. No.'

'Well I definitely heard something.' It was true. She had. This was supposed to be her fresh start – her new house where she would live her new independent single life - but something definitely didn't feel right.

There was a hint of a laugh in Max's eyes. 'Your house isn't haunted Melly.'

She opened her mouth, but stopped herself before she responded. It wasn't Max's fault that she was feeling spooked. He'd been there for her right through the death throes of her ridiculously short marriage. It was he who had braved the former marital home to collect her stuff for her. Apparently, Brett's new girlfriend had been there, shoving her own stuff in the drawers as fast as Max could get Melly's out.

It was Max's spare room that Melly had slept in while she was waiting for the armies of solicitors and accountants to get their paperwork in order and get Brett to stump up the money for her half of the house.

It was Max who'd let her drag him around countless house viewings with estate agents who automatically assumed they were a couple. But the fact that he'd been lovely didn't mean he was right about this. 'I heard something last night.'

He shook his head. 'There's no such thing as a ghost.'

Melly peered around her new hallway. It was going to be really pretty. There were already original 1930s black and white tiles on the floor, and she had brought pots of pale yellow paint waiting to brighten up the walls.

Max was looking around too. 'It's probably rats.'

'What?'

'I'm joking.' He grinned, and then pointed at her left hand. 'Why the torch anyway?'

She felt herself going pink. With hindsight she did see that the torch was stupid; she'd figured that if there was a ghost it'd probably appreciate a nice spooky ambience. 'I was trying to create an atmosphere.'

Max grabbed his coat off the hook at the bottom of the stairs, shaking his head. 'Come on. Pub.'

Melly dropped the torch on the floor and pulled her own jacket and scarf around her. She had promised that they'd be done ghost-hunting in time for the quiz.

Max paused in the doorway. 'I mean we don't have to go to the pub. If you'd rather do something just us…'

Melly shook her head. 'It's ok. A promise is a promise.'

She led the way out into the street. 'Wait.'

'What now?'

She pointed back at the frosted glass in the door. 'The light's gone off.'

'What do you mean?'

Melly was still staring at the house. 'I didn't turn it off. Did you?'

Max grabbed her hand in his.

'What are you doing?'

He frowned. 'I thought you might be scared.'

Melly glanced down at their linked hands before stepping away. 'I'm probably being silly. Come on. To the pub.'

****

Inside the house, Ebenezer Moore sat himself down at the foot of the stairs and shook his head. It appeared to be happening again. This determined-looking blonde girl must be the twentieth new inhabitant. Or maybe nineteenth. To be entirely honest he'd quite lost count. The longer he was here, the faster they all seemed to blur by in front of him. They came and they went. It was a bit upsetting when he thought about it.

Ebenezer reminded himself that he was a calm, beautiful being, and tried to take a deep breath. It didn't help him, of course, but he understood that deep breathing and the use of positive mantras was excellent for maintaining one's inner peace. He'd read that in one of the books the previous one had kept stacked up next to her bed. It sounded like the most incredible poppycock, but he would never want it said that he was afraid to try new things.

Ebenezer stood up and drifted into the living room. He glanced out of the window to the street. The trees that had once been tiny saplings formed bare-branched shadows in the orange streetlight, and the road was empty, as you'd expect on a winter's evening. Ebenezer sighed and looked around the room. She'd got the settee against the wall nearest the door, which made no sense at all. It meant it blocked the radiator and the sun would shine onto the television box that they all seemed so keen on. Ebenezer shook his head. He was quite sure she would work it out – they generally did – but still, having to stand by and watch the same errors repeat themselves time and time again perturbed him.

****

Two nights later, Melly snuggled down under a fleecy blanket on the sofa, glass of wine in hand, and clicked Play on the DVD remote. She flicked through the trailers and onto the main event: *Oklahoma!* This was one of many small promises to herself from the last few months – she would watch all the films that she loved and Brett had hated. Thinking it over, she realised that *all* the films that she loved and Brett hated would be a very long list, but she was starting with her box set of classic musicals – a present from Max, who had shaken his head at the suggestion that he would join her for the viewing. 'Not because I don't want to, but this is your thing. It's about you doing something for you.' Melly smiled at the memory. She knew it was a lie. She had no doubt Max would detest every second of a film like this, but it was the nicest sort of lie.

Melly shivered as the opening tune started up. It was as if an icy finger had run down the side of her face. She glanced around the room. Nothing. She was on her own. She stood up and pushed the door until it clicked shut. A swig of wine. It was just a draught from the door. No reason to be scared. She sat back down and pulled the blanket over her knees. Another blast of cold hit her cheek. This time it felt like somebody, or something, had blown cold air right against her face. She picked her phone up from the table and then stopped. She remembered the last time. Probably rats, he'd said. She didn't want to guess at what he'd say about her calling him over about a draught.

She turned the volume on the film up to drown out her paranoia, and tried to relax. She just wasn't used to living on her own yet. That was all it was. She was sure there were all sorts of odd noises and weird draughts in her previous house. She'd just got used to them. The third time it was unmistakeable though. Not a brush of the fingertips or a waft of air. A hand, a freezing cold hand, rested on her cheek. Melly jumped off the sofa and staggered across the room. There was nobody there. The door was closed. There was no sound, apart from the TV. She was completely alone, only she wasn't. She'd felt the hand on her face. She was sure of it. 'Is someone there?'

There was no reply.

Melly swallowed hard. Of course there was no one there. She could see that. 'Seriously, if there's someone there, come out!'

She froze dead still as an icy finger rested on the back of her hand. She spun around and put a hand out in front of her. There was nothing there. Or was there? A cold spot in the air, perhaps? Ok. Enough was enough. She didn't care if Max laughed at her again. Melly grabbed her phone, hit the speed dial and waited for her best friend to pick up.

****

Ebenezer watched as the new lady's gentleman friend arrived, and listened as she explained loudly, and in some quite unladylike language, that the house was definitely haunted. She seemed quite on edge about the whole matter. Ebenezer wasn't happy about that. It was never his intention to create bad feeling around the place. It was his home as much as anyone's after all. More than anyone, really, when you thought about it.

These young people did overreact so. He'd simply been trying to help. If she realised that putting the settee there was going to be uncomfortable, he'd thought, then she'd move it sooner and be much happier in the long-term. At least that was what Ebenezer had hoped. He took a long look at Melly's shaking hands and red, blotchy face. She didn't seem happier just yet. Ebenezer leaned against the doorway and furrowed his brow. It always seemed to go this way. He tried to help but people never seemed to interpret it the right way.

****

Safely ensconced in the Rose and Crown, Melly managed to get her breathing back to normal and took a big slug of her vodka and coke. She grimaced. 'Is this full fat coke?'

Max nodded. 'Sorry.'

Melly paused. Brett didn't like her drinking full sugar drinks. He liked her to watch her figure. She exhaled slowly before taking another swig. Brett wasn't here. Brett was less real to her now than the ghost in her living room. She looked up. Max was staring at her face. She pursed her lips. 'What are you staring at?'

Max shook his head. 'Nothing.'

She'd caught him looking at her like that a few times recently. It was disconcerting. She kept wondering if she had something on the end of her nose, or stuck between her teeth. 'Max...'

'Yeah?'

'We've been friends forever. Right?'

He nodded.

'So you're not allowed to tell me I'm being stupid.'

He shook his head. 'Actually if you're being stupid, I'm obliged to tell you. Sorry.'

'Please...'

'Ok.'

Melly took another deep breath. She really had known Max forever. He'd been her brother's best friend at nursery school, so technically he'd been an honorary member of the family before Melly was even born. Her brother had headed off travelling as soon as he finished college and never came back, and somehow Melly had found herself with a hand-me-down antique games console and a hand-me-down Max. The games console hadn't lasted the year, but Max was still around a full decade later. If Max wouldn't take her seriously, then no-one would. 'Right. I know you don't believe in ghosts.'

Max shook his head.

'But I really do feel like there's a presence in the house. There's something there.'

Max sipped his pint. 'All right. I think you're nuts, but, for the sake of argument, let's imagine that there is something there.'

'Ok.'

He took another sip. This is what made Max such an amazing friend. He always tried to think about things calmly. When Melly had a moment of weakness last year, and decided she was going to go back to Brett, Max had just got a pen and paper and made a pro and con list. As it turned out, on Max's list, there were an awful lot of cons. 'So if there was a ghost, would that necessarily be a bad thing?'

She opened her mouth to say that of course that would be a bad thing and then stopped. She wasn't actually sure. 'What do you mean?'

'Well, he..'

'Or she.'

'He or she hasn't really done you any harm so far, have they?'

That was true. 'So you think I should just put up with it?'

Max shrugged. 'Maybe you need more information. Knowledge is power and all that. Maybe you need to find out whose ghost you're dealing with.'

That actually wasn't a terrible idea. She nodded. 'Thank you.'

He smiled. 'Anytime.'

He was going to stop interfering. That was Ebenezer's final decision on the matter. A whole life trying to help people was one thing, but after fifty years of trying to do the same in the afterlife he was through. It was time for Ebenezer to start taking care of himself. After all, sometimes it was important that he spent time nurturing his own sacred inner goddess. He'd learnt that from one of those books the previous woman seemed so keen on as well.

He sat down on the top step of the home he'd lived in for more years than he'd actually been alive and tried to think. What would make Ebenezer happy? He didn't have any descendants he could go and visit. Despite his very best efforts during life, Ebenezer had never married and never had children, and anyway he got very weak and dizzy if he tried to go too far from the house. It was something to do with locational resonances, or anthropomorphic frequencies, or some such. Ebenezer didn't remember. There'd been a sort of induction day that explained it all when he'd first passed over, but Ebenezer had been somewhat distracted by the sudden realisation that he was dead.

So what did he enjoy? He enjoyed seeing the people around him being happy. He pushed the thought away. That wasn't the point. The point now was that he was looking after number one. There must be something else. Ah yes. He enjoyed keeping up to date. Ebenezer floated down the stairs and went into the kitchen. He paused for a second and then focussed all his mental energy on the radio on the windowsill. It switched on. He moved through the different stations rejecting Mozart, a radio play, and a station playing swing music before he settled. The DJ's tones seeped into his ears, 'Stay tuned. We're playing all the best music of the seventies, eighties, nineties, noughties and today.' All the best music? That sounded like just the thing to get him bang up to date. Ebenezer leaned on the kitchen door and listened.

****

On the way home from work, Melly stopped. Bill, her neighbour from two doors down, was washing his car on the street in front of his house. Bill had been the first person to introduce himself when she moved in, telling her, very proudly, that he'd bought his house in 1963, when he was just 21 and it had set him back the princely sum of eighteen hundred pounds. At the time Melly had baulked at the knowledge that she'd paid two whole decimal places more than her new friend, but now something else popped back into her head. 1963.

'Bill?'

'Yes love?'

'You've lived here a while, haven't you?'

'I have. 1963 I bought the house. Can you guess what I paid for it?'

Melly felt herself smile. 'I don't know Bill.'

'One thousand, eight hundred pounds.' There was a glint in his eye. 'And not a penny more.'

Melly rolled her eyes. 'I've been ripped off.'

The older man laughed. 'Your young man not with you today?'

She frowned. What young man? 'Oh, Max. We're just friends.'

Bill nodded. 'Right you are.'

What was it that everyone found so hard to believe about that? Her mother wouldn't have it that they were just good friends. Her brother's most recent email from Australia had come right out and asked if he needed to start saving for a flight home for the wedding. And now Bill. She pursed her lips and dragged her mind back to the point. 'I wanted to ask you something about my house.'

Her neighbour splashed his sponge down into the bucket of water and gave Melly his full attention. 'What about it?'

She shifted from foot to foot. 'It probably sounds silly, but did anyone ever...' She tailed off. 'Well did anyone who lived there die in the house?'

Bill sucked the air in through his teeth. 'Well let me see. You bought it from that Jasmine girl. Silly young slip of a thing. She moved to London or Thailand maybe.' He waved his hand. 'One of them places. Before that it was the Cromwells. They went into a home. Then it was rented for a bit. They all came and went.' He sighed and swallowed. Melly waited. 'Then it was David Crozier I think. He sold it to his brother, and it was his brother that rented it out. That's right…'

Slowly the history of Melly's house unfolded. Countless owners and tenants spreading back across the decades.

'It seems like there's been a lot of different people.'

Bill nodded. 'I'd not thought of that. You're right though. People don't seem to stop long.' He shrugged. 'That's young folk for you. Maybe the house is making up for Mr Moore. He was there thirty years or more.'

'Mr Moore?'

Bill shook his head. 'You young ones don't notice anything, do you?' He pointed towards the street sign at the end of the road: Moore Lane.

Melly didn't understand. 'So my house was owned by someone with the same name as the street?'

'The street were named after him, you daft thing. Ebenezer Moore built this whole estate back in the thirties.' Bill took a deep breath. 'Back in the olden days, you see, all this land was owned by the church and they ran a sort of orphanage here. A home for kids with no parents, or whose parents were too hard up to take care of them. Ebenezer grew up there, but when he were older he moved away, made some money for himself. Good money. London money. And I don't know what possessed him, but he came back and he bought the land and built this.'

Melly's gaze followed Bill's outstretched hand and took in the street with fresh eyes. The pretty little terraced houses. The footpath with grass verges before the road, and trees planted here and there. It was a normal sort of street – a come down, she'd half thought, from the expensive newly built house she'd shared with Brett – but through the eyes of a child who'd grown up with no family and no home, the street would have been some sort of heaven.

She turned back to Bill. 'He were an old man, of course, by the time I moved in, but he used to sit out the front and watch the children playing. I reckon he wanted to make a place where families could be proper families, you know.'

Melly nodded.

'Why are you interested?'

Melly shook her head and didn't reply.

'I think he did die in the house though, as it goes. Don't reckon he'd have wanted to be anywhere else.'

****

Inside the house, the radio played on. Ebenezer wrinkled his nose. The song appeared to be about the way in which one could use a flavoured milk beverage to attract local males to one's yard. It made no sense. He was growing increasingly sceptical about the DJ's claim that these songs were objectively the very best of their respective decades. Unfortunately, he was so engrossed in the thought that he didn't hear the front door open.

Melly burst into the kitchen and stared at the radio. Then she turned around and spoke loudly and clearly to the air somewhere to the left of Ebenezer's shoulder. 'Hello. Is that you Mr Moore?'

Ebenezer froze. Well this had never happened before. He coughed politely, hoping to attract her attention in his direction. She didn't move. Well of course not. She couldn't see him. She couldn't hear him either. On reflection, he wasn't entirely sure what response she was looking for.

He watched her as she shrugged and made her way into the lounge. Curious, Ebenezer followed. Melly pulled her mobile telephone out of her bag and hit a couple of buttons. Ebenezer was rather fond of these new mini telephones everyone seemed to have now. He was also quite confused about how little talking people did on them. Melly was talking this time though. From what Ebenezer could tell she was arranging for somebody to come calling. He sat down on the settee, now moved into its proper place opposite the door, and waited.

Fifteen minutes later the young gentleman arrived. It was the same young gentleman that always came around. Ebenezer was starting to wonder why the fellow didn't just move in and be done with it. Hugs were exchanged and bottles of beer were opened. Ebenezer found himself unceremoniously squeezed off the settee as they sat down. Typical. He ought to go upstairs, or at least back into the kitchen. He wasn't taking an interest in people anymore, he reminded himself. Ebenezer had made a change. Ebenezer was looking after number one. He was halfway through the wall when something pulled his attention back into the room.

'I think I know who my ghost is,' said Melly.

Ebenezer watched the young man raise his eyebrows.

Melly ignored the expression. 'There was this man who lived here when the estate was first built. But not just lived here. He built the estate. He was like a sort of twentieth century saint.'

Ebenezer's chest puffed out with pride. He wouldn't say saint, of course, but the beginnings of a memory stirred inside him. Building the estate had meant something. He'd meant it to be a place where people could make happier lives than the one he'd had. He'd sold most of the houses for less than they cost to build, and the few he'd kept back for tenants rented at far below their value. It was the only way he could think of to make sure they went to people who really needed them. That's what he'd been trying to make – a safe place for people who needed it. He swallowed. That was then. The new Ebenezer was all about nurturing his own inner peace in the unified field. No more running around after everyone else.

'Look Melly...' The young gentleman broke Ebenezer's train of thought.

'Don't tell me I'm imagining it.'

'What?' The man was confused. 'No. It's just... I kind of wanted to talk about something else.'

Melly wrinkled her nose. 'What?'

The man cleared his throat. 'OK. Well, you know how we're friends.'

'Yeah.'

'And that's great, but you know how people sometimes think we're more than friends.'

Melly giggled. 'Yeah.'

'Well I was sort of wondering if... you might... I mean, if we might... maybe... if you wanted to...'

Ebenezer shook his head. Oh for goodness sake. The girl hadn't appeared to be stupid, but given that she didn't seem to have a clue what the poor fool in front of her was driving at, Ebenezer was beginning to wonder. What to do? Ebenezer paused. Obviously, he wasn't going to interfere. He definitely didn't do that anymore. Another thought jumped into his head. An image of the children playing in the street, the street he'd built. Helping all those families hadn't just made them happy; it had made him happier than anything else he'd done during his life. Ebenezer smiled to himself and stepped forward.

The young man was still talking, tying himself in tighter and tighter knots as he tried to say anything but the thing he actually wanted to say. Ebenezer leaned towards Melly and reached out a hand. He poked a single icy finger against her back and watched her jump forward. Straight forward, and headlong into the body of the nice, but inarticulate, man. After that it was as if Ebenezer had set off some sort of chain reaction.

'Max,' gasped Melly.

At the same time Max's hand came to rest on her bare arm, and then her fingers moved to his face, and he bent his head to meet her lips. Melly's fingers reached for the bottom of Max's t-shirt and pulled at the fabric.

Ebenezer's jaw dropped open. Right. Things seemed to be moving along quite nicely without his intervention now. He turned, in the interests of propriety, towards the wall and waited a second. No doubt in a moment or two they would either disengage or move the proceedings to the bedroom. He glanced back over his shoulder. Oh no. They didn't seem to be disengaging. In fact, if anything, it seemed to be full steam ahead right there on the settee. Ebenezer had been a bachelor his whole life. He wasn't unaware of the pleasures of the flesh, but had indulged in them rather less than he might have liked. He felt himself blushing, as he averted his eyes once again.

It would make a pleasant change, he thought, to have a housemate who knew he was here, and he would endeavour to be a most helpful tenant, starting, he decided, by respecting his landlady's right to privacy. And with that Ebenezer floated hurriedly through the wall and away.

THE END

Alison May – About the Author

Alison May is a novelist and short story writer who grew up in North Yorkshire, and now lives in Worcester. She worked as a waitress, a shop assistant, a learning adviser, an advice centre manager, a freelance trainer, and now a maker-upper of stories.

She won the RNA's Elizabeth Goudge trophy in 2012, and her short stories have been published by Harlequin and Black Pear Press. Alison now writes romantic comedies for Choc Lit, the innovative independent UK publishing house. Her debut novel, *Sweet Nothing*, was published in 2013.

KEEP IN TOUCH

Twitter @MsAlisonMay .

Website www.alison-may.co.uk

Sweet Nothing True love, tequila, maths, slime mould and a big white wedding...

http://www.amazon.co.uk/Sweet-Nothing-Choc-ebook/

Choc Lit -

www.choc-lit.com/productcat/alison-may/

The Soul Stealer

By
Tina Burton

The Soul Stealer – a short story by Tina K. Burton

It was gone half past nine at night as I walked along the eerily quiet hospital corridor. I'd been to visit a friend who'd had a minor operation, and jokingly chastised her for being in hospital on Hallowe'en instead of out partying.

I should have been kicked out ages ago, but because we were behaving ourselves, for once, the nurse in charge had let me stay.

Rounding a corner, I saw a little girl sitting on the floor ahead of me. What on earth was she doing all alone at this time of night? She saw me coming, got up and ran off with a giggle.

'Oh, you've left your doll,' I called out, but she'd disappeared through a door.

As I drew level with the doll, I thought I saw it move. I tutted, of course it didn't, dolls are inanimate objects.

I bent down to pick it up, and almost screamed with fright. I could have sworn it turned its head towards me. I laughed, and shook myself. I was just a bit freaked out, what with being all alone in a hospital corridor on Hallowe'en night. But, I decided to check, just in case.

'Did...did you just move?' I whispered down at it, feeling both scared and stupid at the same time.

I jumped back in shock as an old lady's voice said, 'Yes I did.'

I looked around, but apart from us, the corridor was empty.

I leaned in closer. 'Did you just speak?'

Oh my God, what the hell was I doing talking to a doll?

A husky laugh came from its mouth. 'Yes. Now, are you going to stand there all night gawping, or are you going to pick me up?'

I rubbed a hand across my eyes. I must be either very tired, or going mad. I'd been working extra hours recently - today was the first time in months that I'd left work early - but surely I wasn't so tired that I was hallucinating?

'Well...I'm waiting,' said the doll, or rather a voice that sounded like it was coming from her.

I suddenly realised what was going on.

'Oh, very clever, you can come out now,' I shouted down the corridor.

The little girl was obviously with someone who could throw their voice. They were probably hiding behind the door at this very moment, laughing their heads off. Great Hallowe'en trick.

I marched down the corridor and flung the door open. There was nobody there.

I walked into the ward and looked around. Nothing. Just the elderly patients. Some asleep, some drinking their late night cups of Horlicks, or whatever they have in hospital these days.

'Can I help you?' a nursing sister asked.

'I'm looking for a little girl, and maybe her relative?'

'There was a lost little girl here a while back; one of my nurses took her to find her mother. Apart from that, there's no-one else, just us and the patients.'

'Are you sure?'

'Positive, I've been on duty for the last three hours. So if you don't mind, visiting time finished long ago.' The nurse stood, hands on hips waiting for me to leave.

'I'm sorry to have troubled you,' I said and fled the ward.

Back out in the corridor, I tripped over the doll.

'Hey, watch what you're doing, you're bigger than me.' She scowled, her little face all twisted up.

'I'm sorry.'

What the hell was I doing, apologising to a doll? I narrowed my eyes. 'How did you get here? I left you halfway up the corridor.'

'Well, you stormed off, so I came after you. I don't want to be alone. Now pick me up before you step on me again.'

'No way! I'm not touching you – no offence, but this isn't normal, dolls don't come to life. You must be possessed or something.'

Oh my God, I was losing the plot. How can a doll be possessed? That's what I get for watching too many episodes of Supernatural in one sitting.

I took a few steps back and looked at her. 'Okay, here's the deal; I'm going to walk to the end of this corridor and out of that door. I am not going to look back, because you are not real. You're a figment of my tired overworked mind. I turned to walk away from her.

'Okay, just leave me in this empty corridor on my own. It'll get dark and cold soon, but never mind, you do what you have to do,' she said, in a sad little old lady voice.

I turned back to face her. 'Don't guilt trip me, that's not fair.'

I looked about to see if we were still alone. If anyone saw me talking to a doll, they'd have me carted away.

'Who said we were playing fair?' she asked with a chuckle.

'If you're just a figment of my imagination, it won't matter if I leave you, will it?'

Her little mouth twisted as she thought about it. Then she got up and punched me on the calf with her fist.

'Ow, what did you do that for?'

'You felt it then?'

'Yes, of course I felt it.'

'Well, it can't be your imagination, can it?'

Oh, very clever, she had me there.

I huffed, bent down and picked her up. 'Right, where am I taking you?'

'How about home with you?'

'You have got to be kidding. I've seen the Chucky films, no way. Uh uh, not on your life.' I shook my head and dropped her on the floor again.

'Ow, that hurt, you can't just drop me. Please take me home, just for tonight. If you hadn't made that little girl run off, I'd be tucked up all warm with her in bed by now. It's your fault I'm all alone,' she wheedled.

I studied her. She seemed harmless enough...for a talking doll. Put it this way, she didn't look anything like Chucky. She was rather pretty, with wavy black hair and blue eyes. I picked her up again. She had on a blue velvet dress that matched her eyes, little white socks, and black shiny shoes. I was about to lift up her dress to see if she had on those bloomer things my dolls used to wear, but I stopped. I didn't think she'd appreciate that.

I made up my mind. 'Okay, I'll take you home with me just for tonight, but once we get there, you'd better tell me what's going on...how come you're...alive.'

She shrugged her little shoulders. 'Okay.'

'And, until we get home, keep still and keep quiet. Got it?'

She didn't answer me.

'I said, got it?'

She still didn't answer me, so I shook her and tipped her upside down.

'Ooh stop it, I feel ill.'

'Well answer me when I talk to you.'

'But you told me not to talk or move, I was merely abiding by your wishes,' she said with a smug little grin.

This doll was far too clever by half, that was twice she'd outsmarted me.

I put her under my arm, walked to the exit and out into the car park.

In my car I was about to throw the doll onto the back seat, when I changed my mind, and put her in the front. I wanted her where I could keep an eye on her.

Should I put the seat belt around her? I tutted aloud at my ridiculousness. What was I thinking? She was hardly likely to die if we crashed, she wasn't alive – well she was, but not like a human being.

That thought made me panic and I tried to control myself. Okay deep breath, it's just a doll, a harmless, pretty doll.

I then remembered that some of the demons in Supernatural weren't all scary looking, some of them were very attractive. What if she really was possessed? What if, there was a whole group of – what was the collective term for lots of dolls? – them, waiting to attack and take over the world.

She sat on the seat, all innocent and cute looking. Nah, I decided, if she *was* evil, she'd have tried to kill me by now, that's what happened whenever characters in films came across evil spirits.

I drove home as fast as I could, praying a police car wouldn't stop me for speeding. I glanced at the doll every now and then, but she just sat there, no movement and no sound. I almost began to believe she *was* just a doll and that I'd imagined the whole thing, but as we pulled onto the drive, she said, 'Ooh, are we home?'

I grabbed her and my bag, walked into the house and dropped both on the sofa.

'Stay!' I ordered as if she was a puppy I was training.

I went into the kitchen and got myself a large glass of wine, then picked up the bottle and went back into the lounge.

'Okay, talk.'

'What do you want me to say? I can recite a poem, tell you a story...'

'How about starting with the truth? How the hell can you move and talk?'

She pressed her little pink lips together. 'You're not going to like it,' she warned me in a sing-song voice.

'I'll be the judge of that, now whenever you're ready, but make it sometime tonight, I've had a long day and would like to go to bed before midnight.'

'I take souls.'

I spluttered on my wine and wiped my mouth. I couldn't have heard correctly. 'Sorry, could you repeat that?'

'I said, I take souls.'

Okay I had heard correctly. 'YOU WHAT!' I yelled jumping up and almost breaking my glass as I slammed it down on the table.

'It's not as bad as it sounds. I borrow them, more than steal them.'

I took a deep breath to try to stop my heart thumping in my chest. It didn't work.

I backed away from her, and must have had a look of sheer fright on my face because she said, 'It's okay, I won't hurt you. I'm not evil or anything, I just need to borrow souls to stay in this form.'

'I don't believe this. Why has this happened to me, and on Hallowe'en of all nights? There I was, doing a good deed by visiting a friend in hospital, and what do I get – a doll who steals souls. Why couldn't someone else have found you? Why couldn't I have got something nice like a... a... oh I don't know... a genie who granted me three wishes?'

'Don't be stupid, there's no such thing as genies who grant wishes,' she said scornfully.

'And before tonight, there were no such things as living dolls, especially ones who steal souls!'

'Well I'm sorry you found me, and the fact that it's Hallowe'en is just a coincidence.'

'Oh, so this happens on all the other days too?' I wiped my hand across my eyes. 'This has turned into one hell of a night.'

'I don't just come out once a year, you know, and I'm sorry if I've ruined your day,' the doll said with a pout.

'Ruined my day? My life will never be the same again.'

'Don't exaggerate.'

'Ha, you ought to be in my position at the moment.'

I sat forward and put my head in my hands, then looked at her. 'You're not staying here, you'll have to go.'

I stood up, grabbed my car keys and picked her up.

'You can't drive, you've been drinking.'

'I've only had one.'

'One very large one, which you've topped up.'

I looked at the half-empty bottle of wine. She was right, I couldn't drive now. I sat down again and took another gulp of wine.

'You might be dangerous, I can't have you in the house, you'll have to go in the dustbin.'

'Oh stop it. I've got a perfectly harmless old lady's soul now, her name was Violet. But you should have seen some of the other souls I've borrowed, especially the one that came out of a witch.' She shuddered.

I stared at her, open mouthed. Did I say I was having a bad day? It had just got a hundred times worse.

'A witch? I know it's Hallowe'en, but you're having me on, right?'

I couldn't get my head around this. Maybe I was asleep and this was all a dream. I pinched myself, hard. No, I was definitely awake.

'Hang on a minute, you told me just now, there are no such things as genies, yet you're telling me there *are* such things as witches?'

'Of course.' She saw my face and quickly added, 'oh don't worry, they died out years ago - well most of them were burnt at the stake - although there may be a few still lingering around...'

'You'll be telling me next that vampires and werewolves are real too.'

She started to speak but I held my hand up. 'I don't want to know. God knows how I'm going to sleep tonight as it is.'

What is it about us humans that makes us curious about the macabre? Why do we enjoy watching horror films, or feel the need to look when we go past an accident?

I don't know why, but I then asked the question I'd been curious about, but was afraid to know the answer to as well.

'So, how does this soul stealing business work?'

'Borrowing if you don't mind.'

'Does it make a difference?' I asked. I wondered how she could be so righteous.

She shuffled her bottom back against the sofa and said, 'Yes it does to me. I don't want to be thought of as a bad person.'

'Person? You're a doll.'

'But inside the doll, I'm kind of a person, one who's recently died.'

Oh heck, did I really want to know this?

'How recently?'

'Oh, very. Violet had only just expired when you found me. The little girl was her great granddaughter. She'd been waiting for her mother to finish visiting Violet. There was no one to look after the little girl you see, so she had to go to the hospital with her mum.'

'Hang on, let me get this straight. Violet was a patient in the hospital, and her granddaughter was visiting, with her daughter, the little girl?'

'That's what I've just said isn't it?' The doll rolled her eyes.

'Yes, but I'm trying to get my head round all this. Okay go on.'

'The little girl was supposed to wait outside, but when she found me I told her to sneak me into Violet's room. I knew she was close to the end you see, and that was my perfect opportunity.'

'To do what?'

'Borrow her soul. You have to wait for the right moment.'

'The right moment?' I echoed.

'The exact moment the soul leaves the body, just after the person's last breath. I saw that Violet was very close to death and waited.'

Dear God on a bicycle, what had I unintentionally got myself caught up in?

'And?' I asked.

'And when I saw the shimmering wisp leave her body, I sucked it into mine.'

'Shimmering wisp?'

'Yes. A soul is a beautiful thing to see, like a silvery wisp of smoke, but it shimmers.'

'And that's all there is to it?'

'Yes, until I need to do it again.'

'Why do you need to do it again, can't you keep Violet's soul forever?' This was getting more and more bizarre by the minute.

'Of course I can't.' The doll looked at me as if to say, any old fool knows that.

'So, how long do you keep it for?'

'Only a month or two; until we know where it's going to end up.'

'End up?'

'Yes. You're not very bright are you,' she said, shaking her head.

'Oh, thanks a lot. I'm not stupid, but this is a lot for me to take in okay, so just bear with me. Now explain what you mean about where it's going to end up.'

The doll sighed and started speaking in an exaggerated tone as if she were talking to a small child or a person for whom English wasn't a first language.

'When - a - person - dies, their soul - leaves their body - and goes to a resting place.'

'I'm not an imbecile, talk to me properly.'

She continued. 'This is for a couple of reasons. One, so that it can recover from the shock of death – it's quite traumatic dying, you know.'

'I should imagine it is.'

'And secondly, whilst Him upstairs decides if it can carry on upwards, or has to go down below.'

'You mean to Heaven or Hell?'

'That's what you humans call it, but yes. That all takes about a month.'

'So, how do you know when the soul you've...erm, borrowed, has to go up or down?'

'It starts to leave. There's nothing I can do to stop it. Once it's been decided where to send it, off it goes. The force is strong, I feel it ebbing away. I get very weak and have to look for another soul to replace it.' She shifted position and crossed her little legs.

I hated to admit it, but I was fascinated. 'So you've got Violet's soul for about a month?'

'Give or take a couple of weeks, yes.'

'How do you know where to get your next one?' I asked.

'I hang around in hospitals when I know the time is close. Then I just look for a little girl, and lay on the ground. Little girls are great, they love dolls.' She grinned. 'They soon pick me up. It's because I'm so adorable you know.' She shook out her head of glossy black hair.

'How do the little girls know to take you to a person who's dying, and how do you know who's dying?'

'That's two questions, one at a time please, I'm old and forgetful.'

'I said...'

The doll tutted. 'I know what you said, I was teasing you. It's easy to know when someone's dying, their soul sings.'

'Sings?'

'Yes, what's the matter with you, are you deaf as well as stupid?'

'Don't talk to me like that or you'll go in the dustbin.'

She sighed with annoyance. 'When a person is close to death, their soul sings. It's a very sad mournful sort of song. Just as well you humans don't hear it - it'd break your hearts. Only another soul can hear a soul's lament. I then ask the little girl to take me to the room with the singing soul.'

'But you just said humans can't hear it.'

'The little girl can't. I tell them what room it's in and they find it.'

I had images of a little girl wandering around a hospital on her own, and her frantic mother trying to find her.

'I know what you're thinking, but once I've borrowed the soul, I tell the little girl to find a nurse and say she's lost. She's soon reunited with her parent again, and they usually get to keep me too.' She grinned delightedly.

I was shocked.

'Whilst I have to admit this is all extremely fascinating, and I've learnt some things I never knew, how can you do something like that, have you no ethics or morals? You ought to be ashamed of yourself.'

The doll had the grace to look a bit ashamed, and her bottom lip wobbled as if she was going to cry.

'You don't understand,' she said.

Too right I didn't understand. I couldn't take it all in. I was also very tired, I looked at my watch and realised we'd been talking for hours. It was almost one o' clock in the morning.

I yawned. 'I still have lots of questions, like, why do you refer to Violet in the third person if you *are* Violet, why not use 'I' or 'me', and why do you have to use a little girl, why can't you just walk into the room yourself?'

'Because I am not specifically Violet, I am her soul. I am the essence of her, but not the thinking matter that made her who she was. And, can you imagine the hullaballoo if anyone saw a doll walk into someone's ward and climb onto their bed. No one takes any notice of a little girl carrying a doll.'

That made sense. I rubbed a hand over my eyes. 'I'd love to stay up and talk all night, but I'm so tired I need to go to bed. What am I going to do with you?'

'Oh, don't worry about me, I'll sit here all night and wait for you to get up in the morning,' the doll said.

'Hmm, you better not budge, I mean it. I want to see you in the same place tomorrow morning. Promise?'

'I promise.'

I went and found the smallest blanket I had, and folded it several times.

'Here, if you want to lie down, use this to cover yourself so you don't get cold.'

'Thank you. Goodnight, sleep tight.'

'Huh, you reckon I will after all this?'

I went into my bedroom and locked the door behind me, then checked that the windows were closed and locked them too. Then, just for good measure, I put my chair under the door handle.

As I undressed, I remembered a verse my grandmother used to say before I went to sleep whenever I stayed with her.

Now I lay me down to sleep, I pray the Lord my soul to keep. If I should die before I wake, I pray the Lord my soul to take.

Well I hoped I wouldn't die in my sleep, I didn't want my soul ending up inside a doll.

I settled down and switched off the light, but sleep evaded me. My mind whirled with all sorts of thoughts. How many dolls were there across the world taking the souls of dying humans? I eventually drifted off, and my dreams were full of vampire dolls chasing me around a hospital. I awoke in the morning feeling even more tired than when I'd gone to bed.

I slipped my dressing gown on, removed the chair and unlocked my bedroom door.

As I entered the lounge, I saw that the blanket was just as I'd left it, and the doll was gone.

I searched the whole flat, but she was nowhere in sight. The bathroom window was open a tad, just enough for a small creature like a cat, or a doll, to squeeze through.

Dammit, I should have locked her in somewhere that she couldn't escape from, like a suitcase.

Where could she have gone? I had to find her. I ran into my room to get dressed, then stopped and sat on the edge of my bed. Where would I look?

She wouldn't be at the hospital yet, Violet's soul had a month at least until it was called away. I picked up my pillow and thumped it in frustration.

She couldn't do this to me, I still had so many questions; like, how long had she been borrowing souls for? She mentioned witches, vampires and werewolves, so it could be going back hundreds of years.

I held the pillow against my face and screamed into it. How could I carry on as if nothing had happened? Yet that was exactly all I *could* do. No one would believe such a far-fetched story; they'd have me down as a nutcase. If someone related the tale to me, I'd think they'd lost the plot.

So, I did nothing.

For years I kept the secret of that night to myself, although I never forgot the strange events, and could recall every detail.

If I closed my eyes, I could still picture the doll, with her glossy black hair, blue eyes and blue velvet dress.

It's the same doll that's here in the arms of the little girl standing by my hospital bed. I smile at them both, and my eyes widen in surprise as I take what must be my last breath, and see a silver shimmering wisp rise up from my body.

THE END

Stranger Than Fiction...? From Tina K. Burton

"When my daughter was about six, we were in the living room and I sent her upstairs to fetch something. She came running downstairs with a look of sheer fright on her face, and said, 'Mummy, who's that man in your bedroom?'

My heart leapt into my mouth because there was nobody else in the house, just me and her. I asked what she meant, and she said there was a man in my bedroom, leaning on my dressing table. She described what he looked like, and what he was wearing and said he had a horrible look on his face.

I was terrified, but, plucked up the courage to creep upstairs. There was nobody there, but my daughter was insistent she'd seen him.

She saw other 'people' too, but thankfully stopped seeing them as she got older."

Spooky.......!

Tina K. Burton – About the Author

Tina K Burton is a freelance writer of articles, short stories, novels, verses, and the occasional Haiku poem - she believes in being versatile! She's sold work to various publications in the UK and overseas. Chapters of Life, her debut novel, is published by Crooked Cat Publishing, she's just completed a light hearted romcom called The Love Shack, which is now with publishers, and she's working on the sequel to Chapters of Life.

Tina has stories on several websites, including Alfie Dog Fiction and Ether Books, and is also in a couple of anthologies. She runs a Facebook writing group, has a blog, and is on Twitter. When she's not writing, she spends her time crafting, relaxing with friends, and taking her recently rescued greyhound for walks across the beautiful moorland in Devon where she lives with her family.

KEEP IN TOUCH

Twitter - @TinaKBurton

Facebook - Tina K Burton

http://tinakburtons.blogspot.co.uk

http://uk.pinterest.com/Quillina/

Stranger than fiction....? From Debbie Flint

"I went to a Sally Morgan (TV psychic) live show in Dorking Halls in September 2009, and lo and behold, my 'dad' came through on the stage – very good it was too – you can see the whole thing from the subsequent Living TV episode on Youtube (search 'derek flint sally morgan dorking'). She got several names accurately listed and a couple of other things happened which made my sister, my daughter and me come away feeling happy, having witnessed some fascinating 'validation.' It's recounted in one of her books too – Life after Death I think.

However, at the end of the show, Sally says to always look out for the little signs and don't be scared of asking spirit a question.

The reading had quite an impact on all of us and I gave it a lot of thought.

I was driving home very late at night about two weeks later, in the driving rain. I was feeling mischievous. Dad was always one for practical jokes and I felt a little of his influence around me, so I said, 'OK Dad, if you're here, give me a sign.'

At that very moment - a split second later, as if in response - the windscreen wiper stopped mid swipe, vertically at the top of the arc. How strange! I thought it must be broken. I turned the switch off, then on again and ... it worked. Weird. It kept working all the way home and the next day and after that. Coincidence maybe?

Then just a fortnight or so later I was thinking about how strange it was, whilst returning home in exactly the same situation again. The rain was pouring, the windscreen wiper was swiping, and I thought there's no way it could happen again. I said out loud, 'If that really was you, do it again, Dad.' And blow me down if it didn't happen exactly as before.

It has never done it since."

Weird....!

Green Man

Rising

By
Litty Williams

Green Man Rising – a short story by Litty Williams

January

Helen smiled at the triteness of the 'Old Macdonald' door chime and mentally added one more item to her to-do list. She ran downstairs and opened the oak front door. A sprightly older lady dressed head to toe in neat pink velour thrust a brightly-patterned cake box at her.

'Hello dear, I'm Janet from next door.' Her voice boomed as though Helen was a battlefield away rather than just across the threshold. 'I thought I'd drop some cupcakes round to welcome you to Hope Cottage.'

'How kind,' Helen said, trying not to flinch at her new neighbour's overwhelming heartiness. 'Do come in Janet, although watch out for all our stuff. The removal van has only just gone so it's a bit of a bomb site. We're just starting to sort out where things go.'

'Well, I won't stay long as you've clearly so much to do.' Janet surveyed the stacks of removal boxes that littered the cottage floor.

'Have you lived in Hurst Green long, Janet?'

'I've lived here nigh on 30 years, though I'm from Scotland originally as I'm sure you'll have noticed. I've seen a great many changes as well, I can tell you.' Janet peered into the living room without asking for permission. 'Lots of comings and goings.' She ran her finger across the curved brass of the door handle then rubbed the film of dust between her fingers. 'Yes, indeed. Much to do.' She turned her gaze back to Helen and adopted a smile, displaying a full set of state-of-the-art dentures. 'It's lovely to see young people joining the community. Most of us are older folk I'm afraid, but we're very active for all that. We have a bowls club and a local history society in case you're interested. And I'm the organiser of our local neighbourhood watch.'

'It's early days yet, but you never know. I'll just get my husband, Pete, from the garden to say hello. I need to ask him where the box with the kettle is anyway.'

'How lovely that you're married. Is it just the two of you? Any children.'

'No, erm... Actually, no.'

'You're still young, aren't you, dear? Plenty of time yet.'

Helen was relieved that Janet hadn't appeared to notice her brief hesitation, busy as she was with lifting the flap and peering into the contents of a half-open box nearby.

'We've three girls ourselves, though of course they're all grown up now with their own families,' Janet continued.

Helen took the box of cupcakes through to the kitchen. Janet followed her, talking all the time, her voice filling the small cottage with a barrage of sound.

'And shall I just come with you to say a brief word of welcome to your husband as well? Then I'll let you get on with the rest of your day.'

Helen led the way down the mossy brick path that led to the lower garden. The winter air was fresh and crisp and Helen paused briefly to savour the tang of damp grass and cold earth. She held back branches of unfamiliar evergreen for Janet. 'Sorry, it's all so overgrown. I don't want you to snag your clothes on these branches.'

'You've a glorious big garden here, haven't you, dear? It's the biggest one around by far. Must be about two-thirds of an acre at least.' Janet's voice reverberated through the glossy dark-emerald leaves.

'Yes - that's what really attracted us to the house.' No need to tell Janet, however, that her plan was to split the garden in two and get planning permission to build a new house in the lower part.

'Such a beautiful big, old greenhouse you have as well. Mind, it will be a full-time job to put everything in order. Look at the state of it. All that ironwork fairly makes my head spin. I've never seen another quite like it.'

And no need to alarm Janet with the news that the greenhouse would probably have to go if her plan for a 'garden grab' succeeded. She definitely didn't want her neighbour to prove a fly in the planning ointment.

Janet carried on in her penetrating voice as they neared the greenhouse. 'You know dear, the old lady who lived here before you was by herself for over 20 years. It was a struggle for her to cope with a garden of this size, especially towards the end, but she wouldn't take any help. Such a very independent woman, she was. And, of course, she was far too sensible to pay any mind to the tales about the house.' She cocked her head to one side. 'Have you heard the sad story? It's a wee piece of local history.'

'Erm, no. I don't think we have.'

Janet beamed in delight. 'Well, about 100 years ago the poor lady who lived here was found dead in her bed. Strangled!' She brought her face close up to Helen's. 'Strangled by her own *husband*. Here, in her bed at Hope Cottage. Just before the First World War, it was. And...' Janet drew herself up, ready to deliver the coup de grâce 'they never found him! He just disappeared did that wicked old Ambrose Pierce and was never seen again.' A smug look appeared on Janet's face at Helen's horrified reaction. She gave a knowing nod of her head and stepped back. 'Well, Ambrose Pierce is all ancient history now.'

Before Helen could reply to this bombshell Janet brushed her aside.

'Oh, that must be your man himself.'

Pete was standing in the greenhouse, running his hand along the wooden slats of the waist-high potting bench that bordered the long structure. He was scooping up crumbs of dried up compost and dead leaves into small piles and smiling slightly. His recent pinched and worried look had been replaced with an expression of calm and wonder, and Helen's heart leaped with joy. It was working! It was what she'd hoped for. This house move would wipe out their money worries and salve Pete's deep wounds from his redundancy.

'Pete, we have our first visitor,' Helen called.

Pete shook his head, as if clearing his mind and took several slow paces to meet them at the door of the greenhouse.

'This is Janet our new neighbour. She's brought us cupcakes.' Janet made as if to enter the greenhouse but Pete stepped out and closed the iron-framed door heavily behind him. As the door slammed a cracked pane of glass near the handle shattered, and tinkling shards fell to the ground. Pete cried out like a wounded animal and cradled his left hand gingerly in his right. Helen could see blood starting to well out of a short gash on the back of his hand. Small drops of blood like holly berries fell onto the threshold of the greenhouse, and the sharp tang of copper filled the still winter air.

After a moment of shocked silence Helen reached for Pete, 'Are you alright?'

Pete drew away from her. Turning his back, he hunched over his injured hand and brought it to his mouth. At first he sucked slowly and then started drawing on it greedily.

'Pete! My God! How bad is it? Do you need stitches?'

Pete pulled his orange scarf from his neck and wrapped it around his left hand. He turned to Helen with a face as pale as ice on a winter pond. 'It's not deep. It'll be fine if I just run it under water.'

'You poor wee thing.' Janet's bray broke in. 'A cup of good strong tea will set you to rights. Your lovely wife told me you haven't found your kettle yet, so let me get you some tea from my own home. And I'll leave telling you more about that old story to another day.'

'Are you sure you're OK, Pete? Do we need to go to hospital?'

'I'll be fine.' Pete smiled with calm certainty down at her.

They turned for the house, Pete cradling his orange-swaddled hand.

'I'm sorry about spoiling your Christmas present, Hells,' Pete said, indicating the blood-stained scarf. But Helen was full of sudden joy. Pete hadn't called her Hells in months.

'Don't worry, my darling. You haven't spoiled anything.'

Despite the shock of the accident, Helen was elated at Pete's calm air of authority, quite unlike his behaviour over past months. Since his redundancy he'd sometimes been clingy, sometimes remote, forcing her to constantly soothe him and manage him, and make decisions for both of them. It was wonderful to see Pete more like the strong man she'd married. Perhaps this could blossom in bed tonight. It had been some time since they'd actually had sex, but it felt right that they should start their new life in Hope Cottage with love. They could even start trying for a baby again.

Pete dropped a quick kiss on Helen's brow. 'But I do think that a cup of tea is a good idea. Now what story has old Granny Macbeth been telling you about our little cottage?'

Pete rolled off Helen and flopped heavily onto his back, making their recently reassembled IKEA pine bed shake. Hands splayed rigidly by his sides he stared up to the ceiling. 'I'm sorry. Oh God, Helen. I'm sorry. I thought I could when you started stroking me. I wanted to … but then, when I was on top of you… I…' His voice trailed off.

'Shh, it doesn't matter, Pete. You know it doesn't matter.' In the faint light from a distant street lamp leaking through the uncurtained window, Helen reached over to cradle Pete's head on her shoulder. 'Perhaps it's just too soon. It'll happen when the time is right.' She stroked the sweat-soaked hair on the back of his head, soothing him as a frightened child.

'I wanted to, and it was wonderful but then somehow I thought about what that bloody Janet told you earlier. About that woman, you know, and what happened to her. And then I was looking down at you and somehow it wasn't you anymore. It was that, her, the other woman. Her mouth was gaping, and her tongue pushed out to the side. And her hair was writhing like angry snakes on the pillow and I just couldn't…'

Helen drew him tighter to her, shushing and soothing, trying to banish this obscene vision and infuse him her strength.

'I'm useless and don't know what to do to make it better. Don't leave me Helen. Say you won't leave me.' To Helen's dismay Pete started crying. Fat tears of shame and misery oozed from the corners of his closed eyes.

Helen's stomach filled with a churning, biting guilt. She had hoped for so much from tonight, but her desperation for a baby had caused her to rush Pete when he wasn't ready.

'Hey there. Hey. I'm not going anywhere. You know I love you.' She raised herself up on one elbow, and stroked his wet cheeks. 'At least we tried tonight - you and me together. That hasn't happened for a long time.' She reached for Pete's hand to bring it to her lips, and as she touched it noticed that the dressing had been knocked to one side. The skin had a heated puffiness, and a slight earthy smell came from the cut.

'You need a new dressing, Pete. And more antiseptic. It's in the bathroom where I put the first aid box. Shall I get it for you?'

'I'll get it. You don't need to get up too.' Pete got out of bed and picked up his pyjama bottoms and sleep T-shirt. He padded across the landing to the bathroom and shut the door. She thought about going after him but he clearly wanted to be left alone. After some minutes, a sudden rush of chilled air invaded the bedroom. Why was Pete opening a window at this time of night bringing the freezing outside air into the warm cottage?

She snuggled down into the covers to escape the cold nipping at her neck and shoulders. 'Pete, close that window and come back to bed, will you? You must be freezing.'

She heard the toilet flush and felt a fresh chill when the duvet was pulled away as Pete got back into bed.

'Did you put on a new dressing?'

'Yes, Hells, I did. My hand's good. Really it is. It's not as bad as you thought, silly. Here.' He reached into the covers and gently rested his cool hand on her warm neck. After her soft murmur of acknowledgement he withdrew his hand and rolled onto his back. 'And then I thought I saw a light moving and bobbing near the greenhouse. I opened the window to get a better look.'

'Probably just a reflection from the street lights.' Helen snuggled further down under the duvet.

'I couldn't see anything, so you're probably right.'

Helen gave in to the drowsiness engulfing her. 'Get some rest, Pete. Lots to do tomorrow,' Helen murmured and abandoned herself to sleep.

Pete lay on his back, holding his left hand against his chest. He lay still for a long time before sleep came, eyes open, tracing the faint swirling patterns of the bedroom ceiling. And as he lay a faint orange glow shone from his eyes. And if Helen had seen this she would have said it was probably a reflection from the street lights.

April

Rinsing the blue and white-striped pottery lunch plates in the sink, Helen looked through the kitchen window and gloried in the sight of nature stirring to life after a long, hard winter. Proud of her newly-gained gardening knowledge, she checked off the plants she recognised. Some lilac bushes by the path, sporting intense purple flower buds. Peonies in a clump near the chestnut tree, their swelling heads almost ready to burst into fist-sized crimson jewels of flower. Some yellow and purple crocuses that dotted the lawn in a mad join-the-dots pattern that she still didn't understand.

She touched her hand to her neck, enjoying the slight tenderness where Pete's stubble had rasped last night, and was deliciously aware of the small tingling spot on her inner thigh where Pete had nipped her. The sex last night had been the best with Pete since he'd lost his job. Such a blessed contrast to that disastrous first night in Hope Cottage.

She made some of Pete's favourite Columbian coffee and poured it into a cream pottery mug with 'HEAD GARDENER' printed on it. The mug had been a cheesy present for Pete but there was a lot of truth in it.

Pete had spent the past few weeks working obsessively on the greenhouse; sanding and painting the cast-iron glazing bars, and replacing cracked and missing glass panes. Helen was sure that Pete's long hours in the winter sunshine had helped banish the depression that had plagued him since he'd lost his job. If only he showed the same enthusiasm for DIY to the cottage itself. She was tired of reminding him about the damp patch on the bathroom wall, and the wonky doors on the kitchen cabinets.

'Pete, here's your coffee', she said as she opened the recently repaired greenhouse door. The smell of fresh paint still hung in the air. Surely he hadn't given it yet another coat of paint? He knew it was probably going to be demolished, for God's sake.

Pete was kneeling down near the far end of the greenhouse. He was absorbed in adjusting something near the intersection where the glass panels met the soil. 'Put it on the bench, will you? I just need to finish this. I think it wants to be right in the middle so it can see everything.'

'What on earth are you doing?' Helen moved closer and peered over his shoulder. Pete was fixing a substantial stone slab into the moist black earth, packing mounds of soil round its base.

'Fabulous, isn't it. I found it stuffed into the roots of the big holly hedge at the back of the garden, almost totally covered in branches and weeds. Must have been there some time. As soon as I dragged it out I knew this was the perfect place for it.' Pete made one final adjustment to the object and turned to her. 'Voila.'

It was a lichen-covered sandstone block about four-feet high with a leering face surrounded by Medusa-like tendrils carved deeply into its weathered surface.

'My God!' Helen reached out to touch it, but pulled her hand back at the last moment. Something about the grotesque face repelled her. 'What is it?'

'A green man. I looked it up on the internet. It's like a spirit of nature - some sort of pagan myth. They even have pubs named after them, like the 'Green Man' down in the village. Amazing isn't it?'

'Well, amazing is one word for it.' And revolting was another. But she didn't want an argument so held back her opinion.

'It's great Pete, but that's not what I wanted to talk about.'

She drew Pete's hands round her waist, reclaiming his attention from the staring stone face. 'I want us to start trying for a baby again, really trying. Last night...last night...' She hesitated and a wave of pink washed over her throat and face. 'Well, it made me feel like a woman again. Like a wife. And I'm sure we can conceive this time round.'

Pete's face tightened and he closed his eyes.

'Oh, Pete. I'm sorry. Is it still too soon? You've seemed so much better recently and I do so want us to start making our future happen.' Her words came out in a desperate tumble. 'You know that once we've sold off the building plot we'll have enough money for a baby. And I'm sure you'll get some freelance work when I'm on maternity leave. It'll all work out. You'll see.'

Pete turned his back, hunching over like he'd received a body blow. He caught hold of the potting bench.

'Pete, what's wrong? Tell me!'

'Haven't you seen how I've worked these past weeks and months? Don't you care? Do you just want to bulldoze all this down?' His questions were low and bitter. He gestured around him. 'Everything I've done. Just wasted?'

Helen couldn't bear the sag of defeat in his shoulders. 'Well... maybe... maybe it won't have to be pulled down. Maybe there's another way?' She tugged his shoulder to get him to face her. He resisted and she felt a flare of exasperation which she tamped down. 'Pete, just think about it.' Her voice was soft and coaxing. 'Maybe we can get the architect to put the new house right at the back, and make the new plot a little bit smaller. OK, so we won't get as much money, but you'll be able to keep your precious greenhouse if it means that much to you.'

Pete's back straightened and he became more alert.

'Pete, I'm talking about a baby. Our baby. It's been our dream for so many years now. And I really think the time is right. It's time for new life.'

Pete's turned to her and his tight expression softened under her pleading gaze. 'I know, Hells. I know it's time for new life. I do love you, Hells. You know that, don't you?' Pete murmured softly.

Relieved, Helen flung herself at him, wrapping her legs around him tightly. 'And I love you.'

At her sudden impact Pete reached out to brace himself and his left hand found and clutched the weathered old stone.

Lost in their embrace they didn't notice the warm air round the ancient stone start to vibrate and the faint orange coating of the lichen gleam with a malevolent sheen.

July

Helen and Pete sat at a small aluminium table in the middle of the large lawn, enjoying a late brunch and reading the newspaper. Helen basked in the heat of the summer sunshine on her face and arms. Pete had done wonders with the garden and she loved its feeling of order and peace; the sweet smell of freshly-mown grass, the faint hum of bees in the flower beds, and the newly-trimmed yew and holly hedges providing privacy and seclusion for their home.

The doorbell rang faintly in the cottage and she smiled wryly at the now familiar sound of 'Old Macdonald'. One more thing she hadn't got round to on her to-do list.

'I'll go.' She said.

The architect was a tall, spare man in his forties, wearing khaki trousers and a denim button-down shirt. He moved some plates to the side of the small table and spread out a marked-up scale plan of their plot.

'I've discussed your case with my partners, and our view is that you have a reasonable chance of getting planning permission for a new build in the northerly part of your garden. You're very fortunate to have a corner plot so you have fewer neighbours to deal with.' He paused and took a deep breath. 'However, I can't give you any guarantees, and the location of the some of the larger trees has made the siting of the proposed new property particularly tricky. There is also the question of access to the main road.' He tapped the plan with his pen. 'But I think I have a solution. The boundary would be here, and a three-bedroom house would be here.' He was looking at the plan and didn't notice Helen's sharp intake of breath.

'By building the new house where the greenhouse currently stands you will maximise your chances of getting approval. This location has direct access to the road in the safest place, and...'

'No.' Pete's interruption was stark and final.

'I'm sorry?'

'I said no. The greenhouse stays. That was part of the brief.'

'I understand it's not ideal, but as I said, there are some particular aspects of your situation which make this the optimum solution.'

Pete stood up sharply, knocking his cup over so the coffee splashed over the architect's plan.

Embarrassed, Helen cut in. 'My husband has spent a great deal of time renovating the greenhouse, and we did say that we wanted to keep it intact.'

'This is bullshit.' Pete slammed his left hand down on the table. 'That's what it is. It's complete crap and it's not going to happen.' He brushed past Helen, banging into her shoulder as he stormed down the garden.

Helen felt like crying but kept her voice level. 'I think it's best if you leave the proposal with me and I'll talk to my husband when he's calmed down.'

'Please don't worry, Mrs Serjeant.' The architect's voice was stiff and formal. 'There's often a process of negotiation - even within families. I'll post you my written report, and then it's up to you if you want to proceed further.'

As she watched the affronted architect's car depart down the street, Helen noticed Janet waving from her side of the low box hedge. Janet was wearing a blue velour track suit and matching gardening gloves, her trowel in her hand as she ruthlessly tended her well-kept front borders. Helen sketched a hasty wave back and closed the front door before Janet could descend on her. Heaven spare her from officious neighbours! She just no longer had the capacity to cope gracefully with Janet's usual overbearing offers of summer shortbread recipes or her intrusive enquiries after Helen's health and that of her "lovely wee man". And thinking of Pete, there was a conversation waiting to be had, and she knew exactly where to find him.

The heat was tangible even though the windows were open to capture any breeze that stirred, and the rows of plants stood like green-clad sentries keeping guard. As soon as Helen stepped into the humid atmosphere sweat started to bead on her upper lip.

Pete stood at the far end of the greenhouse. His left hand was rhythmically stroking the writhing tendrils of the green man's carved hair. His face was a tight mask of anger that echoed the stern face shaped in the stone next to him.

'Did you get rid of him?'

'Somehow he didn't seem keen to stay. I wonder why?'

'I know I embarrassed you and I'm sorry.' His voice was stiff.

'Sorry? Sorry?' Helen's voice rose as she could no longer contain her rage and frustration. 'Sorry doesn't cut it, Pete. It's not the embarrassment although that scene in the garden was pretty bloody humiliating.' Her voice broke with jagged rawness. 'But don't you see? This is our chance, Pete. Our chance for a baby. We said we'd split the garden and have a baby. And now you're spoiling everything.'

Tears fell heedlessly from her eyes. After months of holding it all together - the money worries, the fear for Pete and the denial of her own bone-deep hunger for a child - Helen was defeated and broken. 'And I don't know what to do.' Her cry pierced the air between them. 'I just can't be the strong one anymore.'

The humid atmosphere hung electric between them, like a current had passed through it making everything tingle and vibrate. Like there had been a rip in the mantle of their reality and somehow everything had changed. They stared at each other for several long seconds.

The planes of Pete's face shifted as a passing cloud covered the intense summer sun.

'You don't have to be the strong one anymore, Helen.' Pete's voice was compelling. 'If you don't want to be.'

'I'm just tired, Pete. So tired.'

'I'm here now. I'll look after you. Come to me and all shall be well.'

'But what will we do about the house? About our baby?'

'You'll have your baby. I promise. Now come here to me.'

Unable to resist, Helen took three steps forward, and Pete caught her up in strong arms. He swung her to sit on the wooden potting bench, pushed her knees apart and stepped between them.

She gasped, gripping Pete's shoulders. 'Will this hold me? I don't think I like it.'

Pete pushed the hair back from her neck with gentle fingers and kissed it with warm, dry lips. He eased her cotton skirt slowly up to the top of her thighs. 'I can make you like it.'

'We'll be seen. Granny Macbeth's at home and she'll see us if she goes upstairs.' Her voice quavered with nervousness and anticipation.

'It's just us. Only us.' He stroked the soft swell of her breasts, and sucked lightly on her throat.

Helen moaned and abandoned herself to sensation.

'Now let me slide these down. They're in the way.'

And Helen let him.

Helen slumped forward bonelessly, her sweating forehead resting on Pete's heaving shoulder, her hands cupping the back of his head.

'Wow.' Helen panted, 'Big wow.'

'Was I too rough?'

'No, but I won't be able to walk until tomorrow. You'll have to push me back up to the cottage in the wheelbarrow.'

Pete cracked up laughing and Helen joined in. Their unrestrained laughter caused the potting bench to vibrate under Helen, making her cling to Pete even tighter.

Their mirth resounded through the saturated heat, and the salty musk smell of sex mingled with that of damp earth and new growth. And beneath the sound of their joy swelled the undercurrent of a deeper chuckle. Not friendly. Not happy. Just satisfied.

October

'How much bigger do you want it to be?' Helen watched nervously in the failing autumn light as Pete finished stacking logs, brush and branches methodically into an enormous pile.

'I want it to be the biggest bonfire this garden has ever known. I want the flames to reach the sky. I want to mix sparks with the stars.' He laughed. 'I want to celebrate our baby.'

Helen laughed too, breathing in great gulps of rich autumn air. A strong breeze stirred, bringing her the vinegary aroma of rotting apples, and the rich, earthy smell of compost.

'We've still got six months to go. I don't want to count chickens.' She touched a small nearby log surreptitiously to ward off ill luck.

'Are you sure you don't mind about the greenhouse, after all?'

'It's my plan, isn't it? We keep the new house and sell off Hope Cottage. Simple! And no more leaking bathroom walls!' He moved to the other side of the bonfire to stuff handfuls of dry twigs into empty spaces between larger branches.

'But you still won't have the greenhouse.' Helen raised her voice to make sure Pete heard through the rustle of his activity.

'It doesn't matter.' He shouted back.

Helen took a sip of her apple juice and heard Pete's voice again, fainter this time.

'It will still have us.'

Pete came back to her and took a swig from his own glass. 'What do you think of the juice, Hells?'

'Truly delicious! And all from our very own trees.'

'Told you it would be.' Pete stepped back, and with profound satisfaction raised his glass high to the bonfire in a dramatic toast. 'To the bonfire!'

'Indeed a mighty erection,' Helen remarked dryly and was rewarded by Pete's quick grin and wiggling eyebrows.

'That comes later, m'dear.' He leered at her, laughing.

He moved round the colossal pile, deftly lighting the twists of paper and twigs he'd placed strategically throughout the wood.

Helen was surprised at how quickly the bonfire caught fire. The smoking pockets of tinder joined together to form an unstoppable river of fire that swept over the stack of bone-dry wood.

Pete took her hand, drawing her back from the crackling blaze. The evening light had finally failed, and the orange and red flames dancing in front of them made the rest of the garden seem darker in contrast. They stood a long time together united in their silence.

'It needs to be bigger,' Pete said. He grabbed the large metal spike they'd found in one of the sheds and drove it repeatedly into the base of the bonfire.

Through the roar of the fire Helen thought she heard a low laugh behind her, raw as flayed skin and wicked as a witch's curse. An icy finger seemed to touch her just at the base of her spine. She turned sharply around, but the dark was thick and black as pitch and she saw nothing but the white frame of the greenhouse.

Another strong gust of wind tugged at the bonfire and the whoosh of fire and flame crackled even higher.

'That's more like it. The sparks in the stars,' Pete shouted as he rammed the spike home again and again.

Her face scorching from the intense heat, Helen moved to the far side of the bonfire where there was more room to stand back. And when she did, what she saw was not just the bonfire in front of her but its brilliant reflection mirrored in the dark glass of the greenhouse. And the crackling and popping noises of burning wood were coming not just from the real bonfire, but from the bonfire in the glass as well.

She became aware of Pete standing next to her, frozen in place as he gazed transfixed into the glowing depths of the fire. But then in the greenhouse panes she saw another Pete. This one was leaping and capering grotesquely around. The flickering flames had created deep black lines on this other Pete's hair and face, somehow transforming him into the green man from the pagan stone. This monstrous figure pointed a gnarled finger directly at them, his eyes burning brilliant orange, and mouthed silently but with ancient certainty, 'You'll never leave me.'

A whirling blast of wind struck hard, and the mighty bonfire began slowly and inexorably to topple towards the greenhouse.

Pete roused himself, 'God, no! I didn't mean to! No!' Pete's shout pierced the dark night and he rushed forward, hands extended, as if he could somehow stop disaster from happening.

Helen watched in paralysed silence as the swaying mass plunged closer and closer to the greenhouse, until the bonfire and its reflection exploded together in a mass of burning wood and shattered glass.

'It's never, ever, been like that before.' Helen was in bed. She brushed a hand over her face and eyes, wiping away stinging beads of sweat. One side of her throat felt bruised where Pete had just jerked her closer to him during his violent climax. Her cheeks were scorched all over again, just as they had when she'd watched in appalled horror as the bonfire collapsed onto the greenhouse earlier that evening. Her skin and hair reeked of charred wood and smoke, so deep in her flesh it would never wash out.

She turned her head to Pete and asked hesitantly, 'How did you escape, Pete? I was certain you'd be crushed. Why did you run into the greenhouse?'

Pete dismissed her concern. 'Helen, I'm a survivor.' He rose on one elbow and kissed the place on her neck where bruise marks were beginning to show.

Helen shivered. 'And are you sure it doesn't matter that it's gone? The greenhouse I mean?'

He smiled and drew a soot-blackened fingernail down the canvas of her body from breastbone to navel, leaving a faint white track on her skin.

'We'll be back there soon enough.'

He moved his hand lower and possessively stroked her gently-swelling belly. 'Anyway, he's what's important now.'

'How can you be so sure it's a boy?'

Concentration lined Pete's face so he looked somehow older, like a stranger, and the faint orange glow of the bonfire still lingered in his eyes.

'It's a boy,' he said. 'And his name is Ambrose.'

THE END

Litty Williams – About the Author

I live in Kent with my husband, two teenage sons and a black cat who can open his own sachets of cat food. If only the rest of my family were equally independent! After some (ahem, many) years living and working overseas (in Italy, Hong Kong and Russia) I realised that there really is no place like home and came back to live in the UK.

I am completely fascinated by human behaviour, and my Master's degree in Occupational and Organisational Psychology helps feed my delusion that one day I'll understand how people think and why we do the things we do. I love all my characters, even the ones who are not so nice, and I hope you do too.

KEEP IN TOUCH

Twitter @litty_w

Facebook.com/LittyWilliams

Stranger Than Fiction... from Lizzie Lamb – Leicester, circa 1964

"In 1962, my family –including Granny and the dog all moved from Scotland to live in Leicester in a rambling palisaded villa. Apart from my Granny, all the adults went out to work – Mother in one of the many shoe factories dotted around Leicester and Dad on a building site as a scaffolder.

I was thirteen years old and my siblings ranged below me at eight, six and four years of age respectively. We were rarely alone in the house as Granny was there to welcome us home from school and to give us our evening meal before the adults arrived in from work.

There was something spooky about that house in College Avenue, it had a long dark corridor which led from the front door to the breakfast room, scullery and kitchen at the rear. Other doors opened off the corridor giving onto a sitting room and a gloomy dining room in turn.

Once, the house must have been splendid, in a Gothic sort of way; high ceilings, marble fireplaces, deep cornices and even bells to ring for the servants in each room. But to us kids it was a scary place and we didn't like to be left on our own. In fact, there were certain rooms which the dog wouldn't enter - without its hackles rising.

One day Granny decided to visit her brother in London which meant leaving us alone for several hours until Mother returned from the factory. Granny was very unhappy with this arrangement, but eventually agreed to visit her brother – albeit with the proviso that all four children, plus dog locked ourselves in our parents' bedroom and stayed there until Mother came home.

Granny left, and I locked us in our temporary prison with food, drink, comics, toys, radio, the dog and a chamber pot in case of emergencies! We watched Granny walk to the end of the street and then settled down for a boring couple of hours until Mother arrived home. Time passed slowly and we tried to guess where Granny was on her journey – Luton, Bedford, St Pancras, the underground . . .

Then, the strangest thing happened.

We heard Granny's footsteps climbing the stairs and coming along the landing towards the bedroom. The door knob turned once and then sprang back to its original position. Being kids we thought nothing of it. Ours was an old house and things were always sticking and jamming.

Then, stranger still, we heard Granny calling out my name: 'Betty. Betty,' in her unmistakable Scottish accent.

I looked at my sister Ellen for confirmation of what I'd heard and then walked over to the bedroom door and tried the handle. The door was still locked and the key was on our side, just as I'd left it. I went to unlock the door, but remembering the promise I'd made to Granny to stay put until Mother came home, I changed my mind.

My sister and I sat down on the bed and looked at each other, more puzzled than frightened.

When Mother came home, we were simply glad to be allowed to run outside and play and didn't tell her about Granny's voice, the footsteps or the door knob turning.

Years later I brought up the subject with my sister.

'We did hear Granny's footsteps and her voice, didn't we?' I asked.

'We did,' my sister Ellen replied, emphatically. 'She called out your name, twice and the door handle turned.'

We exchanged a look and shuddered, knowing that, as adults, we were only just beginning to comprehend we'd seen and heard that day.

Had Granny been so worried about us being in the house alone, that she'd projecting her anxiety across the miles from London to Leicester?

Or was it something 'else'; something which wanted us to leave the safety of the bedroom and venture out on to the landing where it was waiting?

The same nameless terror which made us run down the long dark corridor to the safety of the kitchen every time - and the dog refuse to enter the large cupboard under the stairs where we played?

Or, was it the old lady my father (the least fanciful of men) purported to have seen on several occasions standing at the foot of his bed looking distracted and mournful?

You decide.

My sister considers herself a 'wee bit psychic', while I consider myself a complete pragmatist. I know there must be a logical explanation for what happened and I'd feel a whole lot better if someone experienced in this field could explain it to me.

Then I could finally lay this story to rest - where it belongs."

Very very spooky...!

Insubstantial Evidence

By
Tracy Burton

Insubstantial Evidence– a short story by Tracy Burton

How many of these clothes were still being worn just a few weeks ago? Janet wondered as she looked round the storeroom, crammed thigh-deep with stuffed black sacks and carrier bags. The leaflet drop had been a touch of inspiration – Rachel's to be precise – and had been more successful than any of them could have imagined.

Now the hard work would start. Hours of sorting and sniffing, sponging off stains and replacing missing buttons. Finally, every garment would be carefully ironed, priced and hung on a coat hanger – another nearly new bargain for an ever more discerning second-hand market.

Janet had been running the local cancer charity shop for four years now and was proud of her success. There was nothing of the jumble sale about *her* shop: no fusty mothballed overcoats on hangers and a clientele comprising as many teenagers as pensioners, all drawn in by her tastefully coordinated fashion displays. Best of all, under Janet's watchful eye turnover was up month after month.

Rachel popped her head round the door, 'More clothes from Mr Arnold, Jan. Petticoats this time. Oh, and a size 42 girdle that looks brand new – still in the box.'

Janet chuckled. Mr Arnold had been a regular caller at the shop for the past four weeks, always turning up at five fifteen just as her volunteers were disappearing into the night. Rachel had offered to stay late tonight to help, which was why she and not Janet was behind the till.

'My mam used to see Monica Arnold every week down the bingo. One minute she was there bold as brass and next thing they knew, she was gone,' she said now.

'There you are. He'll be getting rid of her things,' Janet responded. 'It can be very therapeutic for the bereaved, donating their loved ones' possessions to charity.'

'But there was no announcement in the paper, my mam said,' Rachel added.

Janet emptied the contents of another black sack on the sorting table. 'He never says a word to me, poor man. Just puts the clothes on the counter with that sad look and scurries off.'

The diminutive Mr Arnold turned up the next day and the next. Janet smiled encouragingly, but he never said a word and always seemed eager to get away. On Friday evening, Janet left work early with a bad cold and it was Vera who took yet another black sack from the elderly man. Inside was a full-length sable coat.

'You could have knocked me down with a feather,' she told the others the following morning. 'And when I looked up to explain that we couldn't possibly accept something so valuable he'd already gone.'

'Fur's *not* valuable,' said Rachel. 'Not no more. No self-respecting woman would wear fur nowadays.'

Janet gave the coat a cursory glance and snorted. 'You're right, both of you. I don't think we can accept this coat and I don't think I'd want to.' She shuddered. 'Will someone please bag it up again? I'll explain the situation to Mr Arnold and insist he takes it back.'

Vera stroked the coat's voluptuous collar. 'The poor man's being so charitable in his grief – couldn't we just hang on to the fur?' she sighed. 'For a few weeks at least?'

Janet thought for a moment, then nodded. 'He does look dreadful and I wouldn't like to upset him further.' She looked sternly at Vera. 'But he *does* get the fur back, do you hear me?'

The problem of the fur coat resolved, Janet turned her attention to the December window display. She suppressed a smile. Thanks to Monica Arnold's untimely demise there was no shortage of decent designer outfits to drape in the shop's windows, most of them hardly worn and all in an 18, their most popular size. Turnover for the month was going to be well above target and all thanks to the benevolence of a grey-faced widower.

The weeks before Christmas were the busiest Janet had ever known. Word must have got around that the cancer charity shop was *the* place to shop if you wanted a designer bargain that looked brand new.

'Monica Arnold will be turning in her grave,' Vera commented. Minutes earlier she had sold a smart peacock blue suit for £7.50 to a sworn enemy of the dead woman.

Rachel bought several outfits for her amateur dramatics group who were performing *The Queen and I* the week after Christmas. 'The Queen is going to look far more regal than we'd ever dreamed possible,' she told Janet happily, patting the bulging carrier bag at her side.

Sales were booming, thanks mainly to the late Monica's extensive wardrobe – though since the arrival of the sable coat, Mr Arnold's visits had ceased. Janet made a mental note to visit him at home in January to thank him personally for his huge contribution to the charity – and to return the coat.

With just days to go and the festive celebrations in full swing, Janet was behind the counter when she heard the scream.

Taking the stairs two at a time, she got to the storeroom door just as Vera was hurling a black sack across the room. She watched as Vera collapsed onto a chair, rubbing her hands furiously against her legs.

'It's horrible, horrible,' Vera stammered. 'It wasn't there before, I'm certain of it.'

Puzzled, Janet retrieved the black sack and glanced into it. 'What do you think you're doing with this coat?' she demanded. 'I thought I'd made it quite clear that it's going back to Mr Arnold.'

'I know, I know. I just wanted one last look,' Vera explained. 'It was always my dream to have a fur . . . when I was young, fur was so glamorous, all the film stars wore it . . . but it's just horrible . . . all that blood on it.'

'Blood? What blood?' Janet demanded. 'Whatever are you talking about?'

Vera pointed to the black sack. 'It's all over the lining,' she whispered tearfully. 'See for yourself.'

Janet shuddered. 'Are you sure?' she asked, picking up the sack and peering inside. 'It looked fine when Mr Arnold brought it in.'

'We didn't check the lining.' Vera's voice trembled. 'There's a massive blood stain. What if he murdered her? She might have been wearing the coat when he killed her.'

'He must have used it to dispose of the body,' added Rachel, who'd heard the scream and followed Janet upstairs. 'You know, laid it down on the floor and rolled her up in it.'

Vera was nodding. 'She's probably lying in a shallow grave somewhere as we speak.'

Janet looked at the horrified faces of her volunteers and burst out laughing. 'Will you stop being so melodramatic, both of you.' She held the coat up to the light. 'I agree, it does look like a blood stain, but that scrawny little man murdering Monica – and getting rid of her body – nonsense! She's twice his size!'

'*Was*,' Rachel piped up. '*Was* twice his size. But I don't get it. If he did kill his wife, he's hardly likely to come here and present us with the evidence, is he?'

'It's a cry for help, that's what it is,' sniffed Vera. 'He killed her in a moment of uncontrolled rage and now he can't live with his guilty conscience. He *wants* us to discover the grisly truth, don't you see? He *wants* us to work it out.'

'Stop it you two!' Janet scolded. 'There's probably a perfectly innocent explanation for this bloodstain. I expect one of them used the coat to take a pet to the vet's or something.'

'Used a sable?' Vera snorted with disbelief. 'Are you crazy? It must be worth a fortune.'

'Maybe Monica Arnold finally caught up with the rest of the world and stopped wearing fur,' suggested Rachel. 'Though, from what my mam says, I doubt it. She's a self-centred cow by all accounts.'

'Rachel!' Janet and Vera chorused. 'Don't speak ill of the dead,' Vera admonished. She lowered her voice, 'especially the *murdered*.'

Janet gave up at that point. Personally she thought it unlikely Mr Arnold had ever trod on a spider, let alone committed the heinous crime of killing his wife, but there was little point in arguing with Vera in her current mood. The woman loved something to gossip about and the more Janet disagreed with her, the longer the Arnolds would remain a topic of conversation.

Ushering her two assistants downstairs, she took another look at the coat's lining. It *was* rather a large bloodstain, elongated in shape;

however, as she'd pointed out, there were all sorts of explanations for it: a litter of puppies (Monica Arnold had owned pedigree poodles at one time), an accidental injury, any number of other possibilities if one had time to stand around and conjecture, which she most certainly didn't.

She jammed the coat back into its sack and vowed to return it to Mr Arnold the following evening. If the removal of the coat from the premises didn't rein in Vera's wild imagination nothing would.

Caught in the whirl of last-minute Christmas bargain hunters, Janet didn't give the coat or its owner a moment's thought the following day.

It was only when she was cashing up at twenty to six, weary and with aching feet, that she remembered her intention to visit Mr Arnold that evening.

'Vera,' she called out. 'Will you come and lock the door or we'll never get home tonight.'

The words had barely left her lips when the bell alerted her to the opening of the door. Looking up, with the words 'sorry we're closed' already formed on her lips, Janet stopped in her tracks, her heart skipping a beat.

Mr Arnold stood in the doorway, gripping a small carrier bag. He entered the shop and, without uttering a word, carefully placed it on the counter. Janet followed his gaze; he was staring at the carrier bag, as if willing her to look inside.

'About the fur coat... it's really very generous of you and I want you to know that your late wife's clothes have made a big difference...' she broke off. The ashen-faced Mr Arnold wasn't listening to a word she was saying but was just gazing at the bag on the counter.

Inexplicably, a shiver ran down her back.

'Vera,' she shouted impatiently. 'Will you please come down here?'

Janet wasn't sure why she wanted someone else there at that precise moment, because Mr Arnold was in no way threatening. Beneath the shabby overcoat, he was an insubstantial little man, browbeaten, broken. She could probably overpower him singlehandedly in the unlikely event he turned nasty.

Goodness, listen to her. She was letting those silly women she worked with get to her. The idea that the frail man standing in front of her was a wife murderer was nothing short of ridiculous.

'The sable coat, it was a very generous donation, but we simply can't accept it,' she said, reaching out for the carrier bag on the counter. 'Now that's cleared up, what have you brought us today?' To her own ears, her voice sounded falsely cheerful but Mr Arnold didn't flinch.

Janet slipped her hand inside and pulled a grubby looking towel from the bag. Her heart hammering, she slowly unrolled the first part and stopped when it began to reveal bloodstains. She heard a gasp and looked up to see Rachel standing there, Vera close on her heels.

Before any of them could say a word, the shop door flew open and a red-faced woman stood panting in the doorway, blocking it with her bulk.

'My beautiful peacock suit!' Monica Arnold yelled at the three terrified women. 'Maureen Perkins told me she bought it here. And Jennifer Tyler's been swanning around in my brand new silk dress. You thieving do-gooders! I'll teach you to sell my clothes!'

Janet was the first to find her voice. 'Mrs Arnold, please calm down,' she said. 'It was your husband here who donated the items to the shop.'

'My husband...' stammered Monica. 'It most certainly was NOT my husband.'

'Yes it was,' insisted Rachel. 'He's been coming here for yonks – ever since you stopped going to bingo.' Vera and Janet nodded in agreement.

'Don't be absurd, girl.' Monica looked as if she was about to explode. 'That's ridiculous.'

'It's true. He's been bringing things in for weeks,' Janet told her, glancing around the shop for him. 'Regular as clockwork,' said Janet. 'If you don't believe us, ask him yourself! He was in here just before you arrived...' It seemed the moment Monica had walked in, her husband had made himself scarce.

'We've made a killing with your clothes,' added Rachel spitefully. 'Sold the lot.'

'Except the sable. Janet wouldn't put it out.' Vera said, then gestured towards the towel. 'And then we saw the...' she shuddered. 'You can take it with you. Along with the sable.'

Monica swallowed. 'My sable?' she eventually managed to stutter. 'H-haaaaaaaow did it get here?'

Rachel couldn't hide her impatience. 'We've already told you. Your husband's been bringing stuff in, regular as clockwork.'

'He was here just a few moments ago,' Janet agreed, but still he was nowhere to be seen. She pointed to the carrier bag and the towel. 'He left this. Let's see what's inside.'

Janet finished unrolling the towel. All eyes were on her as she slowly uncovered a large blood-stained carving knife.

Four pairs of eyes scoured the shop for Mr Arnold but there was no sign of him.

Only a blood-stained knife laying on the shop counter suggested he had ever been there at all...

Monica had gone quite, quite still. If Janet hadn't known better, she'd have sworn the woman was trembling.

THE END

About the Author – Tracy Burton

Tracy has enjoyed putting pen to paper since she was a child; however, fifteen years of media and public relations roles plus a busy home life put her creative writing ambitions on hold for many years.

Now her family is grown and has flown the nest, she is once again pursuing her passion (though her suntan suggests she doesn't spend as much time at her computer as she should!).

She's had several short stories published, including in anthologies, teenage romance magazines and (one) in *Take a Break*. A highlight was being published in the same anthology as the eminent Professor Meic Stephens, her former journalism lecturer.

Much of Tracy's recent writing has been speculative scriptwriting and she is an active member of an international online scriptwriting group. She is currently working on her first novel, *Halter Necks and Cocky Elbows*, set in the sweltering summer of 1976.

Tracy is a keen hiker and runner and, in 2011, started blogging as The Walker's Wife. She has just completed the first draft of a travelogue about her 23-day walk through Wales. *O Fon i Fynwy* will be published in digital format in November as a companion book to her partner's (outdoor writer Harri Roberts) guidebook for the new long-distance trail.

Tracy lives in Rhiwderin, South Wales, with Harri and their cat.

KEEP IN TOUCH

Twitter @thewalkerswife

Facebook - search TracyBurton

Tracy blogs about the outdoor life, running and things which interest (and annoy) her at thewalkerswife.blogspot.co.uk

Website - camau.co.uk

When Dreams

Return

By

Debbie Flint

When Dreams Return – a Short Novella by Debbie Flint

PART ONE

'Ahhh!' Sara shrieked, catching her nail as she nearly dropped the shopping on her driveway. A black tail disappeared into the bush. 'That damned cat made me jump again!' She put a heavy bag gingerly down onto the ground and sucked at one of her fingertips. 'It's made me break a nail. *One more chance, cat,'* she shrieked at it. 'Then I'll be feeding you to the hyenas.'

The cat just tilted its head to one side, peering back out of the bush. Its eyes were piercing green. Not just normal cat-green, but a really bright emerald.

'Shut up Cruella Da Ville,' Chelle replied, looking at her friend's war wound. 'You'll live. Anyway, you haven't got any hyenas.'

'Shhh!' Sara hissed. 'The cat doesn't know that.'

'You're crazy.'

'That's what Gareth says,' Sara replied, peering into the bag checking several bottles. 'At least it was my nail and not this lovely little lot.'

'Well he's right. Now, what do you want to do with this?' Chelle lifted a broomstick out of the silver Mercedes boot, and waved it around.

'Give It here, I'm going to whack the cat,' Sara said, stomping her foot towards the bushes. The green eyes flinched, but the cat stayed put.

'No - if you damage your broomstick, how are you going to do your rounds later?' Chelle teased, tapping her friend on her denim-clad bottom with the brush making her jump. Then Chelle popped it between her legs, and gave a piercing, witch-like cackle.

'Suits you. I should have got you some green face paint after all,' said Sara. 'Go put it on the porch, ta, with the plastic pumpkin and the lights.'

'God you're going overboard this year. That 'cos the husband's still away?'

'Well it'll serve him right. Gareth might hate Hallowe'en but I don't – and there's only so many years I can sit in darkness all evening. And before you say it, yes, I bowed to local pressure. Even got some sweets in for later. Get in the spirit of things eh. Spirit, get it?'

Chelle ignored her. '*Superstitious shite,* I think he calls it.'

'Hates the commercialism of it all,' Sara added, beaming, pulling out three boxes of black and orange swiss rolls, a bag of chocolate pumpkins and some green jelly fingers. She popped one in Chelle's mouth, who took it back out again, made a face and chucked it over the bushes.

'Suit yourself,' Sara said as she ate two more. 'Andy hated it too, didn't he. All the brothers did. I mean, do. I mean, er...' Sara gulped, then hesitated.

It wasn't long ago that a mere mention of Andy's name would have had Chelle in floods of tears. But this last six months, after the third anniversary had been and gone, Chelle turned a bit of a corner. Her huge building project for her new home almost completed, her art had begun to sell again at the gallery, and everything had seemed much brighter.

Even Sara had seemed a bit easier to live with lately. She'd been a huge help, if truth be known. She drew the line at Sandy the Setter, who had had to stay with Chelle's mum whilst all the painstaking restoration work was carried out on the big old Victorian semi backing onto Sara's garden. And now – tonight – it was finally ready to move into. But hey, the little dog had settled in with Chelle's mum who was glad of the company, so there he would stay. Probably just as well. Chelle had to get on with her life and the little chap brought back so many memories.

'Yes. Like brother like brother,' Chelle replied, *in more ways than you know.* She deposited the broomstick on the cute little porch with its pots of autumn flowers and returned to help unload the car. 'What's in the brown bag?'

Sara hesitated, rumbled. 'It's for tonight. The broom isn't the only thing I got whilst you were in the art shop.' Her face was mischievous, taunting. Chelle's eyes widened, and Sara held up a heavy brown paper carrier bag that had been hidden under a coat, and nodded knowingly.

'You didn't,' exclaimed Chelle. 'Is that *the book*? The one behind the glass? You bought it didn't you.'

Sara grinned broadly. 'Instead of that Prada handbag. And it was worth every penny.' She brandished the bag - it had 'Crystals & Cards' written on the side of it in bold red caligraphy. 'This is your last night with me and we're going to do some magic! Your future, my darling, is in this bag.'

'Told you, you're crazy. *She's crazy isn't she, pusscat?*' said Chelle to the flash of black fluff just visible under the rhododendron bush. Suddenly there was a loud miaow. 'Hah! See that? It's official – even the cat agrees.'

'You and your bloody animanls. It's probably just hungry – it's been here since yesterday morning. *Go find someone more appropriate to hang out with, moggy.* Someone like, like...' hearing noises, Sara cupped her hand over her ear theatrically and listened towards the road. As if on cue, two little ghosts appeared in view, and went *Booo!* Sara feigned being shocked, grabbing her heart, and laughed, as a six foot werewolf joined the girls and ushered them on, over to the other side of the street. He turned and raised a giant paw. Sara waved back, then rolled her eyes at Chelle. 'Do you think it's too unreasonable to turn off all the lights and hide again this year? And eat all the treats ourselves?' she whispered.

'And suffer the wrath of the local ghosties and ghoulies? No, you told them all you'd join in, now you stick to it. One year won't hurt. Will it, cat?' The cat miaowed again, right on cue. 'Wow! He really understands me!'

'No-one understands you,' said Sara, and then poked her tongue out and went back to unloading.

'Amazing, Chelle went on, peering downwards. 'You know, his eyes are the same green as Andy's – Gareth's are a bit paler. They had a black cat didn't they? When we were all in high school? I remember it sitting on the piano when I went round for my lessons. All the brothers would be out in the back garden play fighting. I remember their mum keeping it inside and shouting them to *keep the crazy noise down.*'

Sara had put the bottles from the broken bag inside another one and was now struggling to lift it. 'I don't know,' she huffed, as Chelle came round to help her. 'You're the one who remembers all that stuff. I never even noticed Gareth until he got a six pack, remember.'

'Mmm. Too busy dating the football team.'

'Oi! That's just not true!' Sara protested as they both heaved at the bag. 'It was the rugby team. Whilst you and Gareth were at choir.'

Chelle tutted and shook her head. 'Rock choir. There's a difference,' she said, as they both lifted the heavy weight with both hands. 'Not that you noticed.'

'What? He got me in the end, and that's what counts. Oof!' She said, as the handles of the bag broke and several tins went rolling towards the bushes across the driveway. A can of tuna came to rest just in front of the bush. The cat sniffed it and licked its lips.

'Ohhh no you don't,' Sara exclaimed, snatching the can back. 'I'm about to get rid of one house guest who's overstayed her welcome. Don't think you're moving in instead.'

The sleek black ears twitched. The head bobbed and tilted. Listening, watching them.

'Charming I'm sure,' replied Chelle. 'I'm sorry pusscat. Now see that house over the back, there? That's my new home. Come see me over there.' She bent down and stroked the cat. Its green eyes shone brightly at her. At least I'll have one visitor crossing the threshold - madam, over there, is allergic to paint.'

'Yes, well unless you get me a scuba kit to breathe through, the housewarming cake will have to wait till the smell of gloss has gone!' Sara smiled, both girls scurrying round retrieving the remaining cans. 'And anyway, I'm looking forward to getting my house back.' Chelle made a hurt face and Sara continued. 'But you're welcome to pop back anytime you like – as long as you call first. Oh, I forgot there's no mobile signal over there is there? Tut,' she teased. 'Well, whenever the padlock is not on the old iron gate you're welcome to enter my domain once more. Or maybe I'll just forget and keep you locked out!'

'You don't mean it. You've loved having me here.' Chelle said, reaching out a hand again to the cat who scurried away finally. Chelle stood up. 'It's good timing anyway isn't it? What with Gareth's tour ending any day now? By the time he gets back I'll be gone – me and all my – what did you call it? *Bloody rubbish?*'

'Well isn't it time for a clear out? Why take all Andy's old crap into a nice new house? It's not like he'll ever be back for it, is it?' The question hung in the air. '... Sorry, I mean... new start and all that. Well you know what I mean. De-clutter.'

Chelle just pursed her lips, used to her old friend's bluntness. 'It's on my 'to-do' list. Let me get moved in first. It's a big change – I can't believe it's finally finished.'

'Yes well as I say, he'd have been proud of you,' Sara's voice softened. 'Really proud. Next step, you know what.'

'Oh oh, I know that tone. What?' said Chelle.

'I saw the way you looked at Mr Joseph the other day. Time to think about dating again.'

Chelle sighed. *Here we go again.* 'Grant Joseph is just being friendly.'

'*Mister* Joseph over the road is a big fan – did you see the way he hung about the other day after mountain biking? When you were back from your jog? Took forever, standing there in his tight top and his rippling thighs. Hosing down his spokes. It was me that needed hosing down after watching that from behind the curtain.'

'I wondered what you were doing,' Chelle said, closing the car boot. 'Anyway, he's too... nice.'

'He's not that nice. He's got quite a wicked streak if you must know.'

'You still annoyed about the broken summer house windows?' Chelle said, remembering the fuss Sara had made when his nephews's ball had broken the glass. Apparently.

'No, Mr Mansfield's fixing that for me. Taking his time about it, mind you. No, I meant old Bradley Wiggins opposite makes a good werewolf.'

'Oh, that was him.'

'Yes. At least I think it was. Great mask – Hallowe'en's very scary for kids nowadays. In our era it was face paint and black bin bags.'

'Yes, very realistic. I won't be fantasising about *him* any day soon.'

'Don't speak so fast – you never know what changes are ahead of us. Change isn't a bad thing. For either of us.' Sara looked thoughtful for a moment then hunted for her house keys again.

'You'll be all back to normal by tomorrow I bet,' said Chelle, picking up bags and following her towards the door.

'Yes,' said Sara, 'Or whatever normal means.' The last bit was barely audible but Chelle heard it, and noticed the strained look on her friend's face.

Always perfectly made up, always smartly dressed, blonde hair chic and straightened, Sara was a young looking mid-thirties. Whereas Chelle... *well the last two years have taken their toll*, she thought, as she caught sight of her own reflection in the glass panel of the front door - bare-faced, brown wavy hair tied back severely as it usually was nowadays. Several new lines etched into her face. And she'd lost a lot of weight, as her mother was quick to point out. But at least she'd stopped waking up screaming in the middle of the night. Mostly.

'Ahh here it is,' Sara said, producing a key ring with a crystal studded S hanging from it from the depths of an oversized black leather bag with a big gold designer logo on the side. She lifted up the key to the door and then stopped dead. She gasped. Chelle snapped a look at the door.

The door moved. It was open.

'Sara... You – you didn't leave the front door open again, did you?'

'Must have done,' Sara replied, going very slightly white. 'Unless...' she pushed the door open a little further and tentatively peered inside, listening hard. Nothing. 'Helloooo...!' No reply. 'Nah,' she said, reaching inside and switching on the light. 'Nothing. Yes, I guess I must have done.' She chuckled nervously.

'You're such a scaredy cat! And always in too much of a rush, that's your trouble,' Chelle said, narrowing her eyes. 'But you'd better get Gareth to have a look at that lock when he's back. Can't take chances, even in a safe neighbourhood like this with werewolves and monsters on patrol.'

Sara nodded, smiled gratefully and deposited her bags in the hallway. 'Oo, careful with that one,' she said, 'in case you hadn't noticed, there's *champers* in there. We're going to make it a proper send off tonight. And in return, there's a special ritual I want you to do.'

'I'm not watching Mamma Mia yet *again*,' Chelle declared, following Sara's lead and carefully putting down her bags.

'No, silly. It's far more girly than that. I was talking to Mrs Endecott in the shop, and she told me exactly what you have to do,' Sara said as they went back out to pick up the rest of the shopping and spotted some more passers-by. She waved to several four foot Harry Potters and a six foot Hagrid passing by their front gate, patting her watch as if to say *later*. Hagrid nodded and walked on. 'It's because of what's happening tonight. *Tonight*, can you believe it?' Sara said, but Chelle looked blank. 'Come on, what's tonight? Apart from the obvious,' Sara asked.

'The night you finally embraced your inner witch?'

'No. Go on, what's tonight?'

'My last night of being hen-pecked by you?' Chelle replied. 'I don't know, give us a clue.'

'Look at the sky.'

Chelle stopped and followed Sara's gaze up to where a massive white sphere was peering from behind a cloud.

'It's a full moon,' Sara explained, glee in her voice.

Chelle shrugged and made a *'so what'* face. Sara continued. 'Tonight, after our *"Chelle's Sodding Off"* celebration dinner, you, my lovely, are going to start your new era with a dramatic appeal to the universe.' Sara put her arm around her friend's shoulder and gestured skywards. 'As witnessed by the moon.' Chelle slowly raised her eyebrows incredulously but Sara went on. 'Tonight, you'll be conjuring up your man.'

'What?'

'Using a cosmic ordering spell to write your very own ideal man list – then burn it under the full moon. With a spell. Mrs Endecott swears it'll work. Perfect night for magic.'

'No wonder you're doing it tonight then, if Gareth's due back any day now.'

'And don't I know it. It's his fault I have to be so secretive sometimes!'

'Yes I had noticed. Mostly wine-hide-and-seek isn't it?' Chelle quipped and Sara ignored it.

'Anyway, if anyone deserves a new start, you do. And who knows, your ideal man might be just around the corner.' Sara said, then glanced towards the gate again, where Hagrid was trudging back the other way with the raucous group of kids, all Hallowe'en-Hyper from too much sugar, no doubt. Hagrid looked weary. He stopped, cocked his head on one side and held his hands out as if to say *now?'* 'Catch you later Mr Mansfield,' Sara called. Hagrid nodded, and walked on, round-shouldered.

Then Chelle felt something down at her feet. The cat had re-emerged and was wrapping itself around her calves. She bent down to stroke it and the purring noise increased ten-fold.

'Eurgh, make sure you wash your hands afterwards, you don't know where it's been,' said Sara, shaking her keyring at the cat.

'Haha. Perhaps she wants to join in with the magic spells.'

'She? He? IT can be *in* one if it's not careful. As part of the potion,' sniggered Sara, locking her boot and hissing at the cat. With that, it scarpered off into the bushes again. 'Come on, let's go find you a cauldron.'

Chelle made a *'oo, magic!'* face, and started singing, warbling something about flying high defying gravity, as she danced a little on her kitten heels on the way back to the front door of Sara's pristine Edwardian semi.

The girls carted all the bags into the kitchen, unpacked it all, and whilst Sara began preparing the evening meal, Chelle went upstairs to gather the last few of her belongings together.

Ready for the first night in her new house.

Her new home.

A new chapter indeed. Shame though - she'd quite liked the old one.

She picked up an old fashioned scrapbook album, paused, then shoved it into a bag. End of an era indeed.

It had ended just after they celebrated their tenth wedding anniversary, when her husband Andy had gone out to work on the lifeboats one stormy night and never came back. One solitary shoe washed up on the shore was all that turned up. She'd kept it, though god knows why.

Maybe it *was* time to make changes, perhaps Sara was right.

And get back to work. Chelle's sketch book was next to go into the bag. Her career as a promising artist had been killed stone dead as every shred of inspiration dried up. Along with her dreams. She'd been building a reputation as an imaginative contemporary artist, and many of the ideas had been based on crazy imagery which came to her in the middle of the night, when she would wake up, scribble some sketches, then go back to sleep again as soundly as a baby. Andy had thought it endearing. Andy had thought everything she did was endearing.

Then the dreams had become nightmares and she'd sought medication to help. But it got rid of the dreams as well as stopping the nightmares. Now she never woke up in the night, and her whole life felt as though it was in neutral. *Even first gear would be better than this,* Chelle thought. She fished the sketch book back out again but didn't open it, she just ran her hand over the front of it. Then flicked to the back page, where she'd outlines a schedule for the renovation and some notes and drawings. She'd been helped back to a normal routine enormously by the daily distraction of builders and contractors and materials and deadlines. She shivered, thinking about what her life had been like before getting her teeth into this project. And selling up her marital home, to move into Gareth and Sara's till her new home was ready.

Chelle stood up and went to look out the window at the top floor of the century-old building - her building. It was just visible through the trees in the long back-to-back gardens. She compared the view she was looking at, to a sketch in the back of her book. Almost the same. But now there was a faint security light visible through the first floor windows, a warm yellow glow, and it seemed inviting. Kind of. Yes it was empty but maybe Sandy the Setter would be there with her eventually – if she could persuade her mother to give him up. And at least Chelle could play her piano to her heart's content without Sara's jibes about the noise.

As she turned away to continue packing, Chelle could have sworn she saw a strange shadow flicker in one of the attic windows. She did a double take. *Nothing.* Must be the trees. I guess.

Chelle packed the sketch book into her bag and began thinking about the work the house had needed.

It had been slow, but bit by bit, the big house took shape, done up in exactly the way she and Andy had pictured, all the years they'd discussed renovating an old house together. Plus a liberal sprinkling of Gareth's ideas too. And once the work had actually begun, he'd helped her. At least initially. Gareth had been generous with his time whenever he was home on leave, finding solace in spending time with his brother's project. Connection, he'd explained.

Then one stormy afternoon, it had all changed. He wouldn't talk about it so Chelle described to Sara afterwards how Gareth had got upset – which was unusual. She told Sara he'd been telling the builders about his brother, during a tea break, sheltering in the half-finished kitchen from the storm. He'd told them Andy had been inspired to do something worthy after Gareth had joined the army, so he went on the lifeboats. And one night he never came back. If he'd never joined, he'd have been the one helping Chelle, instead of Gareth.

It was no more Gareth's fault than anyone's, but they all blamed themselves anyway. As you do. Maybe the years of bottling it up had just caught up with Gareth, but it was an awkward moment, and Chelle had never seen him like that before. Or since.

Sara looked worried but said she understood.

After that, he'd stopped coming over and had left Chelle to it. Plus over the last year, his job took him away more and more anyway, which was one of the reasons he'd asked Chelle to come and stay – keep Sara company. And anyway – it meant Chelle was right on top of her building project.

It was almost as though, if she could finish the house, then maybe closure could take place. Maybe now, with her mission accomplished, maybe inspiration would return to her. And maybe she would start waking in the night with a head full of ideas again. But at least the house was done. Just a shame it had taken Andy's life insurance settlement to finally make it happen.

But if everything happens for a reason, that was as good as any. *He'd be proud of you,* she thought, remembering Sara's words. Yes, he probably would. Chelle zipped up the bag and left the room for the last time.

When she came back down, with her last remaining bags, a wonderful aroma filled the air, and Sara was busy lighting some candles and laying out the table for two, the champagne already in a big ice bucket. Chelle dumped her bags in the hallway and walked into the dining room.

'Wow, you're sparing no expense here are you?'

'Big night – I'm losing a lodger and gaining a shiny new next door neighbour!' Sara said, a twinkle in her eye.

The meal was spectacular – Sara's cooking prowess had improved no end in the time Chelle had been there – 'the least I can do is feed you right, in the circumstances,' Sara had explained when she'd taken up baking classes. That and bonding with the neighbours. The cake was amazing, complete with little hearts and a marzipan model of Chelle's new house – Sara was top of the class by all accounts. She'd obviously made a huge effort.

'Listen – if I forget to say it tomorrow, thanks again for being a complete star and putting up with me.' Chelle said, smiling at her from ear to ear.

Sara shrugged slightly. 'If I hadn't, Gareth would have had something to say about it wouldn't he! With his baby brother gone, and all that. Had to do all we could to help.'

It was no good. With the emotion of the moment, a tiny tear threatened to appear in the corner of Chelle's eye. She blinked several times and looked upwards. She missed him. They all did.

'So any news about when Gareth's home?' Chelle asked as Sara poured the last of the champagne. 'You bought enough food today to feed an army let alone one sargeant.'

'Major, Sweetie, Major. The answer is, I don't know. I never know.' She paused. 'That's why tonight's the night... for magic!'

'OK where's that spell book? Let's get this silliness out of the way then I can leave you to it, once and for all,' Chelle said, putting her coffee cup down.

'Yay!' said Sara as she got up, 'You won't regret it, Chelle, it won't take long. And, what if it worked – I mean, actually worked? Every woman should have a man to take care of her. You know, someone to cook for her and care for her,' she went on, as she walked backwards to the hallway, gesticulating and rising to her theme. 'And to fix things and to have sex with and...' Suddenly she screamed. A loud piercing shriek which made Chelle jump out of her skin. 'Get out. *Get OUT!*'

Chelle rushed from the room to see Sara kicking out after a black furry object disappearing back through the front door which was once more ajar. 'There's definitely something the matter with that lock. Sod waiting for Gareth, I'm getting Mr Mansfield over tomorrow. Bloody hell,' Sara said, slamming the door again and putting the security chain on. 'Shit.' She rested her back on the door and put her hand on her heart, breathing deeply.

'Are you ok?' Chelle said. 'What was it doing?'

'Nosing around your bags. Nearly scared me half to death! Probably found something stinky in there knowing you,' Sara said, and sat herself down on the bottom step.

'Seriously – you ok?'

'I'll be fine – heart's going ten to the dozen. Haven't been this frightened since that night you screamed the house down. Thank god you got the tablets.'

'Yes sorry about that. Again. Still don't remember doing it. Still very sorry.'

'Well after tonight you can have all the nightmares you want – in your own house. And I won't be able to hear a thing. I'll be on my own. Again.'

'Not for long. He'll be back soon, won't he. Gareth would soon make mincemeat of any intruder with those big muscles of his – he's harder than the average burglar, right?'

'It's not the burglars I'm worried about,' said Sara, under her breath, picking herself up, checking the front door once more, and dusting herself down. She switched off the hallway light, then the porch light, then the front room light. 'OK, let's go find the book.'

'Are you sure about this?' Chelle asked ten minutes later, as they stood in the summer house with its windows now almost good as new. It had been swept clean but still left a lot to be desired. 'Why do we have to do it out here anyway?'

'Mrs Endecott said as far away from atmospheric interference as possible – there's no mobile service here, and you can see the moon. Now, let me see.' Sara tried the lights – no good – so they kept the torches on. They cleared a space on an old wooden workbench and carefully laid out the ancient, leather-bound book. Its frayed corners, barely legible *olde worlde* script with an embossed title, and faded gold-edged pages gave it an other-world feeling. *"The Witch's Journal – charms, spells, potions and enchantments."*

'Do we have to go collect an eye of newt or a hair of dog or something? I might have the dog hair part still in my car?' Chelle teased.

'It's nothing like that, silly. Apparently it's all about putting your intentions out to the universe and really meaning it. That's the most important thing.' She was tracing her finger down the contents. 'Fairy Love Spell, nope... Old Maid's Love Spell...' She looked Chelle up and down. Chelle elbowed her. '...Nope.' Sara was turning the thick, brittle pages slowly. 'Mermaids Love Spell -can't do that one, pond's too small.'

Chelle's mind was taken back for an instant to that day in the attic with Gareth. How things hadn't quite been the same between them since. And the pond, and the sea and the stormy night and the shoe and... Then Sara shrieked in delight. Chelle shook herself back to the present. There was something about the old book that gave her the creeps.

'Aha! Here, see this?' Sara pointed out a paragraph of the ancient text, then bent down to blow away some particles obscuring a couple of the words. She sneezed, then coughed and spluttered a bit, wafting her hand around in the air. 'Bloody dust.'

'Let me see,' Chelle said and held her torch nearer to the page. She read out loud.

"By the light of the full waxing moon, repeat these words.

I call on forces higher than I,
To awaken the dreams I hold inside
Through this connection that knows my need
Grant love's enchantment with all speed."

Seems easy enough. Apart from the lack of dreams inside, but I could always pretend.'

Sara looked thoughtful and nodded, then looked closer, skimming over the rest of the spell. 'Yes, just make some up – imagine what you *would* dream about, if you had dreams. In fact, do it now. Go on, close your eyes and imagine.'

Chelle made a face, then begrudgingly closed her eyes. Surprisingly, images popped into her head straight away.

'From the way you're smiling, I'm guessing that Mr Joseph's thighs might have something to do with it?'

Chelle just smiled and said nothing. Sara continued. 'Right, now, you have to take the list of traits for your ideal man, written in the blood of a lovebird and put it in the container and burn it. It should be a copper cauldron really but you can make do with my metal office bin from Gareth's den. And the red food colouring I borrowed from Mister... from my kitchen as we're clean out of lovebirds. Cat ate them all.' Sara shrugged and Chelle shook her head as if to say *'there's no hope'.* 'That'll do won't it? Modern day equivalent?'

'You sure that'll work ok? With those ingredients, knowing my luck a ginger cyberman will come walking through the door.'

'God I hope not – that'd just about finish me off! Daleks I could cope with, but not the cybermen. Bad enough being here in this summer house – it gives me the creeps out here on my own at night. And I'm going to start wheezing if I stay here much longer. You'll be ok doing the actual spell part out there on your own, though won't you? Mrs *Nothing Scares Me?'*

'Course I will. It's no more scary out there at night than during the daytime. It's all the same stuff, just darker.' She'd hardened up a lot in the last few years.

'Well I'm due a visit from a six foot two hairy giant a.k.a. Mr Mansfield and the cast of the Philosopher's Stone soon, so let's go back inside. You can write the list in the warm, if you want, then find a clearing to burn it. Do it in your own garden though, right? Oooo this is exciting! The highlight of my week!' she said, opening the creaking summer house door and going back outside. 'Can't wait to tell Mrs Endecott at the next cookery class.'

Chelle followed Sara back out into the garden. The full moon was lighting their way almost as brightly as a streetlamp. They made their way up the long narrow path to the house. There was a nip in the air but it wasn't too windy – not yet. Sara put the kettle on whilst Chelle knuckled down and began her list. The doorbell rang and Sara practically skipped out to answer the door with a net-bag of orange foil-covered chocolate pumpkins in her hand. Low voices talked in the hallway for a while, as Chelle found herself strangely carried away with the task of listing her ideal man. It wasn't as hard as she thought. It was as though something was taking over her hand – could it be that strange thing – *inspiration?* She became aware that she was being watched, but not from the doorway. She looked up and there at the French doors was… nothing.

I could have sworn…

Chelle shook her head and took a drink of her tea, furrowed her brow for a moment, then went back to finishing off her list. After what seemed just a few minutes, but it could have been an age, Sara came back into the kitchen. Her face was flushed and she'd obviously been laughing.

'How are you getting on?' she said, popping the second to last chocolate pumpkin in her own mouth and the final one into Chelle's.

'Mmm. Ok. Nearly there. You look happy – looks like joining in with all the Hallowe'en jollities suits you well. Maybe you'll dress up and go out with them yourself next year. If they'll allow a designer witch anywhere near the peasants. Hey, maybe when Gareth's back home for good, maybe he'll relent and join in. He'll have no choice when you finally have a little witch or wizard of your own one day.'

Sara looked thoughtful. 'Maybe. Or maybe not. Now, let me see that list.'

Chelle handed it over and got up to make a pot of tea. As she stood in the kitchen waiting for the kettle to boil, she looked up at the attic room of her house again, just visible through the trees. Looked like there was a window ajar up there, or some sort of shadow from the massive oak tree. Have to check it later. Then, tea made, they both went back into the front room along with a tray of treats in case more Hallowe'en visitors decided to stop by. Suddenly they heard a howl from outside the front window, and a loud bang as a scary face appeared at the glass. Both girls jumped. Then Sara laughed, relieved, as she saw a head with a very realistic ogre type face, pressed up against the pane. 'Go away! I've run out of pumpkins!' she shouted, and threw a marshmallow at the window. 'Bloody Idiot!' she shouted and rolled her eyes at Chelle.

'Stephen Mansfield I assume?

Sara smiled, shrugged, then carried on reading. A couple of minutes later, she put down Chelle's list.

'Bloody hell, you've covered every avenue, haven't you!'

'I got carried away.'

'Well you know who you've described?'

'Andy I suppose.'

'No. Actually.'

'Who?' asked Chelle.

'Gareth.'

'*Like brother like brother,*' both girls laughed.

'Or Mr Joseph with the cycling shorts. Although I'm not sure if he's "imaginitive and generous…" He's certainly tall, dark and hunky. In fact, if I wasn't married…' she tailed off, wistfully. 'It's been a long time.'

'Don't worry, he'll be back soon enough. Gareth I mean,' Chelle said and patted her friend's hand reassuringly. They finished their tea. Sara kept looking at her watch, then over to the window, and back to Chelle. Chelle's departure was obviously bothering Sara more than she was admitting. They chatted for a bit longer, mainly about hunky neighbours. Then the conversation came back round, as usual, to Gareth being away.

In some ways, Sara's life was the life Chelle would have had, if things had worked out differently. And Andy was always away for days on end too. The ladies shared their experiences, compared and contrasted their views on the whole long-distance relationship thing, and consoled themselves with a slice of the cake. Sara put the marzipan house on Chelle's plate. The top was covered in buttercream and very messy.

'He'd have a fit if he saw me munching this lot,' said Sara. 'He knows I'm supposed to be losing weight. We can't all be Mr Health Fanatic – hard-as-iron pecs and perfection 'n rippling muscles and a bitta beefcake. He's a beefcake, my husband, isn't he. Spends enough bloody time at the gym.' Sara had enjoyed most of the champagne. 'He hates all this sugary stuff, and he can't stand buttercream – I'll have to give it away to

Hogwarts before he gets home. Want another piece? Let's make the most of it whilst he's away holed up somewhere in some godforsaken cave inside a...cave in a, mountain - somewhere.' Sara went quiet. 'Didn't even get to say a proper goodbye last time – I woke up and they'd been called away.'

Chelle smiled – it wasn't the first time she'd seen Sara like this in the many months she'd been staying there.

'You know, it's like this...' Sara rambled on. 'You just get used to him being here, and then he's gone. Then no sooner are you used to him *not* being here than he's suddenly back again – can't ever know. You know what it's like... But – we love 'em. And if we miss 'em then we just have to think hard enough... We only have to think of them and they're here... *you* know that better'n anybody. We've got good imaginations you see. Well I have. Yours is... broken. But you'll get your dreams back, Chelle, you wait and see. New start, right? New start's a good things, yes?'

'Yes Sara,' she replied. It was clearly time for Chelle to leave. She packed all of her remaining stuff from the hallway into her car, plus the metal bin and the ideal man list and the copy of the spell.

'Now repeat after me,' Sara said, as she stood at Chelle's car window.

'What?'

'I do solemnly swear,'

'I do solemnly swear...'

'To visit Sara regularly,'

'To visit Sara regularly...'

'But only if I call first.'

'Nut job. I'll probably be back tomorrow morning, don't worry – I'm bound to have forgotten something.'

'Well if you're sure that spending the night in that spooky house won't give you nightm... no, you said you don't get them anymore. Well, whatever happens when you're asleep, I hope you enjoy the new place. Well, sod off then. See you tomorrow. Don't arrive too early!' Sara laughed and Chelle pulled away down the drive on the very short hop to her brand new house.

She wasn't aware of the black shape following along the pavement after her.

A twenty minute unloading session later, and there she was, standing in a clearing in the long back garden, ready to get the final job of the night out of the way before having a long soak in her new roll top bath and going to bed early. She was tempted to just put the list on the woodburning stove and pretend she'd done it, but then changed her mind, remembering all the effort Sara had gone through – all for her. Or all to get rid of her.

The bin in front of her, the list in one hand, and a lighter in the other, she gazed up at the moon, which was behind a cloud. She waited for it to re-emerge, looking around her awkwardly. *This is stupid,* she thought. *Sara's stupid. And she's turning into a pisshead.* Then as soon as she'd said it, she felt guilty. She knew exactly how it felt to be as lonely her friend and a wave of compassion flooded through her veins. Sara clearly wanted Chelle to be happy and get over Andy's death. *Maybe it's me that's been a pain to live with,* thought Chelle. Maybe it was indeed time.

So Chelle sucked it up and focussed her mind on her list. The breeze was blowing more vigorously now, rustling the trees and bushes and catching tendrils of Chelle's hair which had escaped the tight pony tail. Somewhere an owl was hooting, and in the distance, kids were shouting and laughing. She closed her eyes and tilted her face skywards. If there was such a thing as magic, well, why the hell not give it a go.

And then she was ready. She read the spell from the book – well, from a print-out Sara had given her. Then she burned the list in the bin, which made a bright yellow flame that disappeared to nothing quite quickly and lay smouldering in the bottom. Then Chelle stood there looking around her, wondering if she was supposed to feel different, notice anything new… sense something on its way… but painfully, she didn't. The embers still smouldered, the moon still shone and the welcoming glow from inside the windows of her new home still reassured her.

If ever it was time to conjure up a new husband, it was now. The deed had been done and now fate had to step in and take its course. She hoped no one had been watching her, from their back windows in the big old houses nearby. She looked around at them, but nothing stirred, anywhere. She could have sworn…

She came over all embarrassed and felt ever so slightly silly.

Then she gathered up her bits and pieces and turned back to the house, stopping suddenly on the path. *What was that?* She listened, aware only of her own breathing. *Nothing.* If only she could get rid of the feeling that someone or something – was watching her...

PART TWO

'*Jesus!*' Chelle jumped. From several gardens away there was a sudden piercing howl followed by an urgent *bang bang bang* noise. The bushes behind her rustled, and the cat shot out towards her, ran straight past her, and on towards her house, as if fleeing the howl. Then the garden was consumed by the shadows again as the moon went behind a big cloud. 'Bloody hell,' she said to herself out loud. 'I'm getting as jumpy as Sara.' She flicked her torch back on and shone it in front of her feet to help see the pathway. Kids' voices some way off, whined '*let me in,*' then shrieked loudly then banged some more. Chelle smiled and shook her head. *If you can't trick or treat your neighbours, do it to your kids,* she thought, and let out a breath she didn't realise she was holding.

Following the meandering pathway back to the house, she ducked to avoid the overhanging branches of a big willow tree, each step illuminated by the torchlight. The moon was so bright again she hardly needed it, but she kept it trained just ahead of her, just in case of cat's tail emergencies, and finally breathed a sigh of relief when she reached her back door. It was freshly painted and a little stiff, so she pulled it hard. Stepping inside, she turned to look back up at the sky. The 'man in the moon' certainly seemed to be watching over her – luminous, perfect - complete. *Like I will be if this works,* she thought, and then whispered,

'*Whatever happens, if you're up there, Andy, know that it's ok. I'm ok. It's all going to be… fine.*'

Behind her, a dark shape appeared in the doorway to the kitchen. She was still looking upwards.

It approached Chelle from behind, softly, silently; and when it reached her legs, it brushed against them. Chelle gasped. When she saw what it was, she exhaled sharply and tutted.

'I actually think you must have a death wish, cat,' she said, bending down and giving in, petting it, hearing it purr. She knew she shouldn't really encourage it, but liking the feeling of its warm body vibrating away in ecstasy under her hand, as she played with it. Then she held open the door until it went outside. Another sharp tug and the cat and rest of the world was firmly shut out once more. Chelle set about double-locking up and putting the security chain on.

But behind her, something moved. In the background, without a sound, something moved on the stairs.

Oblivious, Chelle poured herself a celebratory glass of wine and took a slow tour of her new home, admiring her handiwork. Every wall cleverly finished, every ornament carefully placed, every colour perfectly matched – apart from the bathroom. And every surface shiny and brand spanking new. She sighed deeply. *Yes, he'd have been very proud of her.*

She went upstairs to run a bath and filled the tub with her favourite bath gel, bubbles already building before she left it to go turn her music on. The reassuring sounds of 1930's melodies filled the air, and Chelle luxuriated in the hot water until her skin was a perfect match for her bathroom. Once or twice she thought she heard a noise in the house, and tried to listen above the music, but there was nothing. *Stop being bloody silly,* she said to herself, and tried to text Sara. 'All good here, apart from a sneaky feeling I'm being watched. Mwahahaaaar! Goodnight and thank you for everything.'

Aha! Some signal! Maybe the atmospherics. It was rare, in this house, but Sara texted straight back, 'Hope you have sweet dreams, or rather have SOME dreams anyway. See you in the morning. Text when on your way over.'

After nearly nodding off in the warm water, and speedily finishing her bathroom routine, Chelle put on a fluffy new robe and settled down with a new book in her new lounge, in front of her new woodburner. *New, new, new.* Unlike the house - which had stood on this spot for over a century. And unlike Chelle herself, who felt *old, old, old.*

A complete contrast to her younger self staring back at her from the photo on the piano across the room.

It was in the corner at an angle, under the window. The piano and the photo were just as they had been in their old house – even adorned with the two little pebbles in the shape of a heart which Andy had given her when they first started dating. That was typical of Andy. He was much softer than hard-nut Gareth. Little gestures, so much more important than expensive gifts.

Noticing the little things keeps romance alive, he'd said.

Like the notes he'd begun hiding around the house for her when they were first married. She'd find them in cookie jars and under her pillow and always when he went off on one of his long shifts. She'd kept some of them, but as always with a marriage, fewer as the years went by. Her scrapbook held the few she had kept – and pictures of significant occasions and the little moments she'd one day wish she hadn't taken for granted. She picked up the photo and sipped her wine. She'd had this frame since forever - it had been Andy's favourite. Sara and Gareth had given it to them as a gift years ago. Then they'd added the latest photo only a year before... 'it'... had happened.

She looked at the photo. It was a group shot, Chelle and Sara on either end, with Andy and his older brother in the middle, their arms around each-others' shoulders. Peas in a pod. Kind of. It was a wonderful snapshot of a moment in time, in a bygone era – younger, happier. Chelle chewed her cheek and played with the pebbles in her palm. She remembered exactly the conversation they'd had just before that photo was taken. A rare heated debate – well, about as heated as it got with Andy. Talking about what to do about whose mother they'd visit first, next Christmas. Only that year, Christmas was cancelled.

How suddenly life can pull the rug from under you – trounce all your expectations. There you are, your life mapped out for years to come, punctuated with birthdays and weddings and Sunday mornings with the papers and coffee, and discussions about holidays and new cars and *one day children...* and then suddenly it's all gone – your whole future, just... no longer exists.

One day you're somebody's wife, thinking about loo roll and eggs and whose turn it is to choose what to watch on telly tonight. Then the next, *pffffft!* Vanished, replaced with an alien world full of new trauma - stressing about where he kept the Philips screwdriver so you can try to change the batteries on the waterproof shower radio he so loved, 'cos it was always his job and now it's yours. Now they're *all* yours. Suddenly even the tiniest, inconsequential task becomes traumatic, and you slump to the floor in tears on a daily basis and stare into space for hours until you realise it's all gone dark and the sun's gone down.

Then just as suddenly it's the painful first anniversary, and you struggle through it, but then you find you've actually been laughing more again lately, even if you have been feeling guilty every time. But you've learned stuff - you do now know where everything is kept, and you've found more logical places for most of it. And by the end of year two you've discovered you can do tasks you never thought possible, like getting the car MOT'd and taxed and working Sara's lawn mower and doing the garden in return for lodging, and becoming generally helpful instead of *helpless*.

Gradually you discover an alien feeling - being just a little bit proud of yourself – as he would have been. 'Cos you're coping, rather than feeling like you're going to drown.

And then a bit more time goes by and people start asking if you'd like to meet their friend, or the guy at work, or the neighbour with the tight cycling shorts...

Chelle smiled. *Actually the thighs HAD looked rather cute.* Progress! And now she'd done her 'man list' and burned it under a full moon, there really was no turning back.

She sat down at the piano and played a few bars of a haunting melody – one from an old time music hall song about being *shy, Mary Ellen so shy*. It had been one of the bedtime songs her nan had sung her when she was tiny. And one she'd played a lot on this piano. Andy, Gareth, Sara and her younger self watched her serenade them from behind glass. She finished with a flourish, and the reverb on the final notes rang round the room and faded into silence once more. Then Chelle picked up the photo, kissed it gently and lowered it towards the piano then stopped, and sniffed. *What was that smell?* She sniffed at the picture frame - *it wasn't this.* She put the photo back down again and wriggled her nose in the air, furrowing her brow. She became aware of an aroma she knew instinctively she had to track down. Fast. She followed her nose and looked around the room, her eyes resting on the curtain by the window. She swallowed – hard.

Something was moving behind the curtain.

That damned cat, she thought. Maybe the window was open and the cat had jumped back in... She stepped towards the curtain, all the while staring intently at the gentle swaying of the fabric. A shiver passed down her spine and she could hear her own pulse in her ears, but she shook herself and got a grip. *It's just the open window,* she told herself. Tentatively her hand reached out towards the curtain and she flung it back wildly... *nothing.* It was just the open window. The wind? *Idiot.* Realising it had rattled her more than she'd care to admit, she took a deep breath - and instantly realised what the smell was. She could feel panic rising in her chest and she rushed into the kitchen, grabbed what she needed and then forced the stiff kitchen door open once more, before dashing outside, without closing the door fully behind her. Then she rushed up the path, knowing exactly where to go.

The smell got stronger – it was something burning. Sure enough, when she reached the little clearing, the office bin she'd used for the spell was now fully ablaze, and the flames were rising four feet in the air. Thick smoke wafted over her on the next breeze and she coughed. Chelle fought with the thing she'd carried out from the kitchen and then suddenly it was spewing white foam all over the flames. She kept going, to be sure. Thank god for burning embers falling from the fireplace at Sara's last weekend, she thought, without which she wouldn't have bought a fire extinguisher, let alone asked the shop for a practise run on how to use one. Something else she could now cope with on her own. However, those flames had been pretty hot and very scary. As she watched the saturated fire snuff out completely, she tried to work out why it would have reignited to that ferocity – she'd definitely made sure it was out before she left it. Maybe something dropped into the metal bin from the trees and caught on the ashes. Something from above? As she looked up at the branches, turning a slow semi-circle beneath the bare boughs, the face in the moon appeared to mock her and the wind got stronger. It was definitely blowing a little bit of a gale now. *Got to be more careful,* she thought. *Better not burn the place down when I've only just moved in.*

As she completed her turn, her gaze settled on the shadows playing on her attic room window again. She squinted her eyes. No, it wasn't shadows.

There was something in the room.

Was that a...? *Oh no, did I leave the kitchen door open?* I don't believe it. She pursed her lips - so much for a relaxing night at home.

Chelle checked the fire in the bin had been extinguished – and couldn't see anything amidst the 'ashes and foam soup' in the blackened, scorched bin – but as she leaned in, there appeared a blob rising to the top of the liquid in the bin – and Chelle jumped when she saw it was a dead mouse, with half its head bitten off. She made a disgusted face, looked up again and heard an owl hoot loudly. She shook her head and hulked the heavy extinguisher onto her shoulder. *I owe you a metal waste paper bin,* she thought, *this one's been through hell and back,* and looked towards Sara's. The iron gate in the her back wall was shut and to her surprise there was already a big padlock back on the gate. *Sara didn't waste any time.* She smiled incredulously, shrugged and turned back towards the house.

Once more she fought with the freshly painted woodwork until the kitchen door closed shut, and thumped the extinguisher back down on the counter top. 'First thing on Monday I'm getting those builders back in,' she said aloud, in as normal a voice as possible. If there was a real intruder, they might scarper if they thought she was with somebody. Fleetingly, she considered doing a male voice and answering herself back, but changed her mind. Her heart was almost beating normally, but she swigged the remains of her wine, down in one, and went via the lounge to investigate what she'd seen.

The soul music was still playing in the background and the lounge had definitely got colder. Chelle shivered. She glanced over at the wood-burning stove – the flames had died right down. Maybe the chimney hadn't been cleaned enough - it shouldn't have gone out *that* quickly. '*And* I'll tell the builders to re-check the flue.' She spoke the words aloud again, only slightly louder this time. Although quite why she thought she had to warn the cat in the attic, goodness only knows. She went over to the window and pulled the latch shut with a hard yank. It thumped closed and she felt it vibrate through her body.

Suddenly there was a crash in the room behind her – she swung round, her heart in her mouth again. The photo frame had fallen over on to the floor. *What the hell…*

When Chelle got closer, she saw that the glass had cracked, right across the centre of the frame, dividing Andy's lower half in two by the fissure. *Dammit.* She bent down to the floor, loosened the back of the frame and separated the photo from the card behind it, then peeled the pic away from the broken glass. Some of it separated and she fumbled, dropping glass onto the floor. Then she stopped and peered at the back of the photograph. There, stuck on the reverse side, was a small handwritten notelet, in Andy's handwriting.

'To my darling forever…'

Chelle just crouched there, staring at the writing, read it several times, swallowed, then stood up and read it again. Then she sank back down to the floor and a tear sprung to the corner of her eye. Through slightly blurry vision she read it one more time – it was short, but sweet, and took her back a million years.

She carefully placed the note and the photo back up onto the piano then gathered the pieces of glass from the floor. Then, she dumped the glass in the bin, made a mental note to vacuum the rest up as soon as possible, used the little remote to turn the music off completely, and made her way to the foot of the stairs, and stood there for a moment, listening intently for any tell-tale signs of pussycat. Nothing. *Ok then, here we go,* she thought.

Every step creaked, playing a spooky rhythm as a perfect backdrop. All she needed was Scooby-doo and Shaggy to appear, she told herself.

As she reached the landing, instead of turning into her new bedroom, she felt a different pull and turned her head slowly upwards. She looked up the next flight of stairs which led to the attic room and held her breath and listened. *Oh god.*

There was indeed a tiny noise coming from the top of the staircase. The hair on the back of her neck stood on end.

She looked around her – there was a lamp with quite a heavy base on the top of the landing nearby, so she unplugged it and wound the cable round so she could hold the lamp upside down as a weapon. Then she caught sight of herself in a mirror on the wall. *Don't be stupid, Chelle.* So she put it down on the landing floor, making a note to push the cable out of the way in case she tripped over later. Then she came over all funny and shook her head to clear it.

When she felt able to continue, she felt the hackles standing on end again. Then she realised why. If she wasn't mistaken, the noise was back, this time accompanied by the last vestiges of the *Mary Ellen* tune she was playing earlier on. She shook herself again, and the music had gone. *It's a cat, Chelle, it's only a cat.*

She steeled herself. What would Sara say if she could see 'Missus Nothing-Scares-Me' now? So, step by step, Chelle carried on up the second staircase to the top floor – to the attic.

On the way up she was thinking about what she would find there. She knew it was bare, apart from a couple of old bits of furniture, so it shouldn't take too long to check. It'd be fine. Would take no time at all.

Really? Yes, really.

Come on girl, have some balls. It might be Hallowe'en but that attic was all freshly painted and bright, not like the cobweb-covered ones you see on scary films. '*So in we go, Chelle,*' she said to herself, out loud.

Opening the door at the top, the most horrendous creak began. She rolled her eyes skywards.

'Note to builders – oil these hinges tomorrow, too.' She spoke the words, as normally as she could, even though she could feel a clichéd nightmare unfolding around her - the door hinges literally could have been a movie sound effect.

Then she reached for the light – nothing. *You're kidding me...*

'And check these...' Surely these circuits had worked when she'd been through the builder's snagging checklist at the handover yesterday?

Chelle clicked the switch on a wall light instead, and the bare bulb came on instantly, so brightly that it briefly blinded her. She took a moment for her eyes to adjust and realised that with the light on, she couldn't see the shadows from outside. She couldn't tell if the movement she'd seen earlier, over by the attic window, was the shadow from the trees after all. Or a cat. Or something else...

There was a sudden whistling, almost a howling. The trees were blowing about quite wildly outside - the wind was whipping up now. It created a supernatural 'wheee' noise as it squeezed through the gap in the window. She walked across to it, tentatively looking all around her. The painter guy whom she'd told to paint over it as she was running out of budget, had ignored her, opened it up to do it 'properly', and then left it slightly ajar to dry. She reached up and began to rock it gently to pull it shut. She'd had to scrimp a little on the top floor. When her art work had sold enough, she'd revamp it all over again, meaning there would be a welcome new project to get her teeth into. Maybe there would even be some new art work soon too, if she got her inspiration back.

Which would happen just as soon as her dreams returned. Maybe it would be tonight – maybe on her first night in her new house? Chelle wondered what else she had to do to make it happen. New era, new home, new ideal man list – maybe she'd done enough already. But if not, she'd just wait it out some more. She was good at waiting.

Baby steps, she told herself. Baby steps.

Meanwhile, let's get rid of this current intrusion threatening to keep her up half the night – she glanced at her watch – it was already half eleven. She didn't really want to be up here when the clock struck twelve, superstition or no superstition.

As she stood at the window, she stopped trying to close it for a sec, and looked out across the bushes and the lawn and the row of trees. This high up, with the branches waving in the wind, she could see into Sara's moonlit back garden.

If Chelle wasn't mistaken, there was someone there, walking down towards the summer house - a shadowy figure, going in, turning on a light and... oh, it was only Sara. Chelle got a distinct feeling of déjà vu, only the light worked this time. She dismissed it, and breathed out heavily. Then Sara looked up her way, and Chelle waved, thinking Sara had seen her. But there was no response, and her friend turned back into the summer house and disappeared out of sight.

Right. Cat.

Chelle finally closed the window, gently this time, after all the rocking to free the congealed paint, then she turned around into the room once more, her back towards the window. The noise suddenly resumed - more clearly now – it was a scratching sound and it was coming from the direction of the eaves.

'Shit, you little idiot, there you are. You've got yourself in the roof space, have you?' Chelle said, and made an irritated 'ugh' sound. 'Right, I'm going to get the torch – you'd better come out 'cos I've had my bath and I'm not coming in there after you!' she said, then turned tail and trotted back down both flights of stairs, to the kitchen. She grabbed the torch she'd brought from Sara's, switched it on and it flickered. She shook it, then turned it off and on again and it shone steadily. Then she started off upstairs again.

As Chelle reached the second flight of stairs, she stopped to listen. The noise was there, above her in the attic room. But as she moved her foot forwards, it became tangled in the cable from the lamp she'd unplugged earlier and she tripped, the torch going flying from her hand as she landed awkwardly on her front.

Bloody typical, she said, dusting herself down and looking at her knee. She'd landed on a nail and a tiny bit of blood oozed slightly from the cut. She wiped it, and sucked her finger, then wiped it again, and it stopped.

She was getting a little bit tired now. And more than a little bit fed up. *Come on, get it over with.*

So with a huff, she grabbed the torch and continued up to the attic, slowly, not sparing a backwards glance.

Had she done so, she would have seen a pair of bright green eyes piercing the darkness within her bedroom.

As she scaled the final flight, the noise got slightly louder. Entering the room through the still-open door, she squinted - the light on the wall was quite blinding after the darkness of the stair well and gave her vision 'white-out'.

She paused, and blinked, hearing her own heart beat. Then she called.

'Pusscat!' She called, 'Puuuussssssy cat!' then listened again. Wind outside, the hoot of an owl and the distant sound of laughter. But nothing from within the room.

The noise had stopped.

She shone the torch under the bare bed in the middle of the room. Nothing. She walked towards the old walnut wardrobe on the far wall, which the painter guy had said he'd buy from her, since it was 'very Narnia.' He'd not collected it yet. *Something else to chase the builders about.* As adept as she'd become with a screwdriver, she didn't fancy dismantling it to get it downstairs herself. It was about all that was left of the artefacts abandoned by the previous occupant when they'd gone into the care home a decade before, and Chelle would be glad to see the back of it. Reaching it, she checked all the doors and drawers – they were still stiff and difficult to open, so she shook her head, and crouched down to flash the torch underneath it, just in case.

Then Chelle heard the noise again. It was coming from... the window? Had the cat got out onto the roof? She pictured the outside view, as she'd seen it from the garden, and as she'd sketched it. There was indeed a little ledge outside, which in her sketch, stretched along all three windows on the top floor. Was the cat out there? On the dodgy ledge? Well if it was, this would turn into a mercy mission rather than an eviction.

She struggled to open the window again so she could look out properly but it was now jammed tight, sticky paint job and all. So she gave up. Instead, Chelle called to the cat again, and flashed the torch out on to the ledge, in case she could see the creature. Nothing – no green eyes, no flash of sleek black fur – only a light from Sara's summer house, and the roiling bushes and branches in an eery half-light from the full moon and a wind gradually increasing to a gale. Then the scratching started again, this time behind her. Coming... from the wardrobe?

Chelle sighed. Some first night this was turning out to be. She walked once more towards the big wooden structure, several feet taller than her. She remembered the builder saying the access to the eaves was behind the wardrobe but that it had been papered over years ago so nothing should have been able to get inside it. Theoretically.

Tentatively, she opened up the door and thankfully after an initial heave, it moved without a creak. The lamp was positioned on the wall directly behind the door leaving the interior of the wardrobe in complete darkness, so Chelle shone the light of the torch inside. And nearly fainted.

There, in the cut-out back, was a whole other room. It was dusty and far from empty. But now she could hear the scratching clearly. Her heart was pounding out of her chest and the torch was revealing all sorts of old dusty suitcases and old kids toys and old costumes hanging on ancient clothes rails, all very decrepit and all very unappealing. They had 'don't come in' written all over them. But the scratching noise was sounding a bit more frantic now, and Chelle was determined to see this through for the sake of peace and quiet. Plus, nothing scared her, right?

So she stepped up onto the bottom floor of the wardrobe, and stepped down again into a room that time forgot.

PART THREE

Chelle did a quick calculation in her head, recalling the sketch of the exterior – three windows. Back there in the main attic there were only two. In here there must be the mysterious third window – oh my god, it had never occurred to her during the handover that there were only two – when it had been full of crap, when she'd first gone in there, she'd assumed the rubbish all heaped up in a corner hid the third. But it was in here. This was, what, a secret room? Did it lead to a back stair case? Was it next door's attic space? What? Only one way to find out, and given how far into this ride she had now come, she took fate in her hands and stepped fully into the room. *It's all the same in the dark as the light, right?*

Amidst the untouched detritus of a bygone era was evidence of a more recent occupation.

She looked around with the torch, across all sorts of old overalls, and old accounts books and storage boxes with illegible writing on them, plus in a space on the floor, a cushion, a fast food takeaway bag and an empty can of cola. There was a light switch on the wall, she saw, so she made her way across, pointing the torch at her feet to make it easier to pick her way around all the junk strewn across the lino on the floor. God this was old. Who uses lino nowadays? If this bit of the house was also hers, this rubbish would be the first thing to go. But how could the builder have missed telling her about it? He'd said it was papered over, hadn't he?

Chelle reached out for the switch, an old one, looking a bit loose. She touched it with trepidation, in case it was faulty. But nothing happened - no light. Just then the scratching sounded, followed by what seemed like a muffled miaow. So she turned around again and saw in the corner of the room a menagerie of stuffed animals, an old fashioned wooden clothes rail with what looked like workmens' outfits, and on top of it, a shelf full of fancy dress. Someone had had a flair for the ridiculous – this was the junk room to end all junk rooms. Even her single shoe and other old stuff of Andy's couldn't compete with this.

And still the scratching went on.

With one tentative step after another, Chelle moved towards where the bright LED torch was illuminating a wide circle of clothing and boxes about four feet across, until finally she was on top of the noise. But then she was stumped. She had no idea what part it was coming from. She pointed the torch at the rail – was it in there? She listened. Perhaps not.

She pointed it at the shelf full of fancy dress and jumped slightly when a clown face came into full colour view. In there? Still no. So her torch reached the menagerie. *Perhaps one of these animal heads was hollow and the silly cat had got itself caught inside somehow and couldn't get out.*

Chelle's torch reached a tall stuffed bear, nearly her height, and pushed it gently – it was lighter than she'd expected and it toppled ever so slightly. The noise seemed to be behind it. She tried to see round. Above it on the shelf was a witch's hat, a very realistic looking Frankenstein head and a dog mask or something. Chelle silenced herself and listened again, trying to hone in on the scratching noise. But it suddenly stopped. All she could hear was breathing. Her own. Or...

Actually she wasn't even breathing – she must stop doing that, she was starting to feel faint. She took a couple of deep breaths and felt her heart rate start to calm slightly. OK, now let's get this done.

Chelle moved closer to the shelf and pointed the torch directly into the mouth of the Frankenstein – if the cat was stuck inside one of these stuffed heads, hopefully she could work out which one and maybe just take the whole thing downstairs and shove it out the back door and let it find its own way out. It was hollow, so no, not that one.

The clown? No, not that one either.

What about the dog... Chelle pointed the torch directly at the realistic jaw and realised there was a drop of moisture on the edge of its muzzle. As she brought the light up for the first time fully onto its face, she realised it wasn't a dog.

It was a werewolf.

And its face turned and looked at her.

Its jaw opened and sharp teeth appeared.

The hot breath was pungent, and smelled like... whisky? Then a black shape launched itself at the furry face with an incredibly loud screech. Suddenly she could hold her breath no more, the faintness that had threatened earlier now took over, dizziness overwhelmed her, and the whole world went black.

She was floating, turning, weightless and confused. No sights, just blackness. No sounds, just a high pitched whistling noise. Then the faces of Sara and Andy and Gareth from the photograph kept coming in and out of focus, replaced with Andy's note and the two little hearts. Then a black cat, one moment with emerald eyes, the next moment the colour dulled slightly and the eyes were lighter, more of a sage colour, flitting in and out of her field of vision. But she knew it wasn't real. So what was?

'Chelle, Chelle,' said a voice in the distance. Chelle felt herself finally coming back to consciousness and someone shaking her shoulder. A glass of water was being proffered to her lips and she sipped it gratefully, feeling a wave of thankfulness that she was ok and someone familiar was there. She felt so weak, like her middle core had been put through a wringer, then left creased and dented. Plus her head ached - really ached. Gradually the world came into focus.

And there before her, was Gareth.

'What a sight for sore eyes you are!' she muttered.

She was down on the first landing again, near the lamp – had she fallen down the stairs from the attic trying to get away? Where was that creature she'd seen in the attic? She panicked and looked round. Gareth was holding her head up, with his arm behind her neck and he soothed her and prompted her to lay back a little.

'Shhh.'

He was close. He smelled good. It reminded her of the old days. She touched her head and groaned, and looked past him - there, in the doorway of her bedroom, was the cat. It had something big in its mouth but Chelle couldn't quite work out what it was, from where she sat.

'Get the cat,' she said, waving her arm. And she saw him turn his gaze towards her bedroom, but then turn back again looking quizzical. She looked – it had gone.

'How's your head?' he asked, concern etched all over his face. He retained that air of institutional authority - he was still in army mode, in fact, still in his army gear. He must have come straight over as soon as he'd got home.

'It's very "ouch" if you must know. Where's the werewolf? And when did you get back? And how did you know to come over? And where was the cat in the end – behind the wardrobe in the secret room? And...' she exclaimed and tried to sit up then clutched her head and leaned back into his strong biceps again. He smiled at her and took a mock deep breath.

'Where do I begin? Er, ok. Not long ago. Sara was out in the summer house, she saw you waving, thought something was wrong. What werewolf? And what cat in a secret room? You've had a nasty knock. It bled a little but I've tidied you up a bit. And myself,' he said, brushing his hair from his face, and she could see some of her blood on his forehead.

'Eurgh,' she said, 'you missed a bit. You'll have to wash again.'

'OK, mother,' he teased, wiped his forehead then brushed his hand on his trousers, smiled, and held up a clean palm.

He pushed back her strands of loose hair from her face, and smiled that warm smile she'd known since childhood. The 'I'll make everything all right' smile. And it usually did. Usually. Although this time her head still ached. And her knee – well, that had magically stopped bleeding and you could hardly see where she'd hurt herself, so he must have done something right. Maybe because he'd propped her knee up on a purple cushion from her luggage in her bedroom.

'You've been busy,' she said, and beamed back at him, looking deeply into his green eyes. They were a little too close to hers – well, his arm was stuck under her head, supporting it. But he made no attempt to move it, or to back away. She thought she recognised the look in his eyes. It was one she hadn't seen for a long time, outside of her dreams.

'It's a good job I arrived when I did,' he said, 'There are no broken bones, but you'd fallen awkwardly, your breathing was restricted. I put you in recovery position and got you some water,' he gestured towards the pink glass on the floor next to the lamp. 'I think you're going to need a trip to the hospital though.' Chelle made a face. 'Just in case!' He said. 'You can never be too careful with knocks on the head – believe me, I know, some of the things I'VE seen. Listen, there's still no mobile signal here, is there, so I'm going to go sort out getting you to your check up. Better safe than sorry. Don't want to lose someone else, there'll only be one of us left.'

'Too...much... information,' she muttered. 'I'll be fine. Tell me simple things – the little things are what matter.'

'Well, here's a little thing for you,' he said, and he leaned down and kissed her gently on the cheek, stayed there, kissed the other side. Then put his lips on hers.

'Mmmmmff,' she protested, and pushed against his chest.

'Chelle?' he said, quizzically, his face still very close to hers.

'What about Sara?'

'You *know* what about Sara.' He replied. 'Don't you remember?'

Chelle's cloudy brain processed what he said and a memory came flooding back – a memory from a day in the attic, a memory from here in this house a year ago – when he'd popped by to have a look round, on his way back to surprising Sara with his earlier than expected arrival home.

Chelle had been on her own in the dilapidated old Victorian semi, having just taken over the property, music blaring, in her dungarees with her hair in a top knot and a pencil in her mouth, when Gareth had found her up in the attic measuring the boarded up windows. They were debating the merits of dormer windows when they'd both spied something outside, through the boards. Something Chelle refused to acknowledge at the time - a memory she'd blocked out for so long - until now. The story she'd told Sara had even begun to be convincing to herself.

And then the recollection hit her like a sledgehammer and she remembered precisely 'what' about Sara. She looked at him, and he seemed to sense the change in her, so he leaned down as if he was going to kiss her again. Headache or no headache, this time Chelle just nodded, and gave in to a sweet surrender, as his mouth met hers and every fibre of her being exploded with longing. She wanted him, just as she had when they were at school together.

'Mmmmm,' she said and the gentle kiss became a very slightly more passionate one. He moved her arms up around his neck and pulled her nearer, and she felt his embrace tightening, pulling her even closer. She kissed him back, visions replaying in her head of what they'd both seen Sara doing, that day in the attic. It interrupted the flow.

What should have been amazing - everything Chelle had wanted, had privately fantasised about when she was a teenager – wasn't quite right.

Something felt strange. She started to feel anxious, so pulled away and looked him in the eye.

'Gareth – what are we doing?'

'We're doing exactly what we should have done, ages ago. What I would have done, if you'd have let me.'

'Two wrongs didn't make a right.'

'But you saw it too, Chelle, clear as day, you were standing right next to me. I know we never discussed it. I couldn't. But I knew you saw too. So who could blame me?'

'I know. And I do remember,' Chelle replied. 'It's coming back to me...' The floodgates had opened on the memory she'd blanked out in the midst of her depression – Gareth and her, standing together, looking out through boarded windows over the back gardens, the pond, the summer house. Seeing – Sara.

And she wasn't alone.

Déjà vu.

She wasn't alone at all, in fact, she was arm in arm with a man, both visible just through the iron gate, thinking they were hidden, at first just standing a little too close for comfort. And then she was kissing him. The man had kissed Sara right back, put his hands under her skirt, and hoisted her up so her legs were around his hips. There was no mistaking the passion between them, as they backed away and disappeared out of view.

Chelle had glanced upwards at Gareth whose jaw was clenched tight, but nothing had been said about it. Ever. She knew Gareth had seen it too, though, as he'd acted very differently ever since. Sure he'd got upset about Andy, when talking to the builders, but that wasn't the real reason.

'It was rebound stuff, hon,' Chelle said, taking another sip of the water from the glass he was offering her. 'And you were confused. And shocked. It was the sweetest kiss, but you know as well as I do that you said and did things that night, which you wouldn't have done had you not seen Sara with...'

'Maybe. Maybe,' he muttered. Then he seemed to gather his thoughts. 'But I've stayed away long enough. You know everything happens for a reason, and there's a reason I'm here now, isn't there? That I was the one who came in and found you tonight. Who listened to your gibberish when you first came round. Honestly - werewolves and hidden rooms! If anyone else had found you, you'd have looked pretty silly when they went to investigate and realised you must have dreamed it all,' he said, looking concerned. 'Only someone who knows you as well as I do would be able to tell instantly that you'd just had one of your vivid dreams.'

'But I haven't had any for so long, Gareth. And it was so real – as real as you are.' She jabbed his arm to prove the point and looked furtively around the hallway and up the stairs again.

'Ow,' he said. 'Anyway, I hate to think how much longer you'd have laid there all twisted up... and it made me realise. Came to my senses. I care about you, Chelle. I always have,' he said, touching her cheek. 'There, I've said it.' She smiled back, but moved her face away slightly - it was her best professional smile. He continued. 'But you haven't changed your mind, have you.'

'I... can't,' she said, still feeling a little wobbly, a little wary, a little like they were being watched. 'I thought you didn't want to see me. And I was so messed up, I just blanked it all, I...'

'I'm sorry I put you in that position Chelle. I guess I missed my chance. I miss *you*. Always did, always will, if truth be known.' And with that he kissed her again and this time she didn't protest. It just felt totally, totally surreal. So right, yet so alien all at the same time. And so familiar – for more reasons than one.

'I've missed you since we were seventeen,' she whispered.

'You are funny, Chelle,' he said affectionately, and she recognised a warmth and intimacy in his voice which she'd first heard way back when - he'd briefly become her very first boyfriend, when everyone else thought they were just attending choir together. They'd kept it a secret, 'cos she didn't want to share him with anybody, least of all Sara. But Sara had been very persuasive, and having no idea what had gone on between them, went hell for leather to bag herself a husband and ride roughshod over the subtle signals her best friend was giving.

As ever, Chelle backed off and left Sara to it, thinking if Gareth really wanted her and not Sara, he'd somehow pull through and come back to let her know. But he never did. He never came back, and told her how he really felt about her. Only in her fantasies.

Instead, he went for the leggy, bubbly blonde. So brother Andy had stepped in to console Chelle and after that it was a whirlwind engagement. Gareth got the message and married Sara. For Chelle, being part of their world, and having Gareth as a brother-in-law, was enough. He'd hardened up from his years in the army and had pretty soon developed quite a hard streak – one of the reasons he kept disappearing - *never get too close.* Was that why Sara had strayed? Was she starved for affection? Whereas Andy was the big softy – with his notes and his attentiveness he suited Chelle better. Not that it mattered. Not any more.

But now out of nowhere, finally Gareth was talking about what had happened - making peace. Maybe there was something in that spell book after all.

Chelle pinched herself to make sure this was real, then reached up and kissed him again. It felt like coming home, it really did. But somehow she knew it was for the last time. Because something was troubling her.

'Did Andy know?' she asked and she could see a little cloud pass over Gareth's beautiful sage green eyes. He nodded.

'Andy told me a long while before that he suspected Sara.'

Chelle bobbed her head up and down slowly, taking it all in, looking at Gareth, seeing the pain in his face. He went on.

'The only person who didn't realise I knew was Sara. Still doesn't. We were going to have to confront her eventually.'

'When the time was right. IF the time was right. But...' Chelle looked at him. He knew what she was about to say. 'But we both know, Gareth, that the time will never be right. Will it? Not now. Not ever. I'll always love you but...' She touched his face with her palm. 'But – no.' He turned his mouth to kiss her palm, then withdrew.

He looked at her sadly. Chelle smiled at him, and he nodded.

'I just wanted you to know,' he said. 'What with Andy and all that. When someone dies, it reminds you of your mortality and makes you realise you have to make use of every precious minute, 'cos there might not be any second chances. Don't waste time, Chelle. Go for your dreams. Preferably not ones with werewolves in.'

Chelle kissed him one final time and he released his arm.

'You have some important things to do,' Chelle said. 'Go – and rest assured, nothing will ever take your place in my heart. Or Andy's.' Gareth looked sad again. 'You missed him too, right?' she asked.

'More than you will ever know,' he said. 'But I'm ok now. I'm ok, at last.'

She raised her hand and put it on his arm. 'I know,' she replied. 'I am too. He's a hard act to follow, though, right?'

'I'm following him as best I can,' Gareth replied. 'Just make sure there's room in that big heart of yours for someone else, if the spell works and the universe wants you to have a new start. That's how you girls say it, isn't it? I must be going daft,' he teased. Chelle laughed. Sara could have kept the spell thing to herself.

'Now, you'll be ok for a while, right? You're stable and warm, and if you just lie still, help will be here soon. I'm going to find a mobile signal – it really comes and goes here doesn't it?' He said, dabbing at his phone to no avail. 'But that bump on your head is pretty big, so you've got to go to the hospital for a once-over just to be sure. Promise? You won't try to brave it out?' Chelle nodded, and reached out to touch him. But as she raised her arm, she felt a weird sensation, like someone had walked over her grave. She was tired – so tired. He left and she lay back and drifted off to sleep.

The next time Chelle awoke, she was on her own. On the landing, the heavy lamp still lay by her side, the cable tangled up in her feet. The torch lay next to her, battery almost flat. The water was gone, and so was the cushion. She couldn't see if she'd kicked them down the staircase - the angle was wrong. She tried to lift her head... Nope, the thumping headache was still there but at least the lump had gone right down. It was hardly there at all in fact. And nothing was broken. She knew that because Gareth had told her.

So where was Gareth?

She began to panic about the werewolf again – perhaps it wasn't a dream after all. Eventually, she got up unsteadily, brushed herself down, and turned to go downstairs. Then she stopped, and pondered for a while. Her knee was hurting again – more than her head. But it was getting light now, and the stairs to the attic looked a whole lot less daunting by daytime. Things felt different. It was the twilight of a New Dawn. And she had to overcome this fear straight away. The compulsion to go back up there was strong – was the cat there? Had there even been a cat?

So Chelle walked slowly up the stairs, gripping the handrail, then into the attic, over to the wardrobe and taking a deep breath, flung it open. All that was in there was an old fur coat. No hidden back exit, no doorway into another room. No Narnia. She closed the door and peered behind the wardrobe, and saw a papered-over hatch into the eaves of the loft.

What the...?

Chelle shook her head. *But it had been so vivid.* Then she went to get dressed.

She washed her face and chose an outfit, then pulled on her jeans and jumper plus a jacket, carelessly throwing everything else onto her bed. Then made her way downstairs and over to Gareth and Sara's. She'd show him she was fine. No harm done. Or maybe she'd agree and let him take her to the hospital. She'd really lost track of time. Had he been gone minutes? Hours?

She went the short way, straight through their back gardens, past the watery slush inside the singed metal bin, with the remains of last night's spell, and down the path to the adjoining wall. Thank goodness Gareth had left the cast iron gate unlocked again, so she nipped straight through. The air smelled fresh, the gale had subsided, and dew was on the early morning grass. There was a light mist hazily covering Sara's pond. And at the back of the pond, in the bushes, a movement. A rustle. Something black? Something... Then Chelle got the shock of her life. And so did Sara, as she appeared out of nowhere, coming out of the summer house, talking. She wasn't with Gareth. The surprise was too much for Chelle's current delicate disposition, and she felt her knees buckle.

'How are you?' asked Sara a little later, handing Chelle another warm mug of tea as she sat back on the bed - up in Sara's house once more.

'I'm feeling strange.' Chelle took the drink gratefully.

'You're always strange,' teased Sara. 'Seriously, it's 'cos you're up too early!' Sara said, breezily, opening the curtains and looking out over the garden at the dawn. 'Never expected you this early!'

'Clearly,' said Chelle, holding the mug of comfort close to her chest and looking at her friend with narrowed eyes.

'Chelle, Mr Mansfield was just finishing up the rest of the, er, lighting, that's what he was doing this morning. And last night, too, when you said you were looking out of your attic room at – what time did you say?'

'About midnight. I wasn't snooping...'

'No, it's ok, really. Yes, it must have been about then. He popped the broom back which his kids had borrowed and came to see what the summer house needed so he could return this morning early cos he's got another job to go to today, out of town.'

Chelle didn't even bother responding to her obvious lies.

'Really? What did Gareth say?'

'I didn't ask him. You won't say anything when he comes back, will you...?' Sara pleaded, a begging look in her eyes.

'He's still not back? Did he really go fetch me an ambulance himself then? I thought he was kidding. He's taken ages. What time did he come home last night, Sara?' Chelle wondered if Gareth had seen something else he shouldn't have, and had disappeared again.

'He's – he's not back yet, Chelle. What are you talking about? He hasn't come home,' Sara said, looking at her friend weirdly. Just then the doorbell rang and Sara got up to go out and answer it. 'You know what I think? I think your dreams are back,' she added. 'You've been dreaming. That's a good sign, right? If your dreams are finally back? Looks like this new house will be really good for you eh?' And with that, Sara left the room to go answer the door.

Chelle felt the strangest feeling of time standing still. She felt drawn to go look out of the window. Something weird was going on for sure. What happened here last night? Before Gareth came over to see Chelle? Or after. What did he see? Had they argued? Was Sara lying? Chelle didn't understand.

She stood at the window looking out into the garden and the hairs stood up on the back of her neck.

There, down by the pond, was Gareth.

He was looking up at her and smiling, peaceful, at ease, crouching down, stroking the green eyed cat. He waved. Chelle just waved back, dumbfounded. Maybe he'd come in in a minute and make a grand entrance. So who was at the door? She pulled on a dressing gown and went downstairs to find out.

There at the front door, were two military policemen. Sara was white as a ghost.

'He was killed instantly,' they were saying. 'Got a nasty knock to his head, probably didn't know much about it.' They filled her in as much as they could. *Good job Sara lived quite near the base, if they could be of any more assistance…*

'Oh Chelle,' Sara cried, dissolving into a heap on the floor. The two policemen had to make a call, so retreated to their car to find a signal.

'What? What is it?' Chelle hissed. Knowing deep down what the answer would be.

'Gareth's dead.' It came out in a whisper, incredulous. 'He's dead, Chelle. Didn't stand a chance.'

Chelle's heart felt like it had stopped. 'When – when did it happen?'

'Around midnight last night, they told me…'

Chelle couldn't believe her ears. If that was Gareth they were talking about then who was in the back garden? It must be a mistake – they'd got the wrong guy.

She turned tail and ran out through the kitchen into the garden, down towards the pond, slippers sliding on the dewy grass and the slimy path. When she got to the edge of the pond, Gareth was nowhere in sight. Just the cat. It was looking at a lump in the water. There, floating on the surface, was Andy's odd shoe. *There WAS a cat in my house,* she thought. *I'm not going mad.* Then she burst into tears, and called Gareth's name, but he had gone, and this time she knew it was forever.

Instead, out of the bushes came another identical black cat, but this one had sage green eyes. It hesitated by the bush, looked at Chelle, seemed to nod its head, and then was joined by the other. Both of the cats vanished into the mist. She would never see them again.

Chelle retrieved Andy's shoe from the water with a twig and went back inside to Sara. She was completely numb, and joined Sara just sitting on the bottom of the stairs. After returning for a few formalities, and knowing Sara was with Chelle, the two policemen left, and the two girls spent a long time just staring into space over the kitchen table as their mugs of tea went cold.

Mr Mansfield turned up again and made himself useful. He was very helpful, as it happened, knocked up some cheese straws and healthy dip, and Chelle bit her tongue about him being around Sara so much. Eventually, Chelle left him in charge of looking after Sara for whom he obviously cared a lot. Sara would need him.

Then Chelle went back to her house, taking the shoe with her. The bump on the back of her head was a lot less bothersome now, but Sara had made her promise to visit the hospital, just to be sure, and had even enlisted the help of 'Mr Joseph' over the road who had seemed more than pleased to offer his assistance to take Chelle to the A&E later that morning. Although he told her to call him Grant. It was only Sara who used surnames around here and no one quite knew why. *To pretend not to know people quite as well as you do, no doubt,* thought Chelle.

Arriving in her bedroom, Chelle half-expected to find a complete mess, since there had obviously been a cat, whatever else was fantasy there had been a cat. And it would have had to go through two suitcases full of stuff on the bed, to find the shoe box with Andy's sneaker in it. And sure enough, a mess was what confronted her, but not much worse than the one she'd left herself late last night. The shoe box was on the top of it all, the lid slightly askew.

Chelle lifted the lid and gasped. The cat hadn't stolen the odd shoe. It had brought her the other one.

She picked up the original shoe and took it into the bathroom with the wet one, placing them side by side in the bottom of the bath. A pair. Whole again. Complete.

She went back into the bedroom and sat and listened. Nothing. Sweet nothing. When she'd changed back into her nightclothes and dressing gown, she felt in the pocket and found the little note from the photo frame.

'To my darling, forever,' it read.

Chelle, you are my life, my light, my day, my night.

Come fires of hell - or high water – I will fight to make things right, or to *partay*! Two hearts, one mind.

Love you baby.

Andy.

X'

'Fire and Water. Certainly had those last night,' Chelle thought to herself. And she folded the note back up and put it in her pocket.

EPILOGUE

'So have you finally cleared out that hidden room, Chelle?'

Mr Joseph – Grant – was opening the door to his BMW so Chelle could get in. It was their almost one year anniversary and he was taking Chelle to a theatre and dinner trip. But first, after dropping Sandy the Setter back with her mum to dogsit once more for the evening, they had a little errand to run.

Sara still wasn't going out anywhere, still hadn't really recovered from the shock of Gareth's violent death. A nasty knock, shrapnel wound to the forehead - Chelle shivered when she remembered her dream, and the blood on his forehead. It was so vivid. It took her months to really believe that he hadn't actually been there. She'd had a shock, and so had Sara.

But Sara had turned a corner and Chelle knew that with Mr Mansfield around – or Stephen as she called him now that there was no more need for formality – she was in good hands – it was looking like he might be a *keeper*. And whilst Sara had finally owned up to Chelle about how she'd been having a string of affairs with various neighbours and odd job men whilst Gareth was away from home, Stephen Mansfield was never one of them. In any case, her shenanigans were made more difficult in the last year or so when Chelle came to stay.

Sara had been having problems with Gareth for a year now, and never quite understood why...

Chelle was discussing the situation with Grant Joseph, who had been the kindly – and quite hunky – soul who took her to hospital for a check-up a year ago, and been by her side constantly ever since.

The whole attic experience – and the vivid encounter with 'Gareth' straight after – a dream within a dream - had been one of the most fanciful sources of inspiration Chelle had ever had, and it had been the catalyst for a whole new collection of art work, with which she was about to relaunch her career at the gallery.

But ironically, after careful investigation, it had been revealed that there *was* a secret room.

The builder had been right, the entrance to the eaves had indeed been papered over, and Chelle and Grant had eventually given in and excavated it. The eaves were full of Victorian rubbish, and one small extra discovery – two small heart shaped pebbles almost identical to the ones Andy had given her years before. They now sat side by side with the other two pebbles. There were, however, thankfully no werewolves, or clowns, or rails of workmen's gear in the real eaves room. Getting tangled in the lamp on the landing and knocking herself out had a lot to answer for, on that fateful night.

It was Hallowe'en once more, and Chelle got out of the car when Grant stopped outside Mrs Endecott's store in the High Street. She went inside 'Crystals and Cards' holding a big battered old book.

'Are you sure, dear?' Mrs E asked, a concerned look on her face.

'Yes, just have it back, I don't want any money. And neither does Sara. I think it's served its purpose well enough. Now it's time for someone else to gain happiness from it like I have,' Chelle said. 'Just make sure they stay right away from the one on page 47,' she said, and left.

As the door tinkled, the cheery faced, grey haired old lady waved goodbye to Chelle and examined the book. She opened it straight to page 47. There on the page was the spell Sara had used once Chelle had left her that fateful night, almost exactly a year ago.

'Now I wonder why she'd say avoid the "Your True Destiny" spell?' she wondered out loud.

Then she replaced it back in its original place, under glass, behind the counter in Crystals and Cards. She'd put the price up, she thought. It obviously did the trick.

THE END

Debbie Flint – About the Author

Debbie Flint is the author of four full length novels, several short stories and this spooky novella. Having been a TV and Radio presenter most of her life, she began paying attention to her writing bug in 2009 with a residential course on how to write a Mills & Boon romance, in Tuscany. Five years later and in summer 2014 she signed her very first publishing deal - her steamy romance series, the Hawaiian Trilogy, was snapped up by UK independent publishing house Choc Lit. First paperback – **Hawaiian Affair** – is due out from early 2015. The three novels will be their first 'hot choc' imprint – 'tastefully spicy!' The trilogy is also available in an alternative 'PG' version, with fewer 'shades of grey...'

Debbie has also written a semi-autobiographical weight loss book about 'Freedom Eating' called '**Till the Fat Lady Slims**.'

She lives in Surrey with her three Labradors, has two grown up children and works on QVC the Shopping Channel where her blog reaches tens of thousands of hits a week. www.qvcuk.com - Presenters' Blogs.

KEEP IN TOUCH

Twitter @debbieflint

Facebook – search DebbieFlintQVC

Go to www.debbieflint.com where you can sign up for updates and get regular newsletters, free downloads and new short stories plus weekly blogs inc *RiWiSi* – Read It Write It Sell It – my weekly look at all things book including advice for would-be authors. Plus links to all her blogs.

Amazon author page is here –

http://www.amazon.co.uk/Debbie-Flint/

Bonus – Stranger than Fiction – 'What's Your True Spooky Story?'

From Facebook posts, September 2014

Princess Louise Jones Well, where can I start, I see, hear, feel and sense spirit I can communicate with spirit. My first encounter was when I was just three when I saw a lady in my bedroom, ever since I had regular encounters. I now work in spiritualist churches at the open circle - every thing I give to people is nearly right. While I'm writing this post I have a young lady I would say around 18 years old and she tells me to say sorry, she tells no she was in accident and 15th January is very significate, and also she's giving me a violin and tulips. And the name laura. So that's my spooky encounter in response to your question this evening...

Laine M Ellery This one wasn't me but my dad, when he was a young boy. When I was a child I was never allowed to throw a ball up stairs and let it bounce down. One day when I was older my dad told me why! In their old house in East London they had a cellar. One day my dad went down there and was throwing the ball up the stairs letting it bounce down. When this black faceless figure grabbed the ball and threw it back to my dad so hard it hit him leaving a huge red area where it hit. Hence I was stopped playing the same game - it spooked my dad so much...

PLUS - for my 40th we went to a Scottish castle. The room we stayed was at the top with a turret. All night I felt I didn't want to look in the mirror for some unknown reason. The following evening we had a meal in the former dungeon, walked up all the stairs to our room and we couldn't get in – it was like the lock had seized up. I said 'oh come on ghostie, I'm too full to walk all the way back down,' and click – it opened and in we went.

..... The next day we had a tour of the castle and were told there's a room where 3 girls left in the early hours because of spooky goings on - yep it was our room. They did tell us a couple of the spooky events - two girls shared the huge and extremely high four poster, the 3rd girl slept in a single put-you-up. One of the two girls woke in the middle of the night, thinking her friend had joined them in the big bed, but it wasn't her... she was still asleep - when she put light on there was nothing at the end of the bed. That night, whilst getting ready, I had something stamp on my foot so hard I yelled out and it left a red mark. The following morning we were leaving to travel somewhere else - luckily - because by now I was actually quite scared. That was very unlike me, as up to then I really didn't believe - am not sure now if I believe but all that happened and I will never ever forget. I still try to look for a logical reason but there wasn't one......gives me shivers x

Susan Skinner My Mum used to keep house for a lovely gentleman who was widowed & she'd mentioned a couple of times that something strange had happened when she was at his home on her own but we hadn't really taken much notice. I was sick one day so went with her. We were both in his front room when the front door suddenly blew open, there was what I can only describe as a gushing sound & footsteps thundering up the stairs. Mum said something like "Oh it's happening again!" She grabbed an umbrella & I followed her up to the landing, we could hear faint sobbing & the atmosphere was electric, I was shaking I am sure my mother was. Again there was a sudden whoosh – straight past us & the door slammed. The sobbing was coming from the front bedroom where this gentleman kept his wife's belongings in a trunk. She was 36 when she died of cancer. I couldn't have been more than 8 or 9 yrs old but I can remember pretty much every detail from that morning! Just telling this again has sent chills down my spine...

Anthony Livesey YES... when I was a baby my other brothers and my sister always used to hear my 'dad' going to the toilet in the night pacing the landing and whistling. When they eventually told him to stop whistling he said he'd never been to the toilet in the night! Then my mum told the lady next door what happened, my parents had only moved into the house about a month prior. Anyway the lady next door said it was an old woman that lived in our house and she was ALWAYS whistling AND she said she always wanted a baby to be brought up in the house when she passed! Everyone said she came to see me and protect me! Anyhow my brothers stayed awake one night and when the pacing and whistling started they peered under their bedroom door and saw a shadow moving on the landing! They opened the bedroom door and the whistling stopped and there was nobody there! Also my mum and dad had been woken to see a shadow at the side of my cot at the bottom of their bed! To this day there are still some bangs in our house (the same house)...usually when I'm out and ALWAYS in my room... I think I really do have a guardian Angel!

Jennifer Kennedy I have an actual pic of a ghost... It's beside my daughter who was 3years old at the time & was recovering from a serious illness. She used to see things & I believed her but when I got the pic developed I couldn't believe how clear it was. Now THAT'S spooky!

Julie Cohen, Author and writing tutor. A couple of years ago I was in France, in Beaune, at a cathedral. I'm not a religious person, but I always light a candle in churches for my dead relatives, and in this one, I lit a candle for my grandmother, who was Catholic and would have loved the cathedral. I said a little prayer for her soul. At that very moment, there was a scent in the air, which was her smell. I can't even explain what it was - it's just that people have distinctive scents, and I definitely smelled her. I knew that she was moved by my candle and my thoughts about her - and that wherever she was, she was thinking of me too.

Michael James Hamlyn Many, many years ago I worked in a newsagents and some of my shifts involved starting at 5.30am to receive the newspapers. One day at about 4am I was getting ready as normal and something drew me to my parents' display cabinet that had photos and holiday nick-knacks etc in.
It's one of those things you can't think is true, and while other smaller things you pass off or forget, this has always stayed with me - reflected in the glass was my aunt Florrie (I think she was my mum's aunt, but she was always auntie Flo to me and my sister). I of course instantly spun around and no one was there. Now I probably would have written it off as tiredness, but when I came home for breakfast I could sense something was wrong and mum sat me down to tell me 'auntie Flo' had died in the early hours of the morning
Like I say there had been other things when I lived at my parents' house that I simply can't recall right now, never had anything since moving out either. But this will forever stay with me.

Gillian Roberts Just after my favourite cousin Barry died, I mentioned to my husband that I wondered how Margaret, his wife, was. At that moment my phone rang and my cousin's phone number showed as calling. I answered it and it was Margaret. As we spoke it appeared that Barry's phone had rung as she walked passed it. As it was showing my number Margaret answered it. I definitely didn't ring her and she definitely didn't ring me! Was it Barry, knowing that we needed to speak, hitching us up? Who knows, but I think so 'cos I can't think of another explanation. My husband, a sceptic, admits my phone was nowhere near me at that time.

Hallowe'en Poem by Joy Padley

Midnight Feast

A knocking is heard on the aged oak door
Trick or treat says the child he knows the score
With mask and cloak and blood congealed
His face is hidden and is well concealed

A treat I say for I want him gone
As he closes his lips around the sugar bonbon
The gate latch clicks he is out on the street
To the next poor soul he is going to cheat

The cold night air becomes misty and damp
But nothing is visible but the old oil lamp
It splutters and flickers casting its shadows around
Transforming the village into a freaky ghost town

The clock strikes twelve the ghouls start emerging
From corners and crevices chilling and bloodcurdling
To strains of Thriller they begin to sway
It's been a year since they came out to play

As daylight emerges from the dark and gloom
The creatures retreat back into their tomb
Halloween has ended a new month arrives
As they roam eternity craving to survive

So what of the child who cheated for treats?
He did too many tricks and ate too many sweets
The spirits have caught him for one last time
They scream and shriek *now you are mine*!

Thank you to all our authors!

Do check out the individual author links - to be found after each short story - for many more titles from our contributors.

Watch out for future anthologies – join Facebook Page 'Short Stories with a Twist.'

Eg – tbc Xmas 2014 –

'Snowflakes and Sleigh bells – Festive Stories with a Twist!'

Email debbie@debbieflint.com for more information

Join our Hocus Pocus Facebook page and enter in the fun!

https://www.facebook.com/hocusPocus2014

Hocus Pocus '14 was edited by Debbie Flint and Mary Jane Hallowell.

Formatted by Yvonne Betancourt - . www.ebook-format.com